MONTAUK CONFIDENTIAL

A FISHERMAN'S MEMOIR

BY PAUL MELNYK

AuthorHouse™
1663 Liberty Drive
Bloomington, IN 47403
www.authorhouse.com
Phone: 1-800-839-8640

First published by AuthorHouse 6/27/2011

ISBN: 978-1-4567-5265-1 (sc)
ISBN: 978-1-4567-5266-8 (e)

Library of Congress Control Number: 2011904484

Printed in the United States of America

Acknowledgements.

To my lovely wife and kids, whom without, I am quite sure I would have left this earth long ago. You have stood by me through all kinds of uncertainty. I am eternally grateful.

To Eugenia Bartell, my editor, who has driven me like a mule to create this book, and in whose tutelage, I have sculpted this into what it is.

To Don Matheson, who was the first person to convince me that I might actually have a talent with words.

To the many characters who grace these pages and have allowed their stories to become part of mine.

I thank you all.

Contents:

Acknowledgements. v
Introduction. ix
The Goog. 1
Fishin' with Crazy Alberto. 5
Obsessive,Compulsive Behavior. 7
Beginnings. 15
Vito and George. 19
Vito Tells a Tale. 25
The Drail. 29
Lumpy. 35
In Between. 39
The Bomb. 43
Snow Day. 49
Rainbow. 57
How To Win... And Lose. 65
I Am The Walrus 105
Spring Fish. 111
Fingers. 121
Crazy Al, Revisited. 125

Jack and Eddie. 133
Charlie.. 139
The Plug.. 143
Melnyk's First Fish. 145
A Fluke. 151
Free Willy. 155
Lights.. 165
The Flash of Silver. 169
Joey "Bag-A-Donuts" rigs an eel. 175
The Montauk Sea Turkey. 187
The Christmas Goose... 193
A Night to Remember. 199
The Mermaid... 203
The Gut. 207
Montauk's Fishing Holes.. 221
Terminal Tackle. 229
About the Author: 231
List of Photographs 233

Introduction.

This book is a window into my world. I have been molded into the person that I am by fate, serendipity and the profound desire to persevere along the edge of personal ingenuity. This is not to say that parts of my life have not been mundane. There are colorless moments in every life. I have chosen to reveal to you the stories and individuals that have molded, challenged or influenced me in dramatic ways. I will also reveal some circumstances and conversations that certain people would rather not see in print. It seems reasonable that some of the Montauk enigma *(other than monsters and mad scientists)* should be brought into the light. C'est la vie. I will leave the common occurrences behind and concentrate on those which I hope will be entertaining.

There are certain individuals and locations portrayed within the pages of this book which may seem recognizable to those who are familiar with the "ins and outs" of our little town. Any similarity to people and places which you may think you recognize are purely coincidental. Being a work of fiction in some respects, this collection is but a concoction of my addled mind, which is somewhat capricious at this point in my life. As far as local history is concerned, I have taken liberties in areas where the storyline would otherwise falter. I do not think the text has suffered from my divergences. From here on, I leave all determination to you.

The Goog.

Let's begin on one particularly bright morning among the rowdy throng of surfmen on a decidedly notorious beach in Montauk. The tide had turned slack and the short run of striped bass during the previous night was over. The men watched as the sun began to grow in the distance, painting a region of purple clouds across the horizon.

The night's fishing had been a disappointment. Even though there were a few linesiders, taken along the adjacent stretch of beach, this illustrious band of pals had not done well. Not a fish had been caught among these fellows. The insomniacs of the group lounged in a circle of beach chairs and lamented on the previous night's action.

"Things just ain't the way they used to be," was one assertion, "Seems like the damned gill netters and draggers have killed all the big bass."

The coffee of the morning soon turned to a bit stronger beverage as the chill wore off, and the sun climbed in the sky, and as the day progressed, happenstance would bring an unassuming figure into this collection of frustrated souls.

"Hey Rocco! Get a load'a this guy, will ya?"

Down the grassy trail that led to their little camp walked a peculiar looking chap. The fellow was of a rather rotund ilk, dressed in a plaid shirt, baggy yellow pants and wearing cheap rubber sandals. On his head, he sported an old sailor's cap which sat awkwardly atop his ample brow as if it had been hastily donned. With a huge toothy grin, he had wandered into this wily collection of hardcore sportsmen. Slung across his shoulder was an old and decrepit boat rod with an ancient conventional 2.0 reel fastened to the butt. He carried none of the other accouterments common to the surf fisherman, such as a tackle bag or waders. This weird exposition of person and gear had at once caught the attention of the group. The crew turned a curious eye towards the stranger.

"*Can you believe this jerk?*"

"Looks to me like he's lookin' for a head boat."

"Easy fellas, it's just another *Googan*."

A Googan. For those of you who don't recognize the term "Googan" I will explain. The word Googan (Goog for short) is a particular epigram with an origin that is often attributed to the surfcasters who ply the waters of Montauk Point. This term is used to describe a certain type of physically awkward individual, usually (*but not exclusive to*) a fisherman. This euphemism is not to be considered complimentary in nature. The designation Goog is often associated with the lack of coordination and experience that would otherwise be necessary to become an accomplished angler. Let's put it this way, even by the most liberal of interpretations, a Goog is to be considered a sorry sort of sod.

On the beach, the shy bumpkin with the funky gear sauntered up to the nearest camper and nervously attempted to open a conversation.

"Hi fellas, how ya doin'?" the little guy asked. A series of grunts ushered from the lazy gathering as they gave the fellow a cool stare. A thin film of sweat seemed to have welled up onto his brow despite the chilled autumn air. "Ummm, any fish around here guys?" was what he finally brought himself to say; you see, he had the distinct impression that he was unwelcome. His flip comment was followed by an undercurrent of twitter.

"You're a little late there bud... the tide has come and gone."

"Ya gonna fish here with *that* rod, pal?" was another remark heard within the chortling throng.

The little fellow unassumingly turned and viewed the congregation. With a nervous smile, he said, "Excuse me?... Hmmm, well . . . I've got a half hour to kill... My wife is doin' the shoppin' thing, ya know?... and ah, well, I just thought I would come down and give it a try." Upon hearing this, a speechless stupor descended over these hardy lads. This upstart had chosen the sanctity of their private little oasis to kill time while doing what? Fishing like a *"know nothin' tourist"!* Rocco murmured into the closest ear. *"Jeeze, what if he's got friends... there goes the neighborhood!"*

Just then, out of this cynical circle of wiseguys, a few kind words issued. Whether these words were in jest, it was hard to say, but the delivery seemed sincere enough. "Let's take a look at what ya got there, buddy." Joe-so-and-so had stepped forward to offer some advice. He turned and gave a wink to his cohorts. Looking over the fellow's antique gear, Joe shook his head. "Well, if yah put a hunka bunker on the end of your line, ya might have a shot at a fish." A snort emanated from a nearby chair and the little fellow turned with a start.

"Gee, ahhh . . . a bunker, huh? What's that? Some kinda bait? Darn it. I thought maybe a worm or somethin'. Do you have any I could borrow? Ah.. You know, bunker, I mean," the wayward hiker asked quizzically. With that, Joe scratched his head, and walked to the front of his camper. He opened a cooler that hung from the bumper, and pulled out a ragged piece of bunker that was stuck to the bottom. "Gee thanks pal, thanks a lot!" Accepting the rancid enticement, off he went to the waters edge to try his luck.

"Did you see that! All that jerk has for a rig is a rusty old hook," Rocco whispered between snickers.

"Looks like a porgy hook."

"That line is as old as the piece-o-junk reel he's usin'!" one of the Rocco buddies remarked.

"All he needs is a wing nut to use as a sinker."

"Jeeze, Joe, *do ya gotta encourage these amateurs*?"

Just about then, the little fellow launched that stinking bunker sky-high with a mighty heave. As it rocketed aloft, it disappeared into the sun, and then returning, the bait landed twenty feet from the water's edge with a dissatisfying *plop*. All in all, it was a lame cast. "Oh darn, I'm tangled!" the exasperated little guy said. He bent over his ancient gear and struggled to pull the loops and knots from his backlashed reel. This caused a muffled chuckle to rumble through the crew, who had been watching. Intrigued by the whole scenario, they were hoping for just this sort of comic relief to liven up the day. As if in acknowledgment to this snafu, the popping of beer can lids could be heard as the infamous group lost interest in the little goog and settled in for an afternoon of indolence. Lazy eyes drifted off into dreamland...

After a brief interlude, the rip of a snarling drag stirred the attentions of the idle clique. *Zzzipp!* Rocco just about fell out of his chair as he scrambled for his binoculars and began to scan the waterline. *What the... but this couldn't be!* The guy, *the Googan*, was scampering down the beach with his rod severely bent! The crashing of a great tail left a rainbow of mist that could be seen by all as the fish breached the surface. Those present heard the little man shouting with vigor as he ran by with the rod and reel in an upside down position. *He was spinning the crank backwards, for cryin' out loud!* He soon receded into the distance.

An exodus followed as the whole congregation became aware of the action! Door hinges were tested as the group dashed to waters edge with renewed enthusiasm. Rods were snatched from their racks and carried off. Twenty souls scrambled into the surf, casting as they pushed their way through the water. Plugs took flight as the front line of sportsmen grew. Popping and jigging, walking and swimming, the fishermen bent in anticipation as they retrieved their lures. It was to be an exercise in futility. Not another sign of life was to be seen upon those fair waters. The experts were skunked.

Maybe twenty minutes later, that funny little fellow came from the distance pulling a stout silver shape towards the campsite of the pros. He had beaten his fish! Furrows of sand were plowed aside by the beast's great weight. The Goog stopped short to wipe the sweat from his forehead. A gaggle of gawkers and tourists closed in to admire his catch. "Boy, that was a lot of work!" the Googan uttered as he patted his brow with a handkerchief. The gathering audience gave off a collective sigh. Suddenly, everyone wanted to talk with this new hero. Someone handed the little guy a beer.

"How did it fight?"

"What did ya get 'im on?"

At first he said nothing. He took a long pull from the offered brew, then gathering himself, he kicked the sand from between his toes. "Jeeze fellas, What kinda fish is this anyway?" he said. It turned out that this was the first time this guy had ever done any surfcasting at all. He had never even seen a striped bass before. "Gosh, look at that! It sure is heavy!" he said, as the fish bottomed out Rocco's handy scale. "Hey, can one of you guys gimme a ride to the parking lot? My wife is waitin' for me... *Boy, I hope she isn't too mad.*"

Fishin' with Crazy Alberto.

There is a sense of camaraderie that is formed between two fellows when on a fishing campaign. A good fishing partner will do wonders for your piscadatious skills. (*Yes, I know, I made up the word...*) A worthy confederate will egg you on and cause you to work harder than ever to out-do yourself and if you have chosen wisely, this pal will shlepp you off to grounds you have never been to before, adding novelty to the adventure of life, a journey as old as time... the hunt.

It is important that you realize your responsibility within this accord. You will have to reciprocate in the sharing of talent. If you can not add to the relationship through ability, knowledge and skill, then you may find that humor, determination and ardency will often suffice. Understand that these mannerisms are not to be depended upon, as these traits are transient in nature and will only prove effective for a short period of time. It is fair to say that donations of beach permits, booze, food and bait will only go so far and sooner or later you will have to exceed your buddy with adroitness.

Alberto Knie and I have had just such a relationship. Alberto compliments my fishing skills, because in my opinion, he is the better fisherman. What my contribution to the relationship is, I can not say. If I provide anything at all to the mix, I am convinced it is a flare towards eccentricity and a sense of maniacal determination.

People always ask why Al is called "Crazy." This is easy to explain. Alberto is deranged in his never ending search for a *bigger fish*. Al has traveled to the ends of the earth in order to catch a record breaker. He has skipped work to fish; weathering the wind, rain and snow, all while navigating the deadfalls of night, just for the chance to indulge his compulsion to possess a cold blooded aquatic vertebrate of phenomenal size. His energy level will endure for periods of forty eight hours or better. Like an addict, one striper of mass and girth, is not enough for Crazy Al. He will continue to fish until hunger and exhaustion overtake him, then, with a small respite of a few hours or so, he is once again primed to repeat the process. This is what makes him "Crazy Alberto."

I can recall one afternoon when the two of us returned to my home to pass some time before fishing the next tide. "Just let me close my eyes for a few minutes, Bubba, I gotta rest up a bit." With that, Al promptly passed out on my living room floor, the nearby couch being, apparently, too comfortable for him.

"Paul! There is a *Chinaman* sleeping on your floor!" my mother-in-law hollered up to me as she made one of her characteristically unannounced visits. I was busy upstairs, changing my clothes.(*You see, Mom had a key.*)

"It's OK Mom, It's just Al." I hollered down to her.

Two hours later, my 13 year old daughter returned home with her girlfriends, intent on having a sleepover party. I was greeted with the shrieks of ten horrified teenyboppers! This finally stirred Al into consciousness and within minutes we were off on our next adventure.

Obsessive,Compulsive Behavior.

As was the usual routine, our quest started with a cryptic call from Alberto. "There are fish in your area, Bub.... I'll be out at 10pm... I'll be in touch..." *CLICK.*

No response from me was necessary. The call may just as well been left on my voice-mail. My choice was to say yes or no and more often than not, I jumped at the chance to join in.

We converged at the rally point, **Paulie's Bait, Tackle & free Coffee Emporium; located just south of the circle on South Edgemire Street, in Montauk....***(Bingo... free bucktail!)* And as I pulled into a parking spot, I noticed Al perusing his vast quantity of tackle and accoutrement which never leaves the back of his SUV. Al saw me pull in and he quickly secreted a magic talisman behind his back.

"Lemme see that!"

"No. It's my secret weapon!"

"GIMME!"

"NO."

"You suck."

There. We had gotten that out of the way, this being our standard greeting. You see, no matter how much fishin' gear you own, you always need to bring something "new" to the current expedition. A cutting edge gizmo will add to the thrill of the hunt whether it is effective or not.

"Where are we goin'?"

"You'll see..."

I suspected I knew where my buddy intended to go, you see, I am privy to the latest intelligence reports delivered by my many "*spies with eyes."* Also, there are only a few places to find fish in Montauk when the tide is dropping and the breeze comes from the northwest which was the way of wind this day. This combination suggested there would be a good bite on the north side at Shagwong Point. With our secret weapons and sharpened hooks, we were off.

The trip to Shagwong was spent nestled within a sphere of steadily building suspense. Cigarettes burnt like fuses on the Fourth of July, as we rolled across the sand at Gin Beach in Al's truck. Alberto pressed for speed and swerved to avoid large deadfalls of driftwood that seemed to jump out of the sand ahead of us. "Big fish out here last night, Bub."

"I know, I heard of a released 35 pounder this morning."

"It's gonna be crowded."

Sure enough, the beach at Shagwong was loaded with surfcasters, all with similar expectations to our own. A slow pass among their ranks revealed an awful truth, not a thing had been caught since sundown, the Point was dead. One of my many confederates walked up to the truck to share the unhappy news.

"Nothin' happinin', dude.."

"Yeah, bummer..."

This is the vernacular of fishermen on the prowl. The facts, please... Just the facts.

We moved out to the end of the Point to make a few casts into the meat of the rip, but after a brief session with bucktails and no luck, we retreated to the truck.

"This sucks...Let's go." We headed east, and away from the crowds. The trip along the rocky beach was uneventful even though we stopped at a few other hot spots like Oyster Pond and Stepping Stones to make a few casts.

"They gotta be here someplace, Bub."

Cigarettes, lukewarm coffee and 3 miles of "make ten casts and run" had brought us to a very productive spit of sand called the False Bar. It was deserted. The wind was in our face here, blowing at from 15 to 20 mph and there was a great sweep of water surging into the shallows as the tide and waves rushed towards the Point. When in search of stripers, these are often considered the best conditions for those *"in the know."* We stepped into the surf, maybe twenty yards apart, and waded into waist deep water. "Put on that secret weapon I gave you...." (*OK. I know you have been dying to know what the magic charm was that night. It was a two ounce Storm shad*). I made a cast and immediately felt a bump.

"THEYA... HEEYA...."

To my right I heard Al shout. *"I'm into big fish, Bubba!"* Al spoke with a peculiar staccato lilt, as he often does when he is in an exaggerated state of stimulus. His clipped words rang like the dialogue of a Samuri film from the 1950s, where the actors seem to bark without moving their lips. My pulse quickened in response to this indicative drawl.

At this point the tip of my rod was dragged into the crest of an incoming swell as a fatty grabbed hold of my lure. We were both drawn down the beach by our fish towards the eastern rocks where we landed them a few yards apart. I looked down at Al's catch, which was the twin of my own.

"My fish is bigger."

"You're so full of crap!"

I trotted back to the sweat spot of the sand bar. Arriving first, I stepped purposefully into the water. Al splashed into the wash behind of me. It was a race.

"Hey! Get outa my spot, you Goog!"

"I don't see no name on it!"

We stood elbow to elbow while we cast, hooking and landing one slob after another for a good hour, all of them being in the twenty five to thirty pound class. By the time the bite slowed down, we each had caught ten fish.

"How many did you catch?"

"Ten, how 'bout you?"

"Twelve."

"No wait... I think I had fourteen."

"Oh, you 're such a dickhead!"

We were both tired and thirsty as we retired to the truck for a breather.

"That was a pisser, man!"

"Yeah, but I think they have moved on, Bub."

"Well, let's not waist the tide, Let's go!"

We drove all the way to the Lighthouse, stopping every few yards and casting. The tide had changed and the fish had vanished. It was amazing how fast they could disappear. "This side is dead. Wadaya think about the flood on the south side?"

Off we went, up the access road, and headed for the highway and the south side of the island. The temperature was falling and a thin layer of frost formed on the inside of the windshield.

"Man, there you go, steamin' up the car, just like a wet dog!"

We passed a fox as we crossed the highway which stared at us with covetous eyes, as if it owned the place.

"Where to?"

"Let's go deep."

Going deep. Deep south. *The Land of the Giants.....*

We drove for several miles and turned off the main road onto an abandoned country lane, at which point we parked the truck and made for the ocean. Fences, gates and "No Trespassing" signs scolded us at every bend in that old half paved right-of-way. Signs! I hate the damned things. I consider the ocean my cathedral. Churches are always supposed to be open, aren't they? A sanctuary, for Christ's sake (*Ha!*). When I see a sign or a fence, I ignore it. These are *my* woods.

We grabbed our gear once again and climbed a fence onto another old dirt lane. "Don't worry, I know this guy," I said as we passed a "Trespassers will be Towed!" banner, as big as a billboard. In truth, I didn't even know the owner's name. We locals *(Maybe it is just me?)* have our own interpretation about private property, especially at 3:00am. You see, I had been passing through these woods for my entire life. As a kid, I walked these glades while picking blackberries and wild apples with my mother. As a teenager my pals and I would raise hell back here. Now, I just don't care about those ridiculous signs and warnings. In the small hours of the morning, they are superfluous and these woods indeed, become my own. Don't get me wrong fellas, my truck is notorious and with easy luck and my Robinhood attitude, I can get away with murder. *You*, on the other hand, will get a ticket, or worse, towed away, so don't get caught!

"*Shhhh... Be vewy, vewy quiwet..... Wew're wabbit huntin'! Ha.a.a.a.a.a.ah!*"

"*You're a lunatic, Melnyk!*"

"Yes! And don't you forget it!"

"The woods are lonely, dark and deep" (*Sorry, I couldn't resist*) as we pushed through the low foliage of a deer trail that headed toward the sound of crashing breakers. The smell of over-ripe grapes and fallen leaves drifted up through the soft loam.

"Ya know what? This sure looks like a good place for a murder."

"*Shut. UP, you Goog...*"

"You know, Knie, I never did like you much."

" *Shhhh! What's that!"* We stopped dead in the path. I heard a soft shuffle moving through the underbrush, heading straight for us. (*I once had a run in with a ten point buck one morning; it was a rather exciting experience).* The brush to our left parted.

"*What the...*" Alberto said, as a spotted fawn about four feet tall popped her head out of the briars. She was a late summer foal. It would be hard winter for this little one.

"SHOO!" I said, as I waved my flashlight and rod at the little beastie. She turned away and danced into the foliage.

"Wow."

"Yeah."

Reaching the bluff, we had to climb down the face of a hundred foot slope. The mist from the surf hit the sheer wall and drifted about halfway up. We took careful steps. The rocks were loose, causing us to slide the last twenty feet to the base. The beach was rocky, and along the cliff stood great spires of solid clay climbing high up the sides, like giant sentinels. *Mon-a-way-tauk* is what the Indians called this country. This translates roughly into "the land of many winds." These cliffs told that tale. A field of weathered boulders extended in every direction at the base of this headland, particularly into the foamy surf. Bass water. At the high tide line the beach was thick with flotsam. Fat gray branches and logs of driftwood were tumbled together at the bottom of the escarpment, competing with seaweed and broken lobster traps, for what little space was available. "*Oh man, does this look fishey*!" I pushed out through the whitewater to one of the far rocks which sat in about four feet of water and began casting a needlefish. The waves would sweep past me, every so often hitting me in the waist, with a high curl. My hands were freezing and I was getting wet.

"Holy Shit! Look down!" Al shouted to me, from his rock, a few yards away. Through the clear green water I saw twelve inch long squid darting among the kelp and boulders below me. The bite was soon to be on.

Sure enough, in a few minutes, we were back into the fish once again. Al held up a bass of around thirty five pounds and slipped it back into the surf. As the sky brightened with the new day we had taken twelve more fish. I came out of the water with a smaller specimen. At this point we were both cold and wet. Al joined me against the bluff where I was busy with my knife.

"What are you doin' with that rat?" (*It wasn't a rat fellas).*

"We're gonna eat it."

"Sushi?"

"Nah, It's chilly, go scrounge up some driftwood and I'll start a fire."

I've been a pyromaniac since I was about seven years old. I never needed an excuse to light a campfire and I didn't need one now, cold and wet as I was. In ten minutes, I had a nice blaze going within a rock enclosure. I stood next to the blaze watching the steam rise from my gloves and waders. I found a flat slate to use as a cook-top at the surf-line. While among the rocks, I noticed fat little squid washing onto a tidepool. They were still wiggling. I harvested a handful.

"Hey look, Al! Calamari!"

The fillet-of-bass was put onto that hot slate and sticks were inserted into our squids and circled like Kabobs around the firepit. Soon the bass flesh turned white and the squid took on a golden brown. Voila! We had a gourmet meal in short order. Al and I picked at the bass like a couple of raccoons, and then chewed at the squidzies-on-a-stick. The mélange of flavor was extraordinary; all that was missing was the bottle of Montrachet!

The blaze was only about a foot high as we completed our nosh and picked our teeth with the fine bass bones.

"The fire is going out, Bub," Al said to me with a maniacal gleam in his eye. (*I think Al is also a bit into fire*).

We dragged over a hunk of driftwood and had a respectable blaze going again in no time. The flames licked against the cliff wall as orange and golden tendrils flickered high into the early light. Great billows of smoke climbed into the sky. I dozed, my waders drying in the mellow smoke of the fire.

Sunrise. The sun began as an orange mushroom on the horizon. Deep purple clouds floated on the vista, their edges tinged in magenta and red stripes. Our fire was roaring now and we were finally dry. Blessed with a second wind, it was time for me to make a few more casts. I waded out to a rock and threw a bucktail at the waves. Nothing. Al watched me cast with his back to the fire.

"***Hey! What the HELL are YOU doing down there! Are you trying to set MY property a FIRE!***"

Uh oh... Ritchie Rich had awakened early, and was now on the war path, in defense of his ultra private country retreat. He shimmied down the cliff and I noticed his expensive Searsucker blazer and topsiders had gotten dirty.

"Are you *MAD*? Do you *KNOW* how much smoke you have made?"

"Hey, HOLD ON THERE FELLA! The fire was started by that googan out there! *I'm just TRYIN' TO PUT IT OUT, T'is all." (Al managed to say this with a straight face).*

In that instant, Alberto had finally become a Montaukett! We don't take NO shit from out-of-townies!

Upon hearing all the commotion, I stepped out of the water and rallied to Alberto's defense. "Is there a problem here?" I guess there must be something intimidating about a 220 pound, muscle bound, balding dude covered in tattoos, because Mr. Rich took a few steps back as I reached the scene.

"Ahemmm... Well.... Put it out before the Fire Department is called." Ritchie stormed away, rather indignantly. His topsiders were now quite muddy and he had scuffed the leather patches on his elbows. Al and I looked at eachother and smiled.

It took us five minutes to dowse the inferno. We had to roll the larger pieces of timber into the surf with push sticks. With an extra nudge at the water line, they sailed like steaming ships as they sputtered away. With the fire extinguished, we hurried up the face of the bluff and made for the truck in double time. We had expected to find the police and fire brigade waiting for us at the road, but Montauk is slow on a Tuesday morning in the fall. We did however find a note stuck under Alberto's windshield wiper that read:

"Marshall, tow this truck to Riverhead immediately, at the owner's expense." Signed; Richard Rich.

At this point we made our get-away. We dove back to **Paulie's Tackle** to pick up my truck. Paulie was there opening up the shop. He is always anxiously waiting for that slammer to weigh in at dawn. A big striper on the scale will add a hearty bit of change to his gross for the week.

"Hey! If it ain't Crazy Al and Schmednick! D'ja get anythin' last night?"

Al looked Paulie, straight in the eye. *"Nah.... It was dead out there, Bub."*

Beginnings.

I am just a man. There is nothing unusual about me, except for a streak of eccentricity which seems to run through my veins. I came into this world as a blank screen until the endless interference derived from the genealogy of my ancestry encroached upon my young, vulnerable ego. I am the mosaic of the people and events that have influenced my actions. Nature, nurture, where it will lead to, I do not know, but within these pages, I have returned to what has been.

I have often thought about the roots of my obsessive behavior and when reminiscing, I am drawn to a favorite quote of my father's, which he passed to me at an early age. You will have be patient to hear these words, as the joy is within the telling.

The reasoning behind my Old Man's 'pearls of wisdom' escapes me now, but I can suspect that it must have had to do with the somewhat frivolous attitudes attributed to the men-folk on my mother's side of the family. Chief among these provocateurs was my mother's father, Walter Rinkiewicz. At the time, Grandpa was in his early seventies and well on the way to fulfilling his life's quest to spend as much time on the water or in the woods as was practical. Papa Rinkiewicz was a stocky man and no more than 5' 6" in stature. He was built like a small bull, with huge ham hock forearms. I can remember Poppa would smile at me *(I was his youngest grandchild)*, through a haze of Lucky Strike fumes, and reminisce over his past glories, much in the way I am, to you, now. When visiting us, Grandpa would sit at the kitchen table and wait for me to get home from grade school. He would stroke his thinning hair and nurse a cup of black coffee while reading the Polish newspaper. On my part, I would hurry home so I could hear more of

Grandpa's off-color stories of a well worn life. "Pavel, come heer and sit vit me, I vant to see how much you grow today. Come, let's see how strong you are!" he would say, as he smiled and placed his elbow on the table in the classic arm wrestling pose. This was our own special greeting and I would always jump to the challenge, grabbing Poppa's hand with zeal. *"Ooh, you are so strong, boy!"* he would say as our arms swayed for and aft in a truly one sided contest. In the end, Papa would let me slam his wrist into the table. "Ahhh! You get harder every day! Come, get me my bottle of Henessey; I need a drink!"

A shot of booze was all it would take to loosen Grandpa's tongue. I would take the lead, inquiring about "the old days," consulting with this great oracle in his divulgences of wisdom. My favorite yarns would unquestionably lead to tales of ships and the sea and he could turn a story so well that I could almost see the world through his words. Of fishing, my favorite yarns were tales of huge tuna, so thick around the boat that all a man had to do to hook one was to dip a baited hook into the water. These fish were of such proportions, Grandpa would say, that it took three stout men with their fishing poles attached to one hook just to hoist them aboard. All three anglers would heave the beast over their shoulders and into an open hold. There were no reels on these rigs and the men would have to perform like a clockwork machine to sweep the fish into the boat in one fluid motion. Papa would explain that the fish would land in a huge tank behind them, where another sailor would promptly slit their throats and remove the barbless hook.

Then there were tales of capsized boats whose crews were swept into the sea. Those unlucky men had sunk to the bottom as their hip boots filled with water, dragging them under. My Grandpa was a hero. He saved four souls during the floundering of an ill fated party boat off Sheepshead Bay, New York early in the twentieth century.

After a few shots, Papa would quietly relate to me how he had buried hundreds of his comrades next to the Volga River in Russia during the dark years of the Great War, (*WWI*) how he rode a white horse into battle like a Kossack, and eventually having to shoot that horse and crawl into its steaming carcass to keep from freezing to death on a frigid Russian winter night. I lived for these stories, and I vowed to myself that I would try to live a life, as full as Grandpa's.

Later on, when my father came home from work, I would ask him what he thought about Grandpa's stories. (*So here it is, my father's favorite saying*) "Don't believe all that crap, Paul. ***It's all bullshit!***" My Father was a sensitive man, a conceptual artist by trade, who worked for a lucrative defense contractor. He was very practical, and spent his days in the company of scientists and engineers within a skyscraper in Manhattan. He did not suffer the slothful. His pragmatic nature was so ingrained into his psyche that Dad often would preach to me about simple truths that today, would be considered quite bigoted. "Do you know who make the best truck drivers, Paul?" Dad said to me one afternoon as we were mired in the traffic of the Long Island Expressway. "*Morons*! Simple idiots make the best drivers, you see, because they have no distractions in their puny minds and will dedicate every nerve cell to the movement of that truck! Why just look at that jerk over there! (*He points to my left*). If he isn't a numb skull, then I don't know what!" As I looked over at the driver, he leered back at me and gave me the finger, at which point I'm sure I turned five shades of red. I was convinced the jerk had somehow heard my old man's callous words.

Dad would impart his opinions as if they were gospel. He was highly intelligent, and would have preferred to be a professor of philosophy or history, if fate had not intervened. Yet he was jaded in some ways, probably by the Great Depression and the effects of life in the Bowery. My father would never discuss his youth on the lower east side of New York City. He seemed to be embarrassed with those years. Although he was an amateur boxer in the nineteen thirties, sports were of no interest to him, and by his standards, out of the question for me. Dad often referred to physical competition as the great panacea of the masses. We spent our time together with Dad teaching me to read engineering drawings and ruminating on the positive and negative traits of mankind.

The greatest jewel of knowledge Dad bestowed upon me was given in a fit of frustration one afternoon when my Mother suggested we go fishing together as something to do as "father and son". Dad took me to the E. J. Korvettes (*the Walmart of the sixties*) to buy my first rod and reel. This selfless act was quite moving to me, as even at an early age, I recognized my father's disdain for the simple pleasures that most men used as welcomed diversions. Later that afternoon, we sat by the shoreline of Rockland Lake and as the day progressed, my father grew restless. Two hours had gone by without a bite when Dad passed down to me the words that would change my life. "Hey

Paul, did you know that Morons and Idiots make the best fishermen? You know what Paul? ***Life is more bullshit than poetry!***" I am not exactly sure which of these two quotes his favorite was. Let's just assume that they were interchangeable. From that moment forward, I vowed to myself, to be a true individualist. No bullshit, and definitely no poetry.

Vito and George.

George is dead, so I feel I can reminisce at this point, without getting my ears boxed, in speaking ill of the bygone. Let's get one thing straight though, I loved George Wade, that old bastard. His constant companion Vito Orlando did, too, but he will not admit to it. If George were here to read this tripe, he would feign anger at these stories, but nevertheless, laugh right along with them. He would always have a good comeback story to retaliate against any ribbing, and everyone understood that he could give as good as he got. George was another old grouch that lived for fishing and hunting. He also loved his booze and could drink brandy by the quart. If you had spent thirty years keeping the scum of the earth in line, (*George was a peace officer*), you would be grouchy, too. They say the only difference between the 'bulls' and the 'cons' in The Joint is that the guards get to go home at the end of shift. I miss the old bastard. He treated me, in his own peculiar way, like a son and I enjoyed every minute I spent with him. He taught me so much about surfcasting that I feel diminished in this world without him. One thing is for sure though; he was a cantankerous son of a bitch.

For a good part of my adult life I owned Ann Breyer's Cottages, a group of small bungalows that I rented to tourists in Montauk. I was privileged to have met many interesting and influential people through my association with the place, though after eighteen years of cleaning toilets and picking up after slobs, I had become a bit jaded with the business. Of all the people I had met while serving the place, Vito and George are the two bums who cause me the most regret after divesting myself of the little gem.

Get a loada these two. I mumbled to myself. It was fifteen years ago when I welcomed two old men into the office, intent on giving them the rush. These guys looked like trouble, incarnate.

I had just shaken hands with the burly, bald headed one and I thought to myself, "*a cop, for sure.*" I had grown up with a detective in the family and I knew the look; that penetrate the soul stare. The other fellow, the one with the hairy eyeball, carried himself like a gangster, full of braggadocio with a good dose of bravado to boot. He wore a sly smile which exposed a snaggle-tooth, like a fang from an aging pit bull. "Sorry, guys, we're all booked up."

"Nah kid, we ain't lookin' for today, we're just lookin' for a place to keep our fishin' club in the fall," Sanggletooth said. The other one just smiled. They were built like a couple of payloaders. Old ones.

Now fishing clubs were my bread and butter and I could smell the dough rising! We started up a conversation and I soon learned about their little group called the "Farragut Striper Club." I also discovered that this was an exclusively surfcasting organization.

"If you play your cards right," the one with the scowl said, "You could book the whole place for the month of October." *Bingo!* In that instant, I decided to give the guys "the run of the place," but it never dawned on me that these two characters would become both my friends and mentors.

I found out what made Vito call George "the ol' Grouch" while helping them as they moved their stuff into the cottages later that October. "Don't touch nothin' in the back of my truck kid!" George said, "and bring that cooler inside. Put it next to the fridge! Don't you eat nothin' outa there, you hear me?"

"Don't listen to that old bastard!" Vito said, "take anything you want outa the truck, It's yours!"

George began to growl like an old dog. This went on relentlessly, until George took out a bottle of Cognac, and poured us each a drink, "*To loosen things up,*" he said.

Loose I was, as I told them all about my style of fishing, that I called "skishing" which is more or less fishing while you swim. They were convinced I was either a nut or a lyin' bastard! As we talked about surfcasting I realized that I had found kindred spirits in the form of these two hoary characters. I soon found George's peculiar mood to be somehow endearing. I grew to expect nothing less. He was like an old dog that growled in his sleep. Vito was the polar opposite of George, being cheerful and gregarious, and together they were great fun, often giving a performance that rivaled Vaudeville

One cool October afternoon, I was sitting with the two guys at one of the picnic tables, I had in front of each cabin. George and Vito always spent their noon-time hour squaring away their gear. We would sit, George arguing about nothing in particular, and Vito laughing at the pointlessness of it all. I watched as truck after truck entered the parking lot, and disgorged bands of men, coming to pay tribute to the 'Deans of the Montauk' surf. Somehow in the process, we got to talking about fishing on Shagwong Point, one of the hottest locations to find trophy stripers in Montauk.

"Hey, you know Charlie Ruger? He was there last night. He did good," Vito said. Vito, being the welcoming type, always received timely intelligence reports from the guys, and Ruger was a notorious crackerjack whose information was golden. George, on the other hand, would stare at people and squeeze them on the neck with his own version of the "Vulcan Nerve Pinch" until he got the information he wanted.

"*Ruger is an asshole.*"

George would call everyone an asshole... but he meant no harm. He would call you an asshole to your face, than stare you down, just to get a reaction. This irked quite a few, though I recognized him for the idiocyncratic old codger, that he was.

"Nah," he said. "They were in there pretty good," said Vito with a cock of his head and a blink of the eye. "Hey kid, why don't you come along with us tonight?"

"*What are you, stupid!* He's gonna tell all his asshole buddies about it! *Paulie, if you tell anyone about this, I'll kill yah!*"

"Nah, he's OK Wade, you old prick! Leave him alone!" Vito said, "Paulie, meet us there at midnight, we'll do good."

Later that night, when I arrived at Shagwong Point, my two tutors were there, already knee deep in the water. Vito came out of the wash to have a chat with me. "The tide is just turnin', there's been a few fish." Somehow, I recognized that by his understated response this session was going to be a productive one. Sure enough, within an hour Vito and George were hammering bass. As for myself, I was having no luck at all.

Just the presence of Vito and George's vehicles would often cause other fishermen to stop and watch before moving on. The two old sneaks would put their rod tips low to the water if they were fighting a fish while the spies were looking on. This bit of trickery would allow very little of the fight to be seen, and often, the oblivious ones would drive away, none the wiser. "*Vito, I swear, if you turn on your light...I'll kill you!*" George whispered out of the side of his mouth as Vito wrangled another fish, while the snoops in the trucks looked on with blind eyes. He let his fish go without taking it from the water, not even causing a splash. The trucks moved on, none the wiser, and we were left in peace for the time being.

By now I had cast my arm off with hardly a bump to show for an hour's work. Vito and George were hooking stripers with almost every cast. "Hey Wade, how many you got?" Vito said from a position off to my right.

"Eight," George said from my left.

"I got nine!" Vito laughed.

"OK! I give up, what am I doin' wrong?" I said, being unable to hook a fish in the heat of a blitz. I had been following the two pro's lead like a dog on a leash. When standing between the two came to no avail, I resorted to snagging George's plug to see what he was using. "*Get outa here!*" he said as I clicked on my light to get a peak at his lure. It was a yellow Musso bottle plug. I was using the same thing! "*You cross me again an' I'll box your ears!* Hey Vito! How many you got now?"

"I got ten!"

"*I got eleven!*"

"*You lyin' prick!*"

You had to know about Vito and George to realize what they were really up to. They weren't fighting; they were playin' with my head. Finally I had enough. I scooted over to George to see what the heck he was doing different. "George, I can't get arrested... What the hell am I doin' wrong?"

George reached over and grabbed the rod out of my hands. "What the... there is something wrong here, Paulie," he said as he reeled my plug to the beach. He reached down and examined the gizmo, calling over to his pal. "*Hey Vito! Get a loada this!*" As Vito looked on, George shook my plug and an ounce of water spilled out of it! "*The plug is cracked you STUPID MORON!*" Sure enough, there was a big crack down the middle of the thing. I must have slammed it into a rock! Vito and George laughed their combined asses off! "Go to my truck and get another one... You owe me breakfast you stupid bastard."

"Are you gonna take that from that rotten old prick, Paulie?" Vito said. His eyes twinkled in the soft light. "Tell 'em to go get bent!"

Yeah, I could take it. I began to catch fish the minute I changed over to the new plug. I did OK for the rest of the night. Later, that morning, we went to breakfast in town. It was on me. They were still laughing by lunchtime as they told the story about how Melnyk had gone fishin' with a submarine.

Vito Tells a Tale.

I arrived at "Mote-ta-hell" (*"motel" to the thick ones among you*) one afternoon to find Vito sitting out at one of his favorite picnic tables. I could see George's truck sitting in its place at the curb. There was a puddle of oil under his front axle gear box. I sat down next to Vito and asked where Georgie was and what was the story with his truck.

"That old drunkin' bastard? I hate that prick! He's sleepin' one off. Look what he did to his front axle! It's all screwed up! Lemme tell you what happened last night!" Vito said this with a huge smile and a twinkle in his eye. I knew I was in for a good story.

Soliloquy: (Vito Orlando)

George starts in on the bottle around four o'clock. I says to him, "Georgie, we gotta go fishin' at the False Bar in an hour, take it easy, you know?" The old prick looks over at me and growls somethin' I can't understand, so I tell him I'm gonna catch the tide, and he should stay and try an' make his head numb. He looks up at me with that drink in his hand and says, "Eat me!" so I rig up and go without him."

A while later I am at the False Bar, and I see his SUV pull onto the beach. He can't even keep it in the tire tracks! Oh boy... I turn my head to take a cast and I hear a big BANG! I look around and I see the dumb bastard has run his truck up onto a boulder!

"Hey, GEORGIE! Good to see you could make it!" I can see his glazed eyes pointed in my direction. He is revin' the motor, and smoke is comin' off the tires, throwin' rocks down the beach as they spin, but he's stuck good an he ain't goin' no place!

I laugh and say, "What did you do, you stupid asshole!" He has some nice words for me and continues to spin his wheels, I don't know which made more smoke, his tires or that stupid cigarette he always has hangin' outa his mouth. Then I hear this big crunch as his truck slips sideways. That's the result over there... (*Vito points at George's truck and I see that the pool of oil under the front end has gotten even bigger.*)

Along comes Stewie in his truck and he pulls up next to Wade. I hear some choice words comin' from the old drunk as Stewie gets out with a chain. Stewie is waving his hand like to say, leave me alone, as he runs the chain around Wade's axle. Then he pulls the "old prick" off the rocks with his truck in low gear, nice and easy like, you know? Wade gets out and yells, "Did I tell you I needed your help, you stupid dope smokin', Rastafarian!" Stewie just shakes his head and gets into the water next to me.

Then the old bastard jumps into the cab, starts the engine, and pulls his truck right back onto the rocks again; I swear he ran it up on the rocks for spite! This time there is an awful crunch as he bottoms out on top of his crankcase! He staggers out of the cab, givin' me and Stewie "*the look*" and stumbles to the back to grab his fishin' gear. The next thing I know I hear him screamin'. "VITO!! HELP ME!!!" I look up and I can't believe my eyes! (*Vito says this with a chuckle and a big smile*) Wade has got himself hangin' from the lift gate. He's all tangled in his suspenders, like a trussed up chicken! He musta slipped on the rocks while tryin' to put his waders on and his suspenders got caught on the door!

So, he is hangin' there, his face turnin' purple with the suspenders wrapped under his chin! "Vito! Vito! Help Me!" he is screamin'. I feel sorry for the dumb bastard so I go over and unhook him. You think he has any nice words for me like thanks for savin' my life, Mr. Orlando? He just stares at me with those blurry eyes of his. Me and Stewie have a good laugh at that and I get back into the water.

So then Wade staggers into the surf, he stands right next to me. He goes to throw a plug and whoop! Dopey goes down! He's so loaded that during his back-cast, he loses his balance and keels over backwards like a fallin' tree! Splat into the wash! Me and Stewie are laughin' our asses off as I try to help him up.

"G-het away fr'm me you cl..ock-sucka!" he stammers and spits as he pushes my hand aside. I say "Screw you Wade" and walk away.

George is now all stinkin' wet. His waders are full of water and sand. He stands up swayin' like a fat goose, and makes for another cast. This time his balance holds for the back-cast but on the return swing, he goes over, face first into the drink, and lands like a sack of potatoes! I'll never forget that splash... it was a belly-whopper!"

So Wade gets up and shakes himself off like an old dog. He don't say a word. He staggers back to the truck with his pants full of salt water, puts his rod in the rack, and drives away into the dusk.

"You gonna make sure he makes it back to the motel, Vito?" Stewie says.

"Hell with him!" I say, "There's fish here, I ain't leavin'! Besides, that old bastard can drive blind."

The Drail.

George scrutinized me with glazed eyes, giving me the stare, the one that leaves you unsure as to whether or not you were about to receive the dreaded Vulcan nerve pinch. "What the hell are you doin' here so early!" he said over his glass. A cigarette hung from the corner of his mouth.

"I wanna learn about drails," I replied. I had come over to the cabin to keep the old man company. Vito had left Montauk for the weekend, (*Vito never fished on the weekends, the crowds annoyed the shit out of him*), and I had dropped in to keep George out of trouble and to pick his brain. Long ago, I had recognized the value of learning through the experiences of the old timers, especially after a few belts.

"You gotta be kiddin'! You interrupt my nap, walk in here and want me to give away my secrets, you little prick! Well... What the hell... Go on! Get my tackle box outa my truck, or maybe you wanna make me go out to get the gear too?"

"Na, gimme the key and I'll get the stuff."

"Here," He threw the ring at me over his shoulder, "the stuff is in the big green box." The back of Georgie's truck was like the interior of a fully stocked tackle shop. Every plug, jig, rod and reel in his inventory was situated in row upon row of neat wooden boxes. There were three green boxes. I grabbed the first one, hoping that I had chosen correctly.

"So, you wanna learn about drails, huh? Well tonight is your lucky night, cause I'm in a talkin' mood. Here." George handed me a glass with three fingers of brandy in it. "Drink up! I hate to drink alone... Look," George continued, "I've been tellin' yah for days that you gotta get your eels to the bottom if you wanna hook a slob. You just ain't gonna get 'em down in that rip if you don't have any weight on 'em." The old man sat at the table in his motel room using a cigarette like a pointer. The dim light from the table lamp accentuated the lines on his face. He eyes smiled up at me, even through the frown of misplaced bravado. I loved these talks with the old prick. Once I got him started, it was hard to stop him. The drink made Georgie's tongue loosen up even more.

"You gotta figure on how much sweep you're gonna get during the first few hours of droppin' water. You should rig up three hooks with different weights. This way you can choose one to suit any condition." George dug into his box and pulled out three torpedo sinkers weighing one, two and two and a half ounces each. The sinkers were oval in shape, with a brass eye at each end. He grabbed a ready made bait rig and held it up in the dim light. This was a thirty inch leader snelled to a 6/0 Mustad hook; an 80 lb. barrel swivel was tied to the other end.

"Now you use the regular fifty pound mono leader, only you cut it at the last third, leaving about two inches for the hook. Then you tie up each end to the drail using a cinch knot, and there you are!" George rigged the hooks up and put them on the table in front of his half full glass. "Simple huh? It is the simple stuff that gets the big one, Paulie. Just be sure to use these hooks on a sandy bottom or you're gonna lose a lot of rigs. And it don't make sense to fish a drail if there ain't no tide, so don't waste your time if there's no sweep to the water." George pushed the rigs over to me. "Here, you go, you owe me a beer!" George poured another finger of brandy into my glass. He pushed it over to me and offered me a smoke. "So where we goin' with your new drails?" he says.

"Shagwong seems like the spot."

"Good choice. The tide will be honkin' in about two hours. We'll take my truck."

Shagwong Point is an exceptional piece of real estate on Montauk's northern shoreline. It is the main promontory on the way up the coast to the Montauk Lighthouse. Big stripers are known to swim the rip that forms there. Some of the biggest catches of the century have come from this parcel of sand. All the pros know that a cow or two will fall to hook and line during the late October nights on Shagwong Point. This makes it a Mecca to the surf rats of the North East fishery. There will often be fifty buggies and a hundred casters plying these waters on a night when the news has spread about a run of fish. Big bass will be left stranded on the beach as the flashing of cameras shatter the darkness.

The ride from the motel would take about a half hour. We climbed into George's Isuzu Trooper and headed out. Darkness surrounded us as we turned onto route 27. I had a hard time seeing over the huge 148 quart cooler George had strapped into a rack below his front grill. The lights from the SUV barely glinted through this conglomeration of gear and paraphernalia. Deer roamed the shoulders of East Lake Drive, threatening to commit hara kari against Georgie's pile of gear. "Damn the fishin', I should'a brought my gun!" George whispered as we passed a ten pointer.

We turned onto the dirt access road and shifted into four wheel drive. The beach to Shagwong passes around a large cove for a mile or so. Wind drifted sand through the high beams and a gust rattled the windows. There was a good swell of three feet or so on the water. "Oh man, there is gonna be a fish for us tonight!" George was excited. It was contagious.

We shut down the lights and coasted onto the Point. Buggies were lined up in neat rows. The club guys were out in force. "Now put on your wetsuit, Paulie, and wade out to the dropoff at the end of the bar. Don't be chicken! The bar goes way out over here. You gotta get the eel out to the fish! I'll stay on the beach and cast a bottle plug. I'll give you the high sign if I am doin' any bass. Don't come back without a fish!" George looked in his cab and pulled out a Musso Bottle Plug. I heard him giggle. "Heh, heh, I got this one loaded with six ounces of mineral oil! I can cast it out farther than those yocks over there!" George walked down the beach to where a cut began and the deep water returned to the beach. I was amazed to see how far the old timer could cast. One fluid motion, over and back and that loaded plug sailed out into the surf. George worked the plug with short little jerks, just barely moving the tip of his rod. "What you waitin' for, an invitation! Get movin! They're out there!"

I made my way up the beach to the sandbar that extended into the sea. I could see the whiteness of the water even in the dark night as the surf rolled over the shallows about 20 feet from the shore. The wind and waves were smacking me in the chest. The bottom here was mostly sand and I managed to wade out about 75 ft, more before I reached the drop off. I stepped over the edge by accident and was treated to a face full of cold water for my carelessness. I made my first cast into a good current. I could feel the eel bumping along the bottom as it traveled down tide, caught within the sweep.

On the beach, I saw Georgie's flashlight blink on for a short burst. He's in! I could just see him landing a fish in the starlight. Nobody was near us. They were all transfixed on the water around 200 yards down the beach from us for some reason. Another blink of George's light signaled that he had a second fish. Maybe I should have stuck to him, but I wanted to try the drails, and I couldn't fish a drail next to George without pissin' him off, even if it was his idea. I watched as a jeep pulled up next to Georgie's truck. Out of it jumped Steve and Windknot Richie, two friends of ours from the Farrigut Club. Richie said hello to the old man and made a few casts. George's light had stopped blinking.

An hour had passed and I had not seen another fish. I was trying to keep from dozing off as I shook the sleep from my head. The wind and waves had let up some even as the rip was screaming along. I switched to a heavier drail and as soon as it hit the bottom, I got my first bump! As I made another cast, I saw Richie wading out towards me. "Hey Paulie, the old man had a fish about an hour ago but since then I ain't seen a thing. There are no fish here; I'm goin' back to the cabin."

"Richie...." I just had a hit. "You should give it a few casts.."

"Aw, you're full of it!"

The tip of my rod took a dip as my eel stopped moving and I waited to see if it was a rock or a fish. "Richie..." I set the hook and almost fell as the rod stopped short in the air. The rod bent in half... and line spun off the spool.

"Richie! I'm in!"

"Your kiddin' me, right?"

With the bend of a slammer in my rod, I struggled to get back to the beach as the fish shook its head, a self defense mechanism designed to free the hook. Stumbling in the sand, I was drawn to my left and as I passed the old man, he got a dig in at me. "What you got there Paulie, an old tire?"

"Georgie..... I got a good fish on here!"

"Well... keep his head up, stupid!" George hollered as I passed him in the night.

The fish was firmly imbedded within the flowing riptide and it was determined to race me down the beach. I was led into a group of casters and I excitedly compelled them to give me some room to fight (*there is no polite way to say get the hell outa my way*). Thank God they were all experienced surf men, (*although I suppose my behavior may have been a bit intimidating at the time*) as they each gave me room for the chase. One after another, they retrieved their gear and let me pass. After about 200 yards, I felt the fish turn towards the beach for the first time. One of George's many lectures rang in my head. "Now when you get her in close, open your drag some 'cause when a slob feels the bottom, she's gonna bolt!" Sure enough, the bass ran as I attempted to coax it over the lip of a sand bar. With room to sprint, the fish shot down tide, but this drive was short lived. The striper was drawn towards the beach as the next swell cut her off and I let the wave send her up towards the tide line. Finally, the tide beached the fish as it flopped in the sand, gills snapping. Dragging that fish down the beach towards the truck was a very gratifying exercise.

"What you got there, Paulie?" George smiled as his light shown on my prize. "You see! I told you they were out there!"

We put the fish on the old man's hand scale and it dipped to the 45 pound mark. Richie came up to the truck with Steve as we slipped it into the cooler. The last bit of the tail stuck out of the half closed lid. "Holy shit!" Richie said.

"Now tell me Paulie, who caught that fish for you?" said George with a big smile on his face.

"You did, Georgie... You did."

Lumpy.

I was born with a strong curiosity and love of the sea and I always felt quite cozy with the ocean pressing me in its welcome embrace. I learned how to swim at an early age. Growing in a suburban environment was confining for us and we often visited my mother's sister in Montauk on hot summer weekends. It was there that I found swimming with a mask, snorkel, and flippers opened a whole new world for me. It came naturally, and I had little fear of those warm Long Island waters. I was soon picking clams, scallops and crabs within the comfort of the 90 degree shallows within Lake Montauk. It became a common occurrence to walk the short distance from my Aunt Helen's house to a tepid lagoon with my Grandma Rinkiewicz to bathe in the summer sun. I was just a kid when gathering little neck and cherry stone clams became a habitual joy between the two of us. We would spend many days digging for these morsels, I, with my trusty trowel, and Grandma with her toes. Grandma was in her seventies at the time and quite eccentric, which is probably another reason I developed the way I did. Nature-Nurture.

Within our close family, we all had a strong love for Grandma and Grandpa. We cherished the days we could spend within their sphere of influence especially my sister Victoria and me. The two of us would often walk from the house our parents rented during the summer to sit at my aunt's kitchen counter to be with them. Grandma would prepare the most delicious snack of fried bananas for us, as we listened to our elders tell stories of bygone times. Grandma and Grandpa would sometimes bicker with each other over some trivial subject, speaking in Polish, which my sister and I found to be hysterical, for some unknown reason. As we laughed at their petty squabble, our levity would bring the quarrel to an end. I would often pretend to holler at Vicky using phony Polish words! The whole room would break out in giggles, hearing such nonsense come from the lips of a little kid. I was a natural mimic.

Grandma was funny and quirky, and we were never sure of the kind of silly mayhem that would develop around her. I recall one particularly memorable episode when Vicky and I were waiting for our grandmother to groom herself before we would all go for a walk to pick wild berries. As we sat at the counter, discussing where we could find the ripest blueberries, we were startled to hear shrieks emanating from the bathroom, followed by gagging!

"O Jezu, wszechmogący!" Grandma shouted, as we rounded the corner to see what all the commotion was about. Looking through the doorway, we saw Grandma hunched over the sink spitting, and wiping her teeth with a hand towel. Her lips were covered with a white concoction which she desperately sought to remove from her mouth. Looking down, we saw that the same awful cream was smeared on her toothbrush. "Oy children, your Grandma is so foolish!" She giggled through her driveling. Next to her glass of water was an open tube of zinc salve, which she had spread on her toothbrush in stead of toothpaste! We all laughed so hard, we were in tears!

Even though clamming was one of Grandma's favorite pastimes, she had never bothered to get a shellfish license, probably due to the fact that the Montauk cops were very lenient towards poaching in the early 1960's. We often would walk to the lake in the afternoon and gather a few little necks. Returning home, my Aunt Helen would collect our clams and sequester them in the Frigidaire. Home made clam chowder would be on the menu as soon as we filled a drawer full. "Moma, you really should get a license. You're gonna get nicked some day!"

"Aw Heleen, Don't vorry 'bout me." In truth, during that short walk from the lake to the bungalow, we met the game warden only once, but this chance meeting left me with a lifelong memory.

I was amazed to see Grandma wiggle her toes into the sand and pluck cockles from the lake. She would giggle with each success. It was common for Grandma to slip clams under her bathing suit, to hide them within her ample bosom. This was her own unusual form of capture bag. On this particular day, as we departed with the booty, we ran right into the Bay Constable strolling down the trail that led to the road. Grandma looked a bit conspicuous as she walked with her arms crossed under her breast to keep her catch from falling through her swimsuit. As the cop approached, Grandma was thinking hard. "Paul, ven he com, you be qviet and let me talk."

The officer sauntered up to us in the way of a cop who has detected something fishey. "What ya got there old girl?" the cop said with a judgmental look. It was a sight to see, this cop staring at Grandma's lumpy old bodice, filled with clams! At this moment, Grandma switched to fluent Polish, babbling incoherently as she worked up a stream of tears. This frustrated the cop to no end. "What the heck is she talkin' 'bout kid? Doesn't she speak English?"

I was now in the position to have to talk to a policeman. I had never spoken to a cop and at the moment, I was dumb struck.

"*Well?*"

Flabbergasted, I could think of nothing and was temporarily struck speechless as Grandma displayed her most innocent look. What was I to do? In a pinch, I did what I thought at the time was expected of me, I began to jabber back in my best imitation of the Polish language! It was easy work for me to create that accented, smooth flowing banter. I was sure it was all gibberish, but it seemed to be working as Grandma smiled sweetly and shrugged.

"Look you two, put those clams back in the water, this instant! And you.... Just go get a license, old girl, or next time it will be a ticket for you!"

Grandma looked at me and I at her. We both shrugged and spoke in tongues once again. I pretended to understand Grandma, but alas, I knew nothing of Polish at all.

The cop pointed at her chest, then down the trail to the beach. Grandma just shrugged, looking quite worried, as though she was being interrogated by the Gestapo! He just stood there taking in the scene. *Those lumpy breasts...*

Finally, he shook his head in disgust, and waving in dismissal, he walked away muttering something about "*These damned immigrants...........*"

When we were sure that he had turned the corner and disappeared, Grandma broke out in peals of nervous laughter. It was infectious! "Pavel, vhere deed you learn Polish?" Grandma said between giggles.

"What do you mean, Grandma? I was pretending!"

"Pretending? Hah! You called heem a *turnip*! Good accent too!"

In Between.

I began surfcasting in earnest the summer of 1973. I was seventeen at the time and spending the summer in our vacation home in Montauk, Long Island.

I made some friends working with the greens crew at the Montauk Golf and Racket Club that summer. Two of my co-workers who became good pals were the Lewis brothers, Bob and Walter. Bob had been fishing in Montauk from the moment he could crank a fishing reel. You see, Bob's parents owned Margie's Cottages on East Lake Dr. during the seventies and Bob Sr. was a notorious pin hooker who fished these waters with great fervor. The old salt stuck to the traditions and folkways of the fishermen of Nova Scotia. He believed that life was a more appropriate teacher than a book. Rarely a smile crossed his craggy, windblown face and he was often quite impatient with his sons, expecting them to inherit his skill through osmosis. Fishing had dominated his behavior and the senior Lewis was renowned among his peers for his unequaled tenacity. He could fill a shipping carton when the other pin hookers were unable to land a thing.

During that summer, Bob Jr. introduced me to the grand addiction of surfcasting. Fishing soon dominated my soul. We were never far from the water during those months, and we packed the season with as much fishing as we could. It was a great diversion and a true life saver for me to gain the knowledge of the sea from my new friends.

Bob and I often spent hours in his basement trying to invent new methods to fool the bass into committing suicide. We experimented with unusual leaders and different plug patterns, generally, attempting to contrive new gizmos to trap those hapless stripers. All that summer of 1973 we would surfcast for the box, making extra money every time we had a chance to slip away for a few hours. We did quite well for a couple of young hacks. I believe Bob and I collected about $3,000.00 in receipts that year, which was a lot of dough at the time. We would pack brown waxed boxes with our fish and ship them once a week from the Atlantic Seafood commercial dock on East Lake Drive. It was here that I saw, for the first time, a sixty pound fish, which was being shipped from one of the boats that pulled up to the dock at sunset. I had no idea before then that these fish could reach such grand proportions and the sight of this monster ruined me. The quest for a fish of massive size became an addiction.

Our best catches were often made while we followed the purse-seiners in the evenings after work. Bonackers held exclusive rights to haul seining in the town. I met and befriended many a Lester and Smith, common surnames for "Bonackers" who were the back woods baymen of Accabonic Harbor in the Springs, which is a remote section of East Hampton township. Their young sons practiced the skills taught to them by their fathers and grandfathers before them. These men's lives revolved around their dories and nets, which when not in use, were tinkered with, or in transit to another hunt. The roads of the Hamptons were often clogged by the seiners, who took great pleasure in driving their contraptions down the main thoroughfares as slowly as possible. This act was often referred to as "forming a bubby line," bubby, being a colloquial tern for Bonacker. We would ride in the back of the trucks, throwing empty beer cans at the impatient tourists who were stuck behind the slow procession. Lending a hand was part of our trade off with the guys who allowed us to tag along. Bob and I would often cast in the lee of their nets. We would take the stragglers of great schools of bass, left behind by the haul. The dories would beach in the churning surf, running full bore for the shoreline to land the boats high on the sand. The men hauled in their catch with the help of large electric winches bolted to the beds of the old trucks. A black Labrador retriever would run to the set and snatch a bass from the spilling net as gulls circled and dove on the catch from above. Seeing a thousand pound haul was another great motivation.

When the bite was on, Bob and I would stay up all night and chase bass. Our pals, who spent most of their time practicing indolence, were left by the wayside. It was difficult for them to understand how a person could become so possessed. We soldiered on through the chastisements of our peers. This was the summer I landed my first fish of over thirty pounds.

As I recall, I woke up at 4am when Bob snuck in my house and kicked my feet.

"Come on! Yah think the fish are gonna wait for you?" Still half asleep, I grabbed my trusty surfstick and staggered to Bob's truck. We drove straight to the Air Force Base where we often began our hunt. The Air Force Base was one of the last bastions of the military left in our town after the demilitarization movement of the Carter presidency in the mid 1970's. In those days, you had to stop at the guard post to sign in. Technically, no civilians were allowed on the base after dark, but this was not a problem for us as we were known to trade a fish or two in exchange for this privilege. From there we ran the back roads of the base to reach the coves and rock strewn coastline of the south side.

There was a chill in the air that morning as we grabbed our gear from the back of Bob's truck, and made for a cove known as the Sewer Pipe, a place where there was a jetty in the water with a thick pipe of rusting iron bolted to the top. We could always count on culling a few fish from this perch.

I fastened an Atom 40 to my leader and headed for the far end of the conduit which extended fifty yards into the cove. Bob was in the lead, and he used his pole as a balance while running along the pipe like a tightrope walker. I followed at his heals. We began to fish, and in no time, we picked a few teen sized bass. We tied them to a stringer that swung from a mussel covered piling.

Sunrise was an event. Golden streamers caused the ocean to shimmer with dazzling light. I noticed a swirl in the calm surf in front of me as a few gulls swooped overhead pinpointing the target. I cast into the center of the commotion and a fish immediately turned on the plug. The sting of the hook caused the fish to breach, thrashing on the surface. I was firmly taken by the fishing bug as I watched my first slob roll at my feet. In my excitement, I slipped and fell into the rocks, filling my waders to the belt with cold surf. This made it impossible to climb the jetty and I had to wade back to the beach with my catch in tow. I sat on the beach, admiring my first slammer.

I am now convinced that it was *the fish* that had *caught me* that morning. My life would never be the same.

The Bomb.

In the summer of 1963, my father had been transferred to Santa Barbara, California from Stanford, Connecticut to keep his position in the company of engineers at AMF (American Machine and Foundry). Dad's job was to draw pretty pictures of the stuff that the company made, as well as drafting, photo retouching and graphic design. Everyone in the world thought the company built sports equipment, but this was just a front for their real profession. It was the hottest part of the Cold War back in '63. Dad's company made the "real money" building Atlas Missile Bases and DEW line radar installations. He drew fancy renderings of multi million dollar defense projects so that the generals in the Pentagon could see what they were appropriating those hundreds of millions for. He had top secret clearance!

The bycatch of our adventure across America was the fact that my sister and I had to make new friends, and be accepted into new tribes of kids, with every move. In the process, I joined forces with some interesting eight year olds. Or maybe it was the other way around.

"Geary, if it does work we could get in Dutch."

"Nah... nothin' in those freight cars but a bunch of ol' orange crates, Paulie. And besides, it's just a little bomb."

We laid the bomb on the tracks. The Southern Pacific Railroad ran the length of California's west coast, and in Santa Barbara County, we were smack dab in the middle of the railway system, a line of steel shimmering in the sun along the bluffs of a small town named Carpinteria, named after the tar that seeped out of just about every crack in the ground along that rocky coastline. It seems that the

Conquistadors used these tar pits to repair their ships. Thus the name, Carpinteria; the place of the carpenters.

The railroad was situated right near the Pacific Ocean on a spit of wild land we called "The Mesa." The place was arid in the way of the high chaparral, but even with the sands and oil that permeated the small plateau, succulent green vegetation and cacti littered the area, fed by the damp ocean mist. We would cross these tracks every day to climb the bluffs to get to the beach, just two blocks from my house.

We kids liked the railroad. Our band of mischief makers would walk the rails every day, looking for shinny stuff, dead things and the magical bric-a-brac that could fall off those moving warehouses. Sometimes we would put our ears to that hot steel like Indians we saw in the Saturday matinees to hear those long trains running. Often these trains would have a hundred cars, all painted in different colors and sporting lettering painted in strange slanting script. The cars proclaimed themselves to be from mysterious and far away places like Chattanooga, Lackawanna and Santa Fe. We would wave to the engineers, brakemen and hobos who rode those long caravans which were pulled by four massive diesel-electric locomotives. These were the beasts of steel, hulking, monsters that shot grease and sparks from under their wheels. We had seen what those wheels could do: the pennies that were flattened under their weight, the piles of feathers and maggots and the flat cats.

We would often stand close to the tracks, daring the gargantuan to grab at our shirttails. Those huge engines blew past at seventy miles an hour, drawing us inward within a strange vacuum, threatening to pull us under their hot wheels. The ground would move under our feet as the sheer mass of the cars flew by.

Pulling.

Pulling.

We heard of a kid that was drawn in by that hungry draft the year before. They found what was left of him a mile away from where he was sucked up. These monsters were seen by us as fair game.

The engineers would blow those ear shattering horns and shake their fists at us when our hair stood straight out as we stood ten feet away from the rails. Some choice expletives would be shouted, in both directions. Geary was from the city, so he taught me some good words, and we could give as good as get! Sometimes we would lie down so close to the tracks that the hot oil would squirt onto our eyes, thrown from the hard steel trucks... Soo close.... That was way cool!

"Look Paulie, don't chicken out! This is gonna be *Boss-Kean*! We got those rolls of caps lined up for a hundred feet on the tracks and when them wheels hit 'em, it's gonna sound like a *Tommy-gun*!"

"Yeah... a Tommy-gun!"

"An' then when it hits the bomb!"

"Yeah! The bomb... You think it will go off?"

"Dunno, maybe..."

We stood, transfixed, watching a signal light that was just down the line. If it was red, that meant the train would come from the south, and that would be a bummer. That ol' bend in the tracks was banked at about a twenty five degree angle, but even so the train would have to slow down through the quarter mile turn. The guys on the engine would see our stuff before they got to it. Today the light had turned green. Good. That meant the train was coming around the rising grade to the north and wouldn't see me and Geary, or the bomb, 'till it was right on top of us!

"Hey, let's step back a bit, just in case it does work." We moved back about twenty feet and lay down on the soft dirt, among the flowering succulents and cinders of the railway easement.

The ground began to roll and we heard the moaning of the horn in the distance.

"Oh Boy! *Here it comes Paulie!"*

Time stood still. We could see the beaming headlight, bright in the noonday sun in the distance. It seemed to take forever, watching as the monster rose from the grade on the horizon.

A hundred feet away, the crack of those fat rolls of caps blasted one after another from behind the locomotives. They went off alright! The reports sounded like a fifty cal. strafing the tracks! Then the first engine hit the bomb.

Thud...

Gasoline will not ignite as a liquid. It is the vapor mixed with air that allows it to burn. The wet parcel, now atomized by the impact of the drive wheels, formed a cloud of spray next to the hot machinery.

KA-BOOM!

Oh, yes, that sucker went off! It ignited like a miniature nuke! The concussion of the fuel-air shock wave was hot as it reached us, searing our eyebrows. A fireball rolled up the side of that big old locomotive in a not-too-miniature mushroom cloud of flame, and smoke, yellow and boiling, just like Hiroshima! It rolled up right past the engineer.

Our ears were met with the shrieking of emergency brakes locked in full engagement.

We ran...We ran like the little mischievous bastards that we were...

...all the way down the block while the train endeavored to stop, with little result. We hid behind the neighbor's fence, laying as low as we could, trying to blend in with the shrubbery.

"PAULIE! THAT WAS SO TOTALLY BOSS!" Geary hissed at me as we peeked through the bushes from an open space near the roots. *"Did you see it? Did you see that sucker go! Boy-oh-BOY!"*

"Holy SHIT! LOOK!"

Soldiers!

Soldiers with uniforms and helmets and *GUNS*! They were now slipping from the freight cars and searching the tracks, even before the train came to a stop.

"Oh man... This ain't good."

There was a collection of GIs standing around the scorch mark on the tracks where the bomb used to be. Other guys were looking around, like it was Korea or something, waving their M-1 carbines around in a semi circle. As the train slowed, we saw a big, double flat car crawl by. There was a big cylindrical shape that stretched across two flat cars, covered with a tarp of some kind. Two rounded lumps made up the rear. The cones of rocket engines swelled into the taught rear end of that tarpaulin! God, it looked like a *missile!* A big-assed-missile! (*There was no such thing as a small missile in '63*). You see, Vandenberg Air Force Base was somewhere just to the south of us, not to far away.

We literally crawled through the back yards and didn't stop crawling 'till we got to the highway. We made it! We had escaped from the *Army*!

"Oh man... that was soooo boss-cool Geary!"

"Yeah, Paulie, super-suckin', freakin'-assed-cool!"

We hid in the woods for the rest of the afternoon. I snuck home and slipped in through the back door.

"So there you are! Where have you been all day?" my Mom said as I stuck my head into the Frigidaire.

"Uh... you know... around."

"Yes, and up to mischief, no doubt."

Nothing was ever heard about a bomb or a train. There were no cops, no MPs. Nothing. It didn't even make the local paper.

A few days later, Geary and I were walking the tracks of that sharp, banked bend in the Southern Pacific Railroad. Someone had chopped through the center of all the railroad ties for half of the steepest part of that turn with an ax. We, being good, upstanding citizens, reported it to the railroad workers who shuffled boxcars in the switching yard of the orange packing warehouse in town. We watched from under the eucalyptus trees above the bend in the rails as black trucks discharged men with suits, who took pictures and searched the brush. Nothing in the papers about this little incident either.

1963 was a very strange year to live in the USA.

Snow Day.

It was a good year for the Bardonia Bombers, which is what we called our little group of pals. The clan was made up of Eugene Wolenczk, Billy Evans and myself. We had been running together since the summer of 1964, when my family moved to Bardonia, New York from California. Like gypsies, we followed the winds of change that rippled through our world after that sad day in the fall, when Kennedy was assassinated. Changes in the Defense Department had my old man transferred again to start a new phase in his career.

The first snowfalls often hit early in our town. By December there was usually a foot or two of snow frozen to the ground. With the snow, our neighborhood became like a feudal fiefdom for us kids, as bands of mischief makers gathered together to incite great snowball fights among the teams that met in the snowy fields. Roaming groups of older boys would ambush the unlucky runt who wandered onto their turf. Sometimes these delinquents would attack the sledding hills and bombard the merrymakers with snow bombs. To stave off these attacks, we would build snow forts to retreat into. A good fort could keep the wolves at bay for a while. Some of these strongholds became obscured in complexity, built like medieval castles. These would be the prime targets for the bullies and their minions. To smash a snow fort was the central objective, especially if it was filled with cowering little squirts.

Snow day! No school for the kids of Bardonia Elementary for what would turn out to be a five day recess! The blizzard blew in on a Wednesday night with giant flakes turning into horizontal streaks. The roads soon became impassable as the wind blew drifts across the open glades. This snow filled the branches of the trees and clung to the sides of the houses. The streets turned into white rivers. By daybreak we all sat around the radio waiting for WMCA to declare a snow emergency for Ramapo Valley School District #2. After this particularly heavy December blizzard, there were two feet of fresh, new snow on the ground! The temperature had moderated a bit so the snow was damp and heavy, perfect for sledding and snowballs! The fighting that week was particularly fierce, even before the storm. The "Big Kids" had taken the initiative and began a campaign to stomp the crap out of us all.

This is about when my ability to think "beyond the box" began to blossom. I would spend Saturday mornings watching shows like "The Little Rascals" on the old RCA Victor black and white TV. These characters from the thirties were always inventing the best "Rube Goldberg" devices: Boats. Go-carts, Booby-traps. All these scenes took root in my brain. I began to build my own neat stuff. Refrigerator boxes became rocket ships, piles of scrap wood morphed into tree forts. So, a week of being pursued and drowned in snow turned into a brainstorm. After getting the tar beaten out of us by hard snow, it was time to fight back. My pals and I would build the ultimate "Snow Fort!"

With me nursing a black eye, caused by a peculiarly solid snow bomb, I came up with a plan. The next day, Eugene, Billy and I began to dig into the side of Cobb's Hill, where there must have been eight feet of snow piled up in a humongous drift. The hill was situated at the rear of what had been a corn field once, but now it was just an overgrown glen where brush and tall grasses sprouted. Cobb's Farm was set on the outskirts of our development, on one of the last islands of the town's rural heritage which lay beyond the woods that were across the street from my home. These woods were filled with swamps. In the winter, those swamps would freeze over and become a skater's freeway, criss-crossing the tree filled acreage.

The guys had all seen the movie "Hans Brinker and the Silver Skates," so it was a given that we would ice skate to the location for our soon to be super-fortress. We set out early in the morning, shoveling the snow from the ice while skating our way on the frozen swamp. The open ice made for the perfect speedway. No one saw us head for the woods, so the fort would be a secret entity for a while. Shovels and buckets were part of our equipment. We dug all day in that snow and fabricated a hollowed out portion in the huge drift of Cobb's Hill. We created a big slit at eye level in the front wall of our new fort. An old plank served as the header for this opening. It took the afternoon to figure out how to install the header without the face of the drift caving in. We slowly made a slit in the wall and slipped the plank within it and then dug below the board until we formed a window about twelve inches high and ten feet long. We kept the walls about two feet thick for strength against the attack we knew was to come. We were proud of our progress and left that evening, after splashing the face of the hill with water from a hole we broke into the swamp. This would turn the face of the hill into solid ice as the temperature dropped below thirty degrees during the night.

The next day we arrived early in the morning to continue the construction of the fort. The front and roof area had indeed turned to ice and we went about improving the design. First we created a protrusion, similar to an eyebrow, over the top of the slit, just as I had seen in pictures of those old German forts of WWII. Inside was a gallery which was an oblong cave five feet high, six feet wide and about twelve feet long that had a round port-hole as an entrance. We rolled a large snowball into a wheel and set it next to the entryway. This could be rolled into place and stand as a door to button us up tight, if the need for a lock-down occurred. As with all rabbit nests, ours had a narrow emergency tunnel, that slipped along that wide hill to a point where the ridge met the woods. Genie and I sent buckets of waste snow down the tunnel to Billy, who used it to make snowballs for ammunition to defend against the war that we were sure would someday befall our fortress. He piled the balls into tidy pyramids and we were pleased at the appearance and neatness of our munitions stash. We let the end of the escape route stop just short of the face of that long drift to a point where the wall became brighter than the rest of the tunnel. This could be pushed through in an emergency and we could escape onto the virgin snow beyond.

Genie created a fire pit and chimney on the interior of the main gallery. Rocks fashioned the fire pit, and a hole in the roof served as a vent for the smoke. It was a work of art. The draft for the fire was good with the open observation slit and in no time, smoke danced from our snowdrift. A fire was a great addition and made the inside of our igloo fort toasty warm. Heat waves from the campfire could be seen flowing out the gallery gun- slit and vent hole.

A tower was made of snow blocks formed in pails and piled into walls, giving cover to the entry hole of our bunker, and stood a good 6 ft. high at the corner of the fortress. There was a battlement at the top of a ledge which could be mounted by running up steps. This allowed our flank to be guarded from a height. The tower was loaded with piles of those pre-made snowballs. Another coat of water was thrown onto our fort as we left through the twilight of the closing day. We all make a pact that evening, and swore not to divulge our fort until we had given ourselves one more day to prepare.

I was always thinkin' and by Saturday morning I had devised a secret weapon for our bunker. Old bicycle inner-tubes attached to vertical sticks were embedded into the front window slit of our fort that day. Water was splashed around the ends of the sticks and the snow that surrounded them was soon frozen rock hard. By stretching the bands to the rear and loading them with snowballs three very potent slingshots had been installed as artillery. By the end of the day, we were slinging snowballs a good 100 feet with accuracy through the narrow slit of the bunker wall. This allowed for a good deal of firepower to be brought to bear while staying inside the safety of our warren.

All this snowball rolling and stomping around made for a distinctly hard and slippery field of fire in front of the fort. Once again at dusk, we gathered buckets of water. For added effect, we poured the water all over the face of the tower and forward battlefield.

Three days of building had created our secret place, but there are no secrets in paradise and during the last day of construction we were followed into the woods by spies. A few choice expletives were all it took to rile up the notorious Dugan Gang, slaughterers of little kids and general juvenile delinquents.

One afternoon, on our way to the fort which had become our sanctuary, we noticed a group of boys moving in our direction. "I think the jig is up guys," I said. "It looks like we're bein' hunted."

We knew those woods better than anyone and the three of us hightailed it into the thick brush. Fallen trees and ice slowed down the pursuit as we wove the beaten trail to the edge of the swamp. We had just enough time to lace our skates and throwing our boots over our shoulders, the three of us skated away. The five goons realized they had been seen and began the chase through the woods, slipping and sliding along the twisting ice trail. Every so often, we would stop to heave a snowball at the pack. Billy had an especially good arm and nailed one of the goons right in the face! This brought a new zeal to the enraged pursuers.

"We're gonna get you, you little shit punks! We're gonna strip yah and roll yah in ice water till your weenie's freeze off!"

Snowballs began to careen in our direction. We took several hits, mostly glancing blows to the back as we flew to the safety of our secret place. The high grass of Cobb's Field did wonders to camouflage the battleground and we arrived a good five minutes ahead of the gang of toughs. The bullies hunkered down, hiding at the edge of the field before engaging their attack, leaving us time to prepare for action and formulate a plan.

The first wave was a strike to our right flank. Two goons each broke from the cover of the field to assault the snow tower in unison. Genie and Billy fought valiantly from the rampart. I was at the slingshots, but I had no chance to fire because of the tight angle between myself and the attackers. I chose not to reveal the secret weapon, and instead, supplied the guys with ammo. My boys were doing a good job from the battlements. Even though the attackers were bringing two balls to bear at a time on the towers, the icy battlements easily deflected this bombardment. Due to the iced up plain, the opposing forces' ammo was limited to what they could carry. After a week of preparation, we were well stocked for a fight. The scrimmage lasted about fifteen minutes, ending with a curse and some sore heads. Huzzah! Our fort had held!

The cry of, "*We're gonna kill you shitters and smash your little sissy club-house, you stupid little dorks!*" initiated their retreat as they disappeared into the woods.

We set ourselves for the upcoming attack. We had the time to light a fire and cook up some soup as we awaited the next wave. Our fortress was invincible! The pride in our accomplishment was energetic and we giggled with laughter as we drank our refreshment. Our defenses had fought them off, two to one, with only the minor damage of a few dents to the rampart. The bully gooks had taken some solid hits. There would be a few black-and-blues on their side. Best of all, there was no need to use the slings, so they were still a secret weapon!

Knowing it would not be long before the mob returned, we spent the time devising a defensive plan. We contrived a cross fire where Billy and Genie would stand on opposite sides and slaughter the enemy with withering blows as I drew them in by lobbing snowballs at the attackers from the tower. An hour later, we saw movement in the woods past the old field, Genie and Billy took their places. The peculiar glint of metal was just visible as the group got closer. I counted the enemy from the tower as they slipped from the woods and into the tall grass. This time there were eight attackers!

As the mob broke from cover, we noticed some clever additions to their paraphernalia. They had shields! The shining we saw in the woods turned out to be old steel garbage-can lids! They charged the field, flinging bomb after bomb. I lobbed snowballs from the turret, which drew the goons in.

"*They got a sissy with no arm*! Charge!"

As they hit the open plain of frozen snow, the guys fired ball after ball at the attackers from their unprotected sides. Many hit home and the gang of thugs slipped and fell on the field. They swung their shields and rushed Genie who sprinted to the fort. He and Billy flung the snowballs as fast as they could grab them, but their projectiles just smashed against those shinny shields!

Five of the kids broke from the pack to move ahead. They set up a defensive wall with joined shields! A phalanx! They must have been taking notes while watching Ben Hur! The three kids in the rear set up a bivouac and rolled snowballs across the icy battlefield to the punks behind the shields. They would not want for ammo this time.

The big kids were making headway. Billy was cut off, but made a run for the fort anyway. Genie covered him the best he could. One of my pitches warmed the ear of a big goon who charged to grab Billy. Slipping this rush, Billy ran the gauntlet but took a ball to the kisser. A trail of blood dripped from his schnoz as he climbed the tower.

Soon the creeps were within the prime range of the slings. The three of us retreated to the safety of the bunker, one at a time. We buttoned up the cave entrance and steadied ourselves for the siege to come.

The first salvo from our powerful artillery slings hit their shield wall with such force that tin lids went flying! We returned fire at a phenomenal rate as Billy diligently fed Eugene and me snowballs. The goon squad seemed badly shaken by the barrage of projectiles flying from the slit window. They never thought we could get snowballs through that narrow crack! With three bombs fired in each volley, we had them on the run. They were beaten back to the woods once again, slipping and sliding on the iced field. Genie let fly an exceptionally good shot to a downed geak and smacked his head with a ball that blew apart on contact. The kid whined and held his face as he staggered into the woods. But the rapid fire of our slingshots had one drawback that we never anticipated.

"Oh man! We are almost out of ammo!" Billy said. The look of dread was upon his face.

"We gotta make more!" I made a dash for some soft snow to our right and was greeted with a direct hit in the face! With my lower lip swelling up, I crawled back to the fort under a barrage of snow and ice.

"We're DEAD!" I shouted as I jumped through the doorway and jammed the giant snowball into the portal, then, packed snow around the gap. We were sealed in, like being in a crypt.

We held off the frontal attack as long as our ammo held out. The back wall of the bunker turned to frozen dirt and grass as we used up what little loose snow was left for ammo. The attackers soon figured the range of the slings and skirted the kill zone. They disappeared to the right, out of view, and attacked us from above and behind.

The tower was the first to fall. The big kids pushed it over onto the doorway. They laughed and cheered, telling us what they were gonna do to us! Eight goons climbed to the roof of our tomb, and jumped up and down. The roof held! The water bath had set the dome into a hunk of solid ice. We had time to contemplate our dilemma, as our tormentors danced and chided us with insults. They threw balls at us through the slit, lining up like a firing squad as we huddled in the corner. The rat finks on the roof sealed the chimney with a big snowball and our bunker filled with smoke; Genie put out the fire with a kick. The last of the steam and smoke billowed out the window and the firing squad was temporarily blinded.

"We're gonna die!" Genie bellowed. "Let's ditch it!"

There was only one escape route left as we squeezed through the getaway tunnel.

"Hey! How did you get ova there! *Get 'em fellas!*"

They rushed us like a pack of wild animals when they saw us make for the woods. Thank God for thick winter coats and snow pants. The kicks and slugs received did less damage than perceived as we bellowed and cried. They smeared snow in our face and hair, down our backs and in our pants! They made us watch as they trashed the snow fort. Rocks and sticks were used to pry the roof off. Our torment was ended when the attention of the ruffians was diverted by the cave in of the drift. We broke the gauntlet with a rush that sent two of the goons sprawling and ran like hell out of the woods. The Dugan Gang laughed and chided us as we sprinted for home. All caution was lost as I ran through the marshlands. My boots broke through the frozen swamp, thoughts of lost ice skates forgotten, and I was soaked as I landed, sprawling in the slush. My hands and toes were so cold I couldn't feel them.

"I'm outa here!" Genie said as he trudged through the snow and into the street. Billy followed behind, sliding on the hard packed sidewalk. I made it home, threw off my wet clothes and ran to the bathtub. My lip was swollen and blue and my teeth chattered.

"Why do I smell smoke?" Mom called out from the kitchen. "Have you been playin' with fire again, Paul?"

I soaked in the hot water for an hour till the feeling in my toes and fingers returned, followed with an aching that had me wincing.

So went the snow battle of '64. I often return to this memory when I am asked how I ever came up with some of the stunts that have made me notorious. Reliving the foibles of my youth has created a well worn path within corridors of my mind. It is here, in those snow covered woods, that my thoughts wander to and I smile.

Rainbow.

The morning started out as another gloomy storm front continued to pound Montauk with blustery winds and horizontal rain. Ever since I was hooked by the fishing bug, I had not been able to sleep past 5am, and so it was for this day as well. I had been fishing consistently since this particular late fall Nor'Easter took hold of the island with my cohorts Joe Gav and Attila. The waters had been unproductive so far and this particular dawn I just couldn't get out of bed. The storm had been pounding the surf for three days now, and what was anticipated of the impending herring run, that often graces the Long Island coast this time of year, had not materialized, leaving me sore and dejected. I peered through the slit of my window shade as the trees of my yard whipped frantically at the overcast sky, and made the choice to skip the drive to the Point.

So, this uneventful forenoon had me sitting in my office sipping coffee and thawing out from the chill of the past days on the beach.

I was dozing from exhaustion when I heard the telephone ring, and I answered with a less than enthusiastic demeanor. It was Joe. "Get down to the bluffs, now! There are fish all over the point!"

"Come on, don't pull my chain, I'm not in the mood for it."

"Come on nothin', I just got a fish call from Attila. He says the fish are bustin' all over the place!"

"Idono..."

"Man, come on, Attila says he sees *broom-sized tails* in the wash!"

It didn't take much to get the "Jones" going. The feeling in your chest combined with a click in the head that chants *this could be the day* had set in as I closed the office and ran home to grab my gear. On my way to the Point, it was obvious that the storm was moving out, the sky was becoming brighter. The storm had caused an early fall of leaves to coat the highway and the fragrance was fabulous as it came wafting through the dashboard vent. It was the scent of autumn, promising an early winter. The temperature dropped to around 36 degrees and the road was a bit slippery. There was a light squall moving through which tossed a fine curtain of spray at my windshield, making it difficult for the wipers to do their work. When I rounded the bend at the Lighthouse, I saw a convoy of buggies making for the parking lot at the State Park. Word of fish on the beach seemed to have spread quickly.

The beach had been battered yet it had rearranged itself. It was high water now, the dirt road into the cove would be impassable. I parked in the upper lot, grabbed my gear and took off down the bluff trail to the beach. Gannets and gulls crashed the surf as I descended the stairs leading to Scott's Cove. The beach was awash with sea foam at the height water line. Long lines of casters stood at the surf. Every shoreline rock had a fisherman standing on it. The sea was pounding the bluffs, literally washing the cliff away. It pulled large portions of rock and clay into the surf. I had a hard time making the trip to my favorite spot, the rip tide pulled at my legs as it swept the narrow rock strewn beach. I was glad to have worn a wetsuit. It was rather cool with all the wind and spray so the addition of a quarter inch of insulation helped to ward off the chill. As I reached the bluffs, west of the lighthouse, the base of the escarpment was strewn with fish. Cow bass lay in rows, behind the cover of the large boulders which stood guard over them. The fishermen were standing in the wash, possessed with blood lust as they threw bucktails and tins into the clouds of birds that ventured in and out with the waves. Every other rod seemed bent with the weight of a striper. In time, I elbowed my way into the mess, weaving to avoid the occasional rod tip or jig that was flipped into the narrow passage between the bluff and the sea where I walked. I soon found my pals, Joe, Attila and Dennis, well placed within the meat of the action and I squeezed in between them.

"Hey! Get outa here you Goog!" This was the welcome I received through their wide smiles; our standard greeting.

"If you cross my line I'll kill you Melnuck!"

"Yeah, I brought my knife too!" Attila jeered. He was teasing me. I always wore a knife, you never know.

"You better know how to use that thing, and by the way, get off my rock you little shit," I hollered back at him as I squeezed between Attila and Dennis on a rock so precarious that I lost my balance with every other cast.

Dennis had hooked up to a fish. It was a slob, which was evident by the severe bend in his rod. He looked over at me with raised eyebrows and a comical "Oh yeah" set to his lips.

"Hey Joe! I got a contender on here!" Dennis shouted to his brother, as he shot him a raspberry. Joe and Dennis had a healthy rivalry that had transcended the years. Hell, *we all did.*

"Don't drop it Goog!" I shouted to my pal. This was a not so secret yearning, fomented, no doubt, by the tournament we were all locked into. Love, hate. *Drop the fish.*

Our crew was both enthused and apprehensive, caught within the grip of the highly competitive tournament season. Everyone was looking for a fish to place on the leader board. Even though we were rife with inveigling taunts, in truth, we harbored no animosity. We would risk life and limb, if need be, to have our brothers succeed in their quest. Even so, we did what we could, without guilt, to psyche Dennis out, while secretly hoping to see him land that winning fish.

We all began singing the theme music for the sixties action show "Batman", which we had agreed long ago, was to be Denny's theme song, having changed the words a little bit to suit his current nickname.

"Dada, dada, dada, dada, dat- *RATMAN!*"

You see, Denny had not landed a fish over ten pounds all season. For us, this was a dream come true. Dennis will own the nickname of "*Ratman*" forever.

Dennis' fish was well hooked, and he jumped from his perch to move down tide, jostling and contorting through all the fishermen and gear that were set as an obstacle course before him.

"*Excuse me- fish on- sorry fellah...*" He shouted as he made his way through the gauntlet.

Of course, being his buddy, I hopped onto his rock the minute he vacated it, and hooked a fish with my first cast. It bent my rod and began to test my drag. I watched for the lull that would prove the fish to be nothing but a strong pretender. It did not come.

Down the beach, I followed up the rear with Dennis in the lead. After a bit of cajoling and an expletive or two, I landed the fish in the rocks, a nice bass in the high twenty pound class, but not big enough to make the cut for the tournament leader board. I released it back into the wash and watched it swim away. I looked around and hoped for Denny to be close behind, but he was nowhere in sight. I walked back to the rock where I saw Eric "The Tree Man," had taken my place on the roost. I felt a covetous pang, but conceded the fact, once again squeezing into a hole in the line and continued to cast. My legs strained as I was jostled by the riptide.

"Hey Paulie! Come up with me, I've got room for two up here!" Joe shouted to me. I turned to see him set upon my favorite perch. This double rock, flat and wide, harbored a deep bowl in front of it. Prime territory. I would have no trouble sharing this rock with my generous pal. I hopped up next to Joe and we wished each other luck.

There was a lull in the action, and I had time to reflect on my surroundings. I could see the storm clouds had begun breaking up. Deep blue holes appeared in the overcast, through which sunlight danced. The rain had suddenly changed to snow flurries which sparkled within sunlit beams, like tinsel. Directly before us a magnificent rainbow arched through the sky. I felt as though I could reach out and touch it.

"Look at that. What an omen!"

"Yeah Paulie, one of us is gonna score big!" Joe said with an air of reverence to his voice. The prism grew in intensity as the sun played between falling flakes. Then, as fast as it had appeared, it dimmed, and then popped out of existence.

We began to hook fish regularly once again, as a flock of gannets moved into our sector. They crashed into the water in front of us from great heights, like white dive bombers. I watched as a bird flew past with a twelve inch herring set within its beak.

"Holly shit! Did you see that?"

"I did, my friend, I did."

From behind us a commotion developed on the beach. I turned to see Dennis within a knot of gathering souls. Dennis held up a bass, which appeared to be over thirty pounds, and he smiled, waving at us.

"I gotta go weigh this fish, save my rock!" he shouted.

"Get outa here you Googan!" I hollered back. Dennis headed away in the direction of the parking lot, his fish bounced along the rock strewn strand.

Come on! It's my turn! Even though it was a phenomenal afternoon, I still did not have a fish on the leader board and I was beset with fish lust. Every nerve was primed to relay the slightest twitch of the line to my consciousness. The waiting seemed eternal.

My rod bent in half and the drag started to sing. The fish gained leverage in the fast rip. I jumped down to chase my fish along the beach once again. It was a brute!

When I finally got a handle on it, I had to drag it across whitewater and up through the wash. Appearing as a great silver bullet viewed along its flanks, it sparkled in the afternoon sun, obscuring my view. A bull of a fish! As I reached to grab the beast by the jaw, a flash of sharp teeth lunged at my fingers.

"*You suck!*" I had not landed a striper, but instead, a huge bluefish. The largest bastard I had ever seen! Clearly, not a contender in a striped bass contest. The chopper jumped and flopped about in the rocks. As I reached for his tail my rod sprang back over my shoulder and the monster had cut himself off, taking my bucktail along for a cruise. I shook my head and walked back towards my friends. On the way, I saw at least twenty bass on display amongst the rocks. A bit further on I passed a pristine herring that had washed up onto the sand. It twitched as a finger of sunlight set upon it. I waded out to the rock and Joe inquired, "Where's your fish?"

"It was just a big freakin' blue-stitch."

"*Aw gee, too bad...*" A driblet of relief could be detected in his voice. I had to replace my terminal tackle which had been mauled by the blue.

The wind and the waves worked hard to delay me and I fumbled as Joe grabbed my sleeve for balance.

"Hey! You fishin', or just takin' up space?"

"Aw, *Shut the Fu...,*" BOOM! Blind-sided and swept from the rock by a wave, I was thrown through the air and dropped on my back. Only a wall of bubbles saved my skin as I landed within its cushioning grasp! I got up laughing as seawater dripped from my sinuses and I was very glad to have missed the boulders which dominated the shoal behind us. I would be hurting in the morning, but I didn't care. Hell man, I was alive!

"That will keep those foul thoughts from your head!" Joe hollered, as he grabbed my hand and pulled me up.

A disturbance and some raised voices wafted through the wind from the beach. "The Tree Man" was in a heated discussion with some broad who had somehow, worked her way under the bluffs and into the fray of men and fish. The two of them seemed to be in the midst of a tug 'o' war over a nice sized linesider. "*You murderer! You should be ashamed! Killing another living thing, one of Gods creatures! This fish deserves a life just as much as you do!*"

"Lady, as it says in the old testament; 'Man shall rule over fish of the sea, and over fowl of the heavens, and over cattle, and over all the earth, and over every creeping thing that is creeping *on* the earth.' With this tidbit of Gospel, Eric grabbed the fish away from the crazed animal rights activist and headed towards me with the bass hugged close to his breast.

"Can you believe that, Paul?" Eric said in passing us. "That nut was gonna throw back my dinner!"

"Anything is possible in Montauk, Eric."

"Hey look! Here comes Richie!" Joe hollered from our perch. "What are you doin' here? Your supposed be working at the deli counter!" Richie was employed by Joe at his famous **Montauk Market, Food Emporium and Bodega**. Rich held the title of chief cook and bottle washer there. Rich jumped up on a nearby rock and tied a bucktail to his line.

"Hey, up yours Joe, your shithead brother just shoved a thirty five pound cow up my ass at the store. He's now in first place on the leader board!" Richie cranked his elbow and made a cast. "Too bad you gotta work," he says to me, "*the cows are on the feed bag at the Point!*" Then Rich gave me a shit eating grin. "So here I am... *Screw work... fire me!*"

With this poignant soliloquy delivered, Rich made his cast and his rod instantly bent in half as soon as the jig hit the water.

"Richie's gotta a ro-ock, Richie's gotta ro-ock!" we all sang in concert.

"Hey, to hell with all of you! Rocks don't take drag!"

Everyone watched as Richie was pulled off his perch by the fish. We all heard the drag scream as he elbowed his way through the Conga Line of casters along the waterfront. *"Hey! Get out of my way! I got a three thousand dollar fish on here!"* The arguing and cajoling followed Richie into the cove where we lost track of his progress.

"Drop it... Drop the fish," I heard Joe mumble under his breath as Richie rounded the corner. I could not be sure, but I think Joe was a bit more serious about his appeal this time.

A quick turn of the head showed me that half the guys fishing were hooked up. A melee of crossed lines and stumbling bodies formed along the shoreline. I watched an old timer get swept off his feet in the undertow and dragged down the beach. He knocked two other fellas over like dominoes before he regained his footing. I made a cast and felt the rod tip sink. A rock. I hauled back to free my bucktail, and the line took off with a spray of mist through the guides. As I stood transfixed, a huge tail slapped the sea where my bucktail had just been.

"Oh God! You gotta slob Paulie!"

All I could do for the first three minutes is hold on as the fish spooled off line from my reel. I turned smiling at Joe.

Joe looked into my eyes and shook his head, "Always a brides mate..." he said.

I jumped into the water and follow my fish down tide, trying to keep free of the other casters. There were about twenty men between me and that fish. I reached the shelter of an open spot in the surf and I stood erect to fight the beast. It had taken about a hundred yards of line from me. At last I was making some headway. It was very heavy. It felt like I was hooked to the back of a bus! The next few seconds burned into my memory for all eternity. There were three big jerks on my line as the bass shook its head and the tip sprang towards the sky. Just like that, the fish was gone. My heart sank. I retrieved my line and examined the terminal tackle. The eighty pound test Duo lock snap had been twisted out of shape and opened, releasing my prize. I made my way back to the rock.

"Hey! Where is your fish Paulie?" my buddies chanted to me.

"Don't ask."

Ten minutes later, we noticed Richie dragging a bass down the beach, followed by a line of gawkers. He posed as someone took his picture. "Hey Joe! I'm goin back to work now! *You can dock an hour from my pay!*"

"*Son of a bitch,*" Joe whispered.

Rainbows and stripers. I don't know which was more awe inspiring that day on the beach. We stayed till slack water; then headed back home. The "*Jones*" had taken hold and tournament fever would plague us all for the last weeks of the contest. No one would out do Richie's "*work day*" fish. That afternoon of rain, snow and rainbows had made Rich a cool *four thousand bucks.*

How To Win... And Lose.

Before I begin this very personal narrative describing the complex relationships and irony of a fishing obsession, please bear with me as I set the stage for the main event.

For years there had existed a singularly prestigious vehicle for garnering bragging rights within the surfcasting confederacy of Montauk, Long Island. This contest was a battle of fishing duelists, which would begin in the late summer and last for an entire fall run. The event pitted friend against friend, rival against rival, in this highfalutin' competition of surfrat deftness known as the Montauk Locals Striped Bass Tournament. It had as its objective the capture of three of the heaviest stripers for the fall run. Those contestants, who were lucky enough to place a striped bass within the leaders, would divide a purse which was often better than $6,000.00. It was quite amusing, for a while, to participate in this communal compulsion to bag a heavyweight. Most of the town believed it was an honor to be welcomed into this fraternity of Montauk locals, as this annual tournament was invitational in nature, and presumably, only the elite were considered as eligible.

I had watched for a few years from the sidelines while these stalwart fishermen chased linesiders across the town's beaches. Often, I could hear these indubitable fishermen on my CB radio as they discussed the locations of bait and fish. Eaves dropping from the sidelines, it seemed as though there was some sort of "secret code" nestled within their banter. To the uninitiated, the communications seemed meaningless. Cryptic phrases such as "third rock from the sun", "the weed bowl" or "wabbits" were broadcast into the airwaves, which few among the uninitiated could decipher. For me, this banter generated a yearning. I felt envious of this fellowship, imagining them to be the closest of friends who were set upon a common goal. I also wanted that code book.

The tournament's contestants seemed to be culled from an elite class of Montauk surfmen. Selection brought with it the implied belief that a contestant was among the cream of the crop. I would eventually realize that within the ranks of the Locals existed a cabal that believed that only they had any real chance to take the grand prize. Other contestants were considered by this group to be donors, the necessary additive for sweetening the pot. Valued primarily for their monetary contribution, the group begrudgingly accepted them into their domain.

I was chosen as a donor in '93, feeling honored by the invitation, I humbly anted up my two hundred bucks, which immediately cast me into the pool of amateurs. There was however one inherent quality that would eventually compel me to prevail. Born with a fierce tenacity, like a tick, I would not let go until I was satiated.

During my first year as a contestant, I did manage to place a fish on the leader board for a few days. That year had been an exceptionally competitive one and there were several high quality fish taken during the fall. My lowly thirty five pounder was eventually downgraded to fifth place. Pleased, none the less at having made the leader board for several days, I felt justified with my donation. The leaders started to recognize my strength of purpose and I was accepted among the "insiders".

It had been a tense competition indeed, that first year. The leader board changed many times within the final days of the competition. This was not surprising in itself. It is often the case in a well matched horse race that a winner springs from behind. What was most unusual were the two striped bass that James Willburt put on the leader board during the final week of the contest. As it turned out, there were some among the contestants who insinuated that a degree of foul play was involved in the entry of those behemoths.

The incident in question occurred the day before the feast, on Thanksgiving's Eve. Jimmy Willburt had deserted his wife's preparations for the extravagant banquet to come in order to pursue stripers in the midst of a full northeast gale. Storm fishing is considered very productive in Montauk and Jimmy found himself under the Montauk Lighthouse as a diversion from his wife's stifling kitchen. Through sheer luck, Jimmy hit a slob of a fish on the head with his bottle plug during that raging tempest. Not quite believing his own luck, Jimmy gathered his catch and shot down Montauk Highway towards a certified scale. Time and weather seem to slow the would-be contender on his trek to the weigh in station. Every minute brought a loss in weight to the fish, as the beast spit up sea and bait in an effort to swindle the fellow out of a his place on the leader board. It seemed to Jimmy as if the trees were scattering branches and leaves along his course in an effort to stifle his progress. Jimmy arrived at Moe's Tackle shop just before closing time and promptly weighed in his catch on the official tournament scale, accepting a firm slap on the back from Moe and thus becoming the leader of the pack. The fish was over fifty pounds.

By 8am the following morning (Thanksgiving) a brew-ha-ha was initiated among the competitors when Pete and Stewie (*two of the more prominent contestants*) repeated a rumor. Someone had mentioned (*that someone else had heard*) that Jimmy had "taken" this fish from a cooler on his boat in the middle of the night, not from the beach at the Lightouse.

"How could he have landed a slammer in this gale?" was murmured among a select few envious opponents. Somehow a third party, Gary, "the Toad" Stephens, had been insinuated into this controversy as being the originator of the rumor and by being in the wrong place at an inopportune moment.

Gary Stephens was obsessed with fishing that season, as is often the case. He is an eccentric character who often said things out of compulsion, with little concern for other people's opinions. In many ways it seemed as though he had a yen to be the center of attention. Needless to say, he is often the individual mentioned when it comes to some obscure or contentious event. He frequently finds himself in the leading role when blame is being cast.

Back at the setting for this altercation, an element of conspiracy was added to the mix as three fellows met on that cold and blustery morning in the parking lot of Joe's Delicatessen. It was an easy thing, to cast a shadow upon Jimmy's now questionable accomplishment. You see, Willburt was not well loved by certain types among our little community, and any excuse to foil his plans, or tarnish his reputation was acceptable within a singularly exclusive bunch of characters. Jimmy Willburt was known to be the town dogmatist. He had little patience for Hebrews, herbivores, homosexuals and humanists who felt compelled to flaunt their differences while in public. Jimmy would often expound his own peculiar philosophy using the most derogatory terms as he spewed his commentary within the editorial section of the local newspaper.

I was present that morning outside Joe's Market and watched as the proverbial "shit" hit the fan.

"*Toad seen the fish come off his boat...*" Stewie whispered, as we all stood around the front door, waiting for the storm to abate.

"That Willburt is sneaky," said Pete. "But I wouldn't go that far."

Toad was the next to arrive on the scene, and barely had time to jump down from the cab of his truck before the situation developed into a full fledged brouhaha. We all looked on with wide eyes as just then, Willburt flew past the store in his 4x4, throwing great torrents of water asunder and causing a tsunami in the pond sized puddle that formed in Joe's parking lot. Toad was unlucky enough to be within striking distance.

"*Screw you, yah lyin' asshole!*" were the words Willburt shouted from his vehicle at the hapless frog prince. Willburt flew from the cab of his Ford Bronco in a rage, first throwing open, then springing the driver's side door. "*I took that fish fair and square you stupid, addled shithead!*"

"You've got a big mouth, Jimmy, *Let's see if you have big balls!*"

"*You lowlife, sow fed, bastard! I'm sick of this crap! If I catch yah on the beach anywhere near me, I'll... KILL YOU, yah prick!*"

What ensued was a pushing match that had the observers hustling the two combatants away from the market. No real blows had been struck, but bad feelings drifted within the gale winds. By noon the smear of bullshit had spread throughout town. Pros and cons were issued; the latter prevailing. The quiet murmur of impending disqualification for Jimmy's fifty pounder had been whispered among the players.

Jimmy sat at home brooding as his Thanksgiving guests arrived for the feast. Jimmy stewed as he sat alone in his living room chair while his friends and family gaily greeted each other. How dare those bastards steal his glory and deprive him of the thrill of shoving the great fish up thirty five envious arsses? Why, he had already commissioned a taxidermist and sent the carcass off to be mounted! *Damn*, he was livid! Wheels of exculpation spun in his now "tournament addled" brain. With dinner and guests around the table, Jimmy took off on a mission, supposedly to buy a gallon of milk. Excusing himself from his questioning guests, off Jimmy went into the storm. He was not seen again for three hours. His wife could only sigh in disbelief and make lamenting excuses to her guests. When he finally returned, Jimmy had brought home *another* Montauk sea turkey. You see, Jimmy had gone for that container of milk with a slight detour to the Montauk Lighthouse, and in doing so, had hit another fifty pound striper on the head within that still raging storm. There were witnesses this time to confirm his feat of prowess. It was on the up-and-up. Wilburt had another cow to laud.

Jimmy took the tournament that year with his two fish over fifty pounds, garnering both first and second place. It was a forceful win, two grand cows being caught back to back at the very end of competition. One man had taken both purses! Those who would belittle went mum. The dough was his and he took it. Screw 'em all.

That winter, Jimmy created a monument to himself. He stuffed those two bruits and mounted them upon his living room wall, swimming within a huge undersea mural, complete with illustrated rocks and surrounded by teeming bait fish. He had paid an amateur artist to render the watery scene, garnished green and gaudy. To Jimmy, it was a lovely relic. Jimmy's wife was mortified.

****

One year later, the 1994 Tourney was being prepared for with rampant optimism. All the characters assembled themselves with great flourish. Tribes of warriors met at Moe's Tackle to sharpen their hooks. Indeed, it appeared to be coalescing into a good year, with many mid-sized fish blitzing the beaches as the summer waned. Being quite enthusiastic about the whole affair, I had the determination to get on the leader board in earnest that season. Little was I to know that I was destined to poke the proverbial eight hundred pound gorilla in the eye with my fishing pole.

The autumn had been a glorious thing. Warm breezes prevailed in Montauk for weeks as high pressure dominated the month of September. It was as though the summer would not end. I spent many mornings casting at the Lighthouse. The rocks of the reef were very active, holding fish for days on end. Parrot colored darters were the lure of choice for me, as I hooked bass after bass within the sweeping tides. Although the stripers were plentiful, in general they were rather small. More often then not, the fish were in the "teen" class (*fish of thirteen pounds or better, but not breaking twenty*), and the leader board for the Locals Tournament remained vacant for the month of September and most of October. Then began a good run of twenty pound class fish, on Shagwong Point, a shoal known to hold good sized stripers. It seemed as though the entire body of aspiring contestants would show up during those dark evenings of waning light and chilling temperatures. It was a massed school of mullet that had brought in the fish to the promontory, and quite soon we were all catching those fat linesiders.

Bass in the twenty pound class are at the stage in size and aggressiveness where they are capable of making a decent fight of it. This was great fun. If hooked in the mouth, these fish could fool you into believing that they were even larger than they actually were. I happened to place my darter in front of a nice fish one night and beached it. No entries were on the leader board as of yet, so I brought that smallish fish willingly to the scale at Moe's Tackle Shop as the day turned, just for the sake of being number one on the leader board.

It seemed a degree of snobbery was prevalent within the confines of the tournament, as the big shots considered it rather gauche to enter a mediocre fish. At the time I was not savvy to this fact, always assuming that a fish over twenty five pounds was a good fish, and thus, I had stepped into a contemptible situation. To the high hookers of the competition, it seemed to be a joke of sorts.

Moe was there to meet me, as I greased the highway, and confronted the reaper of the scales. "Don't you come in here in your waders! And what is *that? A stinkin' rat!* Take it to the back, *if you must."*

In the rear of Moe's shop is his scale, a rather elaborate triple beam arrangement, with the capacity to weigh fish of over one hundred pounds. My fish went on the scale and Moe started with the balance weight at thirty pounds. The beam didn't budge. *"Jesus Christ, you shoulda let it go..."* Moe grumbled as the scale finally leveled at twenty five point four pounds. "Well, this puts you on the board in first place Melnyk. Don't get to comfortable there. *I doubt this rat will hold for a day."* I took my weigh slip and walked away feeling rather dejected. I did, however, submit the entry and indeed had the thrill of witnessing my name on the board in first place, even though by some people's standards this fish was unworthy.

As tournament fishing goes, when it comes to placing an entry in high standing, it is not comfortable to hang a fish of questionable stature. You see, my striper was seen as a minnow, nothing but a subtle shade of a fish. To the anointed ones this linesider was deserving only of contempt. In the ranks of the Forties and Fifties that were hung in past competitions, this entry was a mere piss-ant.

"How dare Melnyk enter a rat like that!"

"He is a Goog, and that fish will never hold!"

Yes indeed, I was uncomfortable with this entry and woke each day expecting to be cast off the board with this pip-squeak of a fish. It was a good thing that I had my own business because I was often late for work after over sleeping. From that moment on, I would be fishing throughout the nights. I had been convinced that my contender was no contender at all. The poor thing was just "a flash in the pan" a non-event, a laughable diversion to be forgotten shortly, a grease spot on an otherwise spotless leader board. Thus driven to fish, I stood a constant vigil at the waters edge, hoping for a real striper to grace my hook. That was the state of affairs, until November the 11th, when another fish at last bounced that "small-fry" into second place..... Once again, it was my fish.

Shagwong Point was producing for another round and I had found my place surrounded by frantic contestants, each vying for a shot at *"Melnyk's Minnow."* My arms were quite sore from long nights of endless casting and I was just about to call it quits, as this particular night was shaping up to be another slow tide. BANG! My lure was attacked from the depths as a strong fish ran sideways down the line of hapless casters.

"Get out of the STINKIN' WAY! I got a CONTENDA HEEAH!" I shouted through an emotional maelstrom of pent up frustration and perceived aggression. To their credit, all those I confronted used proper etiquette, and made room for me. Upon landing the beast, I was convinced that this fish was over forty pounds. I ran to my truck as my pals leered at my prize in the dimness of a moonless night. Imaginary hounds from hell were chasing me as the truck flew through the ruts and minefields of driftwood that graced the long beach trail back to civilization. I arrived at Moe's Tackle only to realize that it was 3am! Moe would not open until six... I tossed and fidgeted in the cab of my truck until I finally passed out from exhaustion around 5am. I awoke to find Moe in another one of his moods.

"*What the hell is this? Another stinkin' RAT!*" Moe looked from the fish and back at me with disgust. "So I bet you wanna weigh-in slip.... Well.... At least it is bigger than the last runt you brought me... *HA! 28.8 pounds! I don't believe this.*"

So there I was, on the board with both first and second place fish, paltry little wannabes of no significance at all. November had arrived. We all remembered Willburt's late season fish of the last tourney. *Now those were some fish!*

Every night I fought with myself and my tormentors. As a gag, my pals had taken to waking me in the afternoon with news of being bounced off the board; subterfuge of the worst type, for no larger fish had yet been entered. Believe it or not, no one had even entered a third place fish. It would be too embarrassing. Any day Melnyk would be shot down... *Any day now.*

Thus passed November. My nerves were shot as I was getting only two hours of rest and sleepwalking during the daylight. The nights I fished were spent listening to my detractor's cat calls on the CB as we all rallied and drove as a convoy to the next hotspot. "*Hey Melnyk, Markley just weighed in a Fifty! You're out, pal!*" Oh, did they have such good fun at my expense! I am afraid that it all came to a head on the last morning of the tournament.

That morning was rich, crisp and full of potential. We started the hunt on Jones' Reef, a collection of muscle shoals located on the north side of Montauk Point. An entire platoon of contestants was present, pulling fish after fish from a blitz of stripers. It was hard to believe, but out of all those fish caught, none had been larger than twenty pounds.

"Hey Joe! Look over at the Point!" someone shouted.

We all turned to see a cacophony of birds and splashing fishtails exploding among the rocks of the Lighthouse abutment.

It was like a race as twenty surfcasters high-tailed it for those rocks. In the midst of this forced march, and locked within the confines of my waders, my constitution began to fail me and I was stricken with a case of the cramps. I remember doubling over as I charged into the reeds at the base of the Lighthouse, shedding my waders just in the nick of time to pass a royal shit. No paper... *damn.*

Upon cresting those rocks under the Lighthouse, I found little room to maneuver. All the good perches were taken! Tails as big as brooms were sweeping bait in the waters below, and my stomach turned another knot. It was a school of big fish for sure. Gannets dove into a surf teaming with bait. *Herring*! Everyone seemed to be being dragged along the jetty, pursuing their fish. It was a ruckus scene of mass hysteria as lines tangled and the linesiders fought. Making my first cast, I immediately felt the weight of a good fish, which ran down the rocks towards Scott's Cove. I held my rod overhead as I jostled and cajoled my pals into showing me quarter. My luck seemed to be holding as I reached the cove and saw the fat silhouette of a fish in the water. It looked as though I had hooked a real contender for sure, until I beached the freakin' thing. It was a *stinkin' bluefish!* The Chopper had shredded my leader! *Fuck.* Now I was forced to re-tie my terminal gear before re-entering the fray.

As I returned to my rock I met Willburt standing in my place. "Hey Willburt, *get off my rock!"*

Somehow, this moment seems to be the birthplace of a deep animosity Wilburt held toward me from that point on. "BITE ME ASSHOLE!" He shouted at me with a sneer.

"Look *Dick weed*, Move your ass or I'll move it for you!"

"*Hah! You, and what army?"*

What army? "I don't need no stinkin' army *Willey-burt!* **I'm an army of *ONE!*"**

"Paulie, *cool it. Its just a rock..."* Joe said to me from a perch below.

Etiquette. I was loosing my cool. My buds had gone through calisthenics to give me the chance to land that stupid bluefish, so I had to accept the fact that I would be a spectator for a while. I was forced to sit it out as I watched Willburt hook up. As it pulled him to the waterline just off to our left I scrambled for the perch, taking back my high ground, a not too kosher move, but what the hell.

"*You're a looser, Melnyk!*" Willburt hollered up at me. In return, I gave him the finger.

I made a cast and at the end of my swing I watched as the tip guide on my rod went flying off. *SHIT*! The glue had come loose! Willburt was right there with some choice words. "***Ha! You broke your tip off!***"

With all those fish in front of me, I could do little to rectify the situation. I made a tentative cast and my line broke as it caught the bare end of my rod tip. I lost a bucktail. Things were spiraling out of control as equipment failure became my bane. As I reeled in what was left of my line, I noticed the screw for the bale-spring on my reel was loose. I used my thumbnail, trying as best as I could to tighten the thing. It was not good enough.

"*HEY MELNYK! Your off the board! I got the winning fish in my hands, asshole!*" Looking down the row of fishermen, I took notice as my pal, Richie Michelson, hollering with joy, held a fish over his head. It was big. Richie ran off to weigh in his prize.

"Well, you knew it couldn't last, Paulie." Joe said to me from my right as he cast into the bait below us. I went numb. Another wave of nausea swept over me as I made my final cast. PING! *What the hell?* Oh my GOD! That bale screw had backed out completely and sprung with a pop, into the surf.

"***GOO-GAN!.. GOO-GAN!.. GOO-GAN!..***" Willburt chanted, seemingly, quite pleased with himself.

That was the clincher. I turned my rod around and began to use the piece-of-shit reel like a sledge hammer, bashing it on the rocks below my feet. Joe's eyes bugged out of his head as he witnessed my emotional breakdown. Pieces of metal sailed past his face as the reel came apart with a satisfying crunch!

"*What the hell, Paulie!*" Joe gasped in shock at my performance. It was a good performance at that... one of my best.

I had lost it. "***Later dudes!***" Turning, I climbed the rocks and began the walk back along the jetty, towards the truck. Back to the sanity of home. At the foot of the sea wall I bumped into Dennis, Joe's brother. "Hey Paulie! *Where you goin'?*" He looked down to see what was left of my rod hanging from my grasp. "*There ain't no fish here Denny!*" was all

I could think to say. Dennis took a look at the birds and tails churning in the sea, and seemed to shiver. *"No fish?"* he said, as I turned and walked away. I *was* shaking when I reached my truck. My guts were killing me and I was sure I would shit myself. I can remember the hypnotic strobe of the sun as it flashed between the winter-bare trees along Montauk Highway. It was over. I was dejected. I slept until 1:00pm, a fitful sleep of bad dreams filled with visions of sharks breaching the Point rocks and dragging me down. When I finally stirred, I couldn't bring myself to rise and call Joe to find out the score. Who had bested me in that blitz? Richie? Dennis? The tails... *The tails...* At 3:00pm, the phone rang, waking me from those fitful dreams.

"Paul?" it was Joe. "What *happened* to you, pal?"

"Nothin'. What happened under the Light?"

"Richie weighed in his fish... It was only twenty four pounds... You won pal, *first and second place*, just like Willburt did last year! Congratulations."

Was I still dreaming? How could this be? I had witnessed those broom sized tails in the surf at the Lighthouse. I could not fathom that out of all those fish, *which I saw with my own eyes*, nobody could land a striper larger than my two stinkin' rats! Two months of hell were over... *Yes!* I had taken the Montauk Locals Tournament with a record that I suspect will last forever. ***I had taken the purse with the two smallest fish to ever win the Locals contest!***

Bones of contention cannot be buried in frozen ground. The plot continued to twist. The night after my win, Willburt called a *"special meeting"* of the tournament committee in an attempt to extend the contest for two more weeks! The vote was close. My friend Joe was the deciding vote. The contest was certified over. *Those damned little fish.*

The awards dinner was anti-climatic. The prizes were given to grumbles of discontent as I was handed the $4,000.00 that was my share of first and second place. I gave an acceptance speech, as is customary for the reigning champion. I can remember it to this day.

"I am the egg man, (*I pointed to myself*). THEY are the egg men! (*I pointed at the congregation*). ***I AM THE WALRUS! GOOG, GOOG, ACHEW!"*** This went completely over their heads, and they stared at me with moon eyes.

Along with my prize money, another special award was to be presented. A beautifully wrapped box was presented to me. Inside were the bent and broken remains of my busted up reel. It seems my buddies fished it out of the rocks for me. This was the booby prize- "*Goog of the Year.*" The audience jeered. I took my winnings and ran before they made me give it back. As I walked out the door, I heard Wilburt mumble, "*Drop dead, Melnyk.*"

So, in '94, I was the lucky Googan that won the Montauk Locals Bass Tournament. Through the following winter I was subjected to the effects of the discontent that continued to prevail among a certain crew. There was even an attempt to shame me out of the cash. The suggestion was made by a certain committee member that I donate the winnings to a proposed youth division. I bought a **Van Staal** reel, custom rod, and put the down-payment on a new pickup, instead! This shadow over my triumph became like a thorn in my side. I was mortified that my friends and associates would attempt to change the tournament to suit their personal vanities by contemplating extending the match for another two weeks. With a good deal of introspection, I came to the conclusion that I needed to make a better showing in the next contest. Next season it would be a goal of mine to become a truly accomplished surfrat. I would put a few cows on the board next year for sure! With a new attitude, I went about learning how to target the larger striped bass.

****

Pope Noel was there along side of me out on those far rocks, which we would eventually learn to conquer. Now let me tell you about Pope.

Livingstone Pope Noel the third, to be exact. Yes this *is* his given name. A moniker of this sort could not be a fabrication. Our friendship began one cold November night in 1993, during another one of those howling Nor' Easter's. I had decided this was my moment and off I went to pursue the quest. Through cold mist and flying sea foam, I turned the corner towards the rocks of the Lighthouse. I could just make out the shape of a person standing at my favored fishing perch and I intended to roust him, but he would not capitulate this "choice" piece of real estate and we stood together as close as clams. We both could sense that big stripers would be there during this cold night and we refused to give eachother any leeway, as we cast for the same piece of structure known to sit within the waters ahead. We were uncomfortably close. The place was lonely; just the two of us to brave the surf and bitter cold. After what seemed endless silence we did converse. I had snagged his lure and in my zeal to banish this invader, I cut his line and his lure was lost. Whether I did it by accident or on purpose, I can not recall, Let's just say the lure was stuck in the rocks and I pulled on his line *a bit to hard*.

Through the darkness, he loomed over the rocks like some mythical gargoyle, guarding the gates to the Cathedral. He carried a six foot four inch frame, and I could just make out his face as he glared at me through the sweeping Lighthouse beacon. "*You dickweed...*" I heard as the giant mumbled under his breath. It is amazing how the mind can pick out certain things through the crashing of waves. I thought better of my 'lost lure strategy' as I surveyed my options. The bastard was big. Prudence was called for. "Jeeze fella, I'm sorry."

I just discerned the phrase "*You better be...*" through the wind. Discretion. I reached into my bag and brought out a brand new darter, still in the packaging. "Look.... that was my fault... Here."

"You sure?"

"Yeah, no sweat..." My act of supplication had broken the ice. At first I found it difficult to relate to this big Texan. He spoke with a Gulf Coast drawl that was out of place under this bluff. "What did you say your name was? *Poke?*"

Louder this time...."Naw, not *Poke*, ***Pope...*** Pope Noel."

"Post?"(I actually thought I had heard ***Dope****, but that, I would not dare repeat to a six foot, four stranger, being alone, in the dark...)*

"Not Post! *Pope!*..... P-O-P-E spells Pope!" (*I heard two "pops" as he emphasizes those 'p's*). "You know... ***like the old guy in Rome.......***" (*implied: "you dimwit!")* I gave it up completely, when it came to his last name.

As the night progressed and through the ensuing bull session, I connected with this guy. I was in the presence of a kindred spirit. The fact that we bagged several jumbo stripers made it evident that there was a positive aspect to the providence of this new association. I soon found out that Pope was quite insane. "I spent two tours in 'Nam in the door of a Marine Chinook," Pope said. "I seen my buddy git his nose blowed off one day. *Damn near the funniest thin' I ever seen!* Two weeks later the chopper crashed and they all got killed, 'cept me. *Didn't even get a scratch... He he he!...*" Pope's laugh was like that wheezing dog in the old Hanna Barberra cartoon, Muttley; not a laugh as much as a wheezing series of H's all strung together.

Another time, when I needed winter money, Pope hired me to sling a brush for his painting company. Pope was a house painter by trade. We were working in an estate in Bridgehampton in the dead of February. As we were discussing the work necessary to finish the master bedroom, Pope decided to relate a peculiar yarn to me.

"Paul, (*When Pope says my name, it often sounds like P-hall).* keep yer eyes on the job not the clients stuff, she is a friend of mine. Met her in A.A. (*Pope is a recovering alcoholic; Montauk is a town full of recovering alcoholics).* She's a *real looker,* man! I come in here one day to talk about paintin' her bedroom. I got here early... *by chance, yah understand?* I go into the bedroom to look around, an' there's a pair of her knickers on the floor. I look around, no one's there, so I put the things over my head. Don't know why really, seemed like the right thing tah do, at the time... So there I am with my ears stickin' out the leggin's! I take a deep breath, like this...(Pope breathes in deep through his nose, like a bird dog sniffing the ground.)... *and in she walks!* She stands there, lookin' at me, makin' this weird face, an' she says,"*Pope... You're really screwed up!*" He, he, he... !(*that wheeze*) 'en she shakes her head an' walks out! I got the job the next day! He, he, he...!"

Yes, I have no doubt. Pope is insane.

Another character to bring into this equation is none other than that outlandish surf rat by the name of Jack Yee. Jack is considered to be the elemental extreme surfcaster, having pioneered wetsuiting and rock hopping in the early sixties along with "the Professor" Jack Frech.

I had seen Jack cruising the beaches in his old truck for years but I had never really had a good conversation with him. He would greet me as "Melznick" as he still does to this day. I take no offense at this, for at first I thought that Jack was a bit deaf and couldn't twist my name around his tongue. I later figured out that Jack had a 'special name' for each person in his life. This slur of my name is not offensive to me and I now accept it as another one of those famous Montauk "terms of endearment." Jack is also crazy. Jack has been known to chase people down the beach with a hatchet. This is quite comical when you realize that Jack is five foot two seventy years old and with a bad case of emphysema.

Last, but not to be minimized, as this individual has held a unique position in my life, is Dominique, to this day, one of my best friends. I met Dom in 1967, when we were both 12 years old. I had learned that summer, through the superintendence of Grandpa Rinkiewicz, to hunt for "*Da leetle rabbets*." Thus, I would stalk the vermin each morning at dawn, slinking up and down the silent lanes of Montauk, like the comical character, Elmer Fudd ("*Shhh! I'm wabbit huntin'!"*). During one of these forays, I was approached by a sedan, a Citroen to be exact, inside of which was a kid of my stature, and an adult. Immediately, I threw my 22 pellet gun into the bushes, but the jig was up, I had been caught!

"Hey! Kid! Wacha doin'!" said the kid through the passenger window.

"Aw, I ain't doin' nuthin'...."

"Sure you are!" says the kid, "You're HUNTIN'!" Now I was cornered in deceit.

"Nah... I was just takin' a walk."

"With za gun? You arrr 'unting*!*" Now the adult was involved. He spoke with a distinctive *French* accent. Busted. I looked around for a place to run. I was trapped a mile away from home with this kid and some old French guy (*his Pop?*) I had no doubt, I was going to jail.

"Hey look kid. *I'm huntin' too!*" With that the kid held up a shiny new Crossman 704 air rife... with a telescopic site! "Me and my dad are crusin' around, shootin' rabbits from the car!" *Shooting rabbits from a car?* With an adult! This could not be true! "Yah! I love to shoot rabbits! We eat 'em!"

"Zey arrr very tender zis year!" The father added.

Wow, this kid eats the little bunnies! Hell, I just kill them and cut off their feet. I was curing them and selling the things to my pals as good luck charms. (*I had always found this rather ironic*).

Well, as the worm turned, we became fast friends that summer. We hunted rabbits every morning, sometimes filling a ruck sack with them. We decimated the rabbit population that year, the two of us stalking the rodents along the roads and fairways of the Montauk Golf Course. The local gardeners were pleased to find their vegetables unmolested, thanks to our diligence! It was a good trade between us. I would get the feet and the skins, and Dom would get the meat. You see, Dominique was decidedly French by birth, along with his folks and his mom could make the most delicious rabbit stew. It is quite true, dear reader, it tastes like chicken.

Thus began a friendship that has lasted over forty years. Even to this day, Dom will find his way to Montauk (*sometimes by way of Charles De Gaulle Airport*), in the fall, to join in another manic episode, fishing included.

In the fall of '95, Dom was ensconced in Unit #7 at my motel, Ann Breyer's Cottages, of which, I was the proprietor and guardian. His willing participation in the events to follow is uncontested.

****

Well as it went, Pope and I began to press the outer rocks during the early summer months of 1995. We tried the best we could to find the more productive of the far rocks, but it was apparent that we were in need of some instructive assistance.

"Paul, that old "Chinee" Jack Yee said he would show me all the secret rocks for a hundred bucks! You wanna come? We'll split it!"

So with a bribe paid, Jack took on two protégées. I do feel we got our monies worth. Mr. Yee supplied a great deal of input for those hundred bucks. Through Jack, Pope and I learned the finer nuances of wet suiting, as well as the locations of the best of the perches.

As the summer of '95 progressed, the two of us began to move toward the mid-water rocks, with Jack gaining vicarious pleasure as he watched from the beach. Jack's better days had come and gone. Even back then, Jack would only fish from places he could drive to.

I would often leave my work at any hour to fish. You see, in running the roost at **Ann Breyer's Cottages**, a collection of tourist bungalows located at Montauk Harbor, I was afforded an abundance of free time. I took advantage of this freedom during the weekdays. I would often go on long solo fishing safaris and thought of myself as quite proficient at several productive fishing spots in and around the Lighthouse.

It is a fact that in Montauk there are certain locations that can be counted on to hold fish with regularity. The best of these spots are located in deep waters surrounding the Montauk Lighthouse. There is one rock in particular that changed my life and literally caused me to re-think my style.

I often spent my afternoons chasing what few stripers I could cull from the late summer surf. For me, the concept of using a wetsuit had not yet sunken in and I was still frequenting the north side rocks in neoprene waders and a dry top, standing with the crowds that competed for the honey holes along the shoreline.

It was a haze filled evening the first time I realized what could be accomplished by casting from those *really* far off rocks. Standing on one of my favorite perches, under the concession stand at the Point, my bucktails were being lost within the rocks on a regular basis that afternoon. The bass were scarce and the sun was poaching me in my waders. Then I happened to noticed a fellow in a wetsuit heading into the water. Being curious now, I watched him enter the surf from the cove, an area I thought to have no fishable rocks. He waded deeper until, amazingly, he began to swim for the open sea. There was a bit of white breakwater forming in the ocean where the guy was headed. Before long, the swimmer had jumped up onto a submerged platform a good seventy yards from the beach! As he stood, his legs remained under water to about mid thigh. Now this was intriguing! It took no more than two minutes and three casts before the wetsuiter had a fish hooked! From where I stood the striper looked to be a big one, and his sucess was followed by another hookup and then another! I had been fishless for the last two hours and was quite frustrated while watching this guy. I spent another hour scrutinizing the fellow. He must have caught twenty fish.

Stumbling back to my truck, I drove off the beach, intrigued. The performance from that sunken rock had made a lasting impression on my eager cranial synapses. It seemed quite clear to me that what the wetsuiter had accomplished was not at all difficult. By God, I was gonna find out for myself what was going on out there!

The next afternoon I returned to the cove with my own scheme for acquiring the rights to the distant rock. It was a slack tide, and through these still waters, I stumbled into the surf, dressed in neoprene waders, cleated boots and carrying a fishing rod and plug bag. Once again, I noticed a lip curl as each passing swell slipped over that coveted platform. Piece of cake! I waded out into the cove and headed toward the turbulence ahead. When I got within ten yards of the rock, the bottom of the sea dropped out from under me and I had to float the last few yards as the tide slung me onto the rock. With the help of a swell, I floated right on top of the thing and stood up. This would be the easiest location that I had ever been to!

I made a few casts with a bucktail jig and was graced with the strike of a nice fish. In a few moments I had a twenty pound bass at my feet. Wow! This *was* a honey hole! Three more casts and I had landed two big stripers, as simple as that!

The tide had picked up. It moved between my legs and threatened to sweep me away and I had to lean into the current to regain my balance as I cast. About ten yards ahead I saw a plug float past. Wow! Maybe I could snag it and get a freebee! I cast towards the lure and just missed it. In the corner of my eye I noticed more objects drifting in the tide. Look! More plugs! Some schmuck musta dropped his tackle box into the surf! This time I reached into the drink and grabbed a particularly expensive plug. I knew this because I had just bought one like it. Hmm... just like it... Looking down into my bag, I now figured out who the schmuck was! The latch must have been loose on my bag when I waded out. My plugs bobbed within the forming rip. ***No way!*** The thought of how much it would cost to replace my gear compelled me to jump into the drink and I grabbed as many plugs as I could reach. I snagged maybe three. *Oh well...* As I turned to climb back up onto the rock, I found that it was disappearing into the distance. *What the hell...* Swimming my ass off, I could not make it back to the perch as the building force of the forming rip dragged me away. It was no easy task, trying to swim in waders and cleats. The waders float you up and the cleats drag you down.

The bottom was nowhere to be found as I stretched my legs trying to find some purchase. Water began to leak passed my cinched belt and I realized that straining for the bottom was a bad idea. I struggled to reach for other rocks as they flew past. I was so tired that all I could do was claw and kick at them. No way to stop. It appeared that I would drift out to sea. Pure panic set in. I was in waders, I was physically exhausted and it seemed as though I was going to drown. I tried desperately to reach the bottom with my toes. Thrashing and kicking seemed to bring me a bit closer to the beach, and I threw up a frenzy of spray as I crawled along, scratching at the surface of the sea. I finally made it into some shallower water as a wave slammed into me, tumbling me in the wash. Coughing and spitting water, I was caught by a rock that ripped my waders. The last wave threw me onto the beach, spitting me out like a bad piece of meat. I dragged myself out of the surf and collapsed. A tourist came up to me to see if I was still alive. "Hey! You OK Buddy?"

"Oh yeah, I'm fine... no sweat." Thus waving him off as I struggled to catch my breath.

My plug bag was gone. My waders were ripped. I had a lump on my head the size of an egg. Staggering down the beach, I collapsed into the truck. As I sat, rethinking my experience, my thoughts focused on the fact that I was able to hook three fish in fifteen minutes. It was then that I decided to tell Pope about the adventure. Maybe he was interested in accompanying me for the next jaunt out to Weakfish Rock.

It was a delicate task for the two of us, swimming to that rock. This table like structure was set within the deep water at the meat of the Point rip and showed itself only as a standing wave in the current at mid-tide. Of course this was when we needed to be there, so on this next attempt we would truly press the envelope of fisherman's luck. It occurred to us that it was probably better to swim in dive gear so Pope and I set out one afternoon to purchase wetsuits. In no time we were ready for another shot at it.

We started the swim, this time wearing wetsuits and cleated shoes, in a place we were sure would give us a good chance to drift to the rock. The idea once again was to grab hold and stand up. Not a problem.

I was the first to attempt the trek, since I already had some experience. Confident now that I was dressed in thick neoprene, I set off into the cove and walked halfway there before being forced to swim. I drifted towards the boulder as the current took hold. Pope provided support and body-English.

"More to the left you Moron! OK, you got it! Just grab a hold!"

The throne of the thing was a good five feet across, big enough for the two of us to stand comfortably side by side and I reached for a sharp ledge on the perch, attempting to grab it. The rip current caught hold of my legs and my shoulder was jarred as the edge of the rock slipped from my grasp and I began to head towards Block Island.

"Aw.. You're done fer now boy! He, he, he.... I'll be readin' 'bout you in the papers!" Pope cheered from the beach.

No doubt, I *was* screwed. I tried to swim inshore but instead, I was drawn further into the Point rip even as I pulled frantically with my free arm. If I passed the Lighthouse, I would be lost... I sought a way out of the mess, clinging at the straws of hope. I began to bump into things along the bottom with my feet. These were submerged boulders just visible as small ripples on the current. As I neared another, I kicked out with great force and the tenacity brought about with a surge of pure adrenaline! A lucky strike sent me several yards closer to the beach.

"**USE YOUR POLE, MORON!**" Pope was shouting as he chased me down the rock strewn shore line.

"WHAT!"

"**YOUR POLE!**" Pope pantomimed a rowing motion. "**LIKE A DANGED GONDOLIER!** ***PUSH YOURSELF WITH YOUR ROD OR YOU'RE A GONNER!***"

It was worth a try.......The pole went completely under before I felt the bottom. It just caught the reef as I held the last two feet of it between the tips of my outstretched fingers. I attempted to push with the butt against the rocks. The rod tip bent dangerously, threatening to snap, but I did seem to move closer to the shore. With each push, I made headway towards the surf zone until a wave took hold of me. I rolled around in the wash like a wounded seal and finally managed to stand; thoroughly exhausted.

"*What you lallygaggin' 'bout there boy? Yow-ee! That looks like some fun! It's my turn now!*"

I got to watch Pope's eyes bug out as he, too, attempted, and failed to secure Weakfish Rock.

"Use your pole YOU IDJOT!" I yelled. (*It felt good.*)

"SHUT the HELL UP!"

On the second try, one of us caught hold of that rock and managed to stand up. We figured out that you could grab hold of your buddy as he went sailing by and soon we had it licked.

That summer became the summer of "Weakfish Rock" for us. People took to calling us Pope-Paul, as we were a regular fixture on the horizon for many evenings. We would bail one slammer after another out there while drifting eels in the rip. It was crazy. We took to experimenting with methods to swim out, and were soon using fins to power through the tide. Pope figured he could glue a set of spikes to the bottom of his flippers, instead of trying to change into cleats upon arriving out there on the rock. I developed the final design which used stainless steel screws sunk through the soul of high density polyurethane dive fins to act as spikes. These fins could be slipped on and fastened to your feet with one smooth motion. We soon took to calling any fish less than twenty five pounds a "Weakfish Rat." They were all big fish that summer. We were also attracting an audience as the guys on the beach watched us toss keepers back one after another.

"This keeps up; we got the Locals Tourney all sewed up, tight-like!"

Sewed up.

Before long, fall was upon us and once again the Montauk Local's Striped Bass Tournament was on our agenda. Pope and I were determined to place among the contenders on the leader board, if not win outright.

The Locals Tourney had begun, along with all the mayhem that was to follow. Pope and I swam to Weakfish Rock on the afternoon of the first day of the tournament, thinking about nothing more than testing our luck. The two of us were not very enthused as the water had been quiet and there had not been many fish in the last few days. After a time, we amused ourselves with mindless banter.

"Don't STOMP yer feet on the rock, Moron!"

"Lay off, will ya! My feet are cold."

"You're scarrin' the fish!"

"Fish don't scare like that!"

"Do Too! I seen 'en spooked in the river back home."

"Then why do they put rattles in lures? *To scare the fish away?*" I then felt a pickup and I set the hook. The fish was not a fighter.

"Your feet ain't no rattle! Hey, wacha got there?"

"I don't know, but it's commin' right in."

"Anyways, the damned fish are spooked by... *Well will you look at that, HOLY-SHIT*!"

I looked down at the water that was now up to our knees and saw the bass. *A great, mighty slob of a fish!*

"HOLEE-SHEEEIT! DAMMIT BOY! YOU JUST WON THE LOCAL'S TOURNEY ON THE VERY FIRST DAY!" At arms distance from me swam

the biggest striper that I had seen all year, probably a fish in the mid forty pound class, if not bigger. It had come in like its belly was sitting on a skateboard. No fight to it at all. It was securely fastened to my line, the hook having been swallowed so deep that I could almost see it hanging out of its asshole. "*I don't believe this...*" Pope said as he shook his head.

"*YEE-HA*!" I hollered at the top of my lungs as I grabbed the beastie's lip. "*Scares the fish does it*! Damn! *I'm stompin' my feet from now until Christmas!*"

A strange look came over Pope. It was a look of both dread and determination. Staring me in the eye, he declared, "*Let it go, Paul...*"

"ARE-YOU-NUTS?"

"Let it go. You can't keep it!"

"Why the hell NOT!"

"*If you keep it, then nobody 'ill enter the damn tournament. There are only ten guys signed up right now and the others are all late comers!*"

You see, during those years, the Local's Tournament had a clause in the rules that any would-be contender could anti-up anytime during the three months of the contest. The one stipulation was that there would be a day's grace period in which a contestant was exempt from entering any fish. Most of the entrants were lazy and hedged their bets, not entering until the fall run was full on and the fish, thick. Last year had a bumper crop of donors in October because of those two lowly twenties of mine. There had been thirty two entries in total; a bumper crop. Now Pope told me that there were only ten contestants entered to date.

"I AIN'T LETTIN' IT GO!"

"YOU'RE A SELFISH PRICK! YOU"RE GONNA RUIN THE TOURNEY FOR EVERYONE, KEEPIN' THAT FISH!"

"I -AIN'T- LETTIN'- IT -GO!!!!"

"***YOU SUCK!***"

"NO, YOU SUCK!!!" In the distance a dragger chugged past us, drawing a crest at its bow as it pressed for the open sea. I picked the fish from the water and held it in my arms. God, it was a big one. I was positive it was my personal best to date. I had my rod tucked under my arm as bigger swells began to slap into us, caused by the dragger's wake. My fish was picked up by a following wave. As it slipped from my grasp, it began to slowly swim away. No worries. The beast was soundly hooked by the tonsils and it was not going anywhere. I grabbed my rod and began to reel her back in.

Something was not right. The crank wouldn't turn and my rod was starting to bend as the reviving fish took to swimming hard for a change! I watched as the rod bent in half... *What the hell...* I opened the drag on the reel and things began to go wrong in a big way.

"*What the hell you doin' boy? Yer fish is runnin'!"*

I tried to pull line from the reel, *but nothing happened!* As hard as I tugged, no line would come off the spool. With three more big pumps of her tail the fish strained at the line. *PING!* Gone.... I watched her slowly sink into the depths. Free.

"YOU ASSHOLE!"

I looked at the reel. What could have gone wrong? Wait a sec...*Shit*, my thread thin line had *wrapped* itself around the bailess roller bearing, probably as I held the fish in my arms. It had tied itself in a knot.

"*YOU ASSHOLE! YOU JUST WON AND LOST THE TOURNEY IN THE SAME BREATH!* YEE-HA! *You are a dumb bastard... Wait 'til I tell everybody*!"

And he did tell everyone. He positively beamed; my pal did, describing how I had dropped the winning fish on the first day of the contest to anyone who would listen.

****

It was during the following week, and the day before the opening of the Montauk Surf Classic Tournament, that I decided to make another trip out to Weakfish Rock to see how the fishing was going to fare for the contest. Another trial run. Within the previous weeks, Pope and I had figured out how to use flippers to swim to the rock with relative ease and I felt prepared to make a solo trip. A rare celestial event had made for interesting tides. The sun and moon had conspired to create a lunar eclipse within the next twenty four hours. As I arrived, I saw that the water was the lowest I'd seen yet, and the far rocks were sticking high above the water. I literally walked right out to Weakfish Rock for the first time in my life that afternoon. I put my flippers on as I climbed the rock, just in case, and began to fish.

Because of this unusual full moon tide, the afternoon flood was higher then normal. The water had risen up to my ribs as the rip reversed and ran full tilt back into Scott's Cove. Thank God the sea was fairly calm, because a stray swell lifted me off the table just as an especially large cow pulled me from the perch and set me adrift. I found myself attached to a slammer while being pulled around in ten feet of water. Within moments this fish had flipped me upside down when it swam straight at me and then, under my legs. I never thought of myself as a quick study, but at that moment I learned to fight from the water, freestyle. After the initial shock of being manhandled by this fish, I began to gain the semblance of control. With a moment of serendipity, I figured out how to kick with my flippers to keep my balance. I managed to steady myself in the water as I battled with the beast. It made a dash for the open water and pulled me along in the current. After a few tense minutes, I lost the brute, which broke my line. I had fought my first striper from the water! Even in losing the fish, I was enthralled by this unique experience. This was that moment of quiddity that soon became my singular compulsion, the birth of skishing.

Skishing is a verb that I am proud to say I have originated. It is also an anagram, roughly formed by the conjunction of two words, skiing and fishing. I named it so because of the innate ability for large fish to fight so fiercely and they will pull the swimmer through the water. With stronger beasts, it is possible to be dragged to the extent of creating a wake. The true definition of this technique is swim-fishing, but somehow the combination of these two words *(swishing)* just did not seem appropriate at the time. Skishing it was.

Fool that I am, I ran home and told my pals Joe Gav, and Attila about how much fun I had fighting a fish while treading water, and how, exactly, this technique worked. Attila was, at once, intrigued. My buddy Joe, to his credit, shook his head and suggested that I should keep it to myself.

"Paul, if this gets out, a lot of people will be upset."

I explained that I had no intention of swimming through the tournament. Joe said to keep quiet, all the same.

The following day was the clincher. The Montauk Surf Classic would open at noon. The Local's Tournament had begun the weekend before. The two contests coincided with eachother for the next three days. This overlap was an opportunity to fish two events simultaneously. *I was psyched!*

Promptly at noon, I took to the surf, this time without my fins, but instead, wearing a pair of Korkers over boots. I walked out to the rock at the very bottom of the tide. I cast live eels from Weakfish Rock all afternoon during the flood with fanatical persistence, but to no avail. The fish seemed to avoid my bait. Then finally, at the end of the incoming tide, I hooked and landed a bass of almost thirty pounds. The beach was full of enthusiastic contestants at the time. I had quite an audience. Not only did this fish give me the win in the Montauk Classic, but this same fish also made the number one slot in the Montauk Local's competition. Once again, I was the first person on the board.

I am quite fond of big bass bragging rights. I find it almost as satisfying as catching the darned things... I pursued this aspect of my obsession with considerable vigor, and I spent the whole evening showing off my fish. One of the last bums to have the fish shoved up his anus happened to be the person who would eventually become my nemesis, Jimmy Willburt.

"Hey Jimmy! Guess what? I'm on the leader board of the Classic with a thirty pounder!"

"Ha, hah! Yah, I heard about that Melnyk, you were swimmin' again, weren't you?"

"No ***Jimmy***, I was standing on Weakfish Rock, and as a matter of fact, I walked there."

"That ain't possible. That rock is in ten feet of water!"

"Not today it wasn't." I smiled.

"Not what I heard."

"I've got a hundred witnesses."

"I heard you were swimming and hooked a fish using fins and a wet suit."

"That was yesterday, I caught the thirty today."

"Ha, ha, ha! We'll see about that!"

"What the hell are you talkin' about?"

"We're havin' a special meetin' later this weekend, you will be the main event!"

Willburt was a member in standing on the Montauk Local's Tournament Rules Committee. In fact, Willburt was one of the founding members of the game. There were a total of six members on this committee, most of whom were my pals, including Joe and Pope.

****

That night, as the tournament committee met, I went to the

Lighthouse to collect my winnings with Dominique. My little incident with Willburt had been wearing on my mind and somehow I felt as though the proverbial sword was hanging over my head.

"Hey Paul, don't let that asshole Willburt get to you! You got the dough Dude!"

"I don't trust that guy, Dom. You remember what he tried to do to me last year."

"To hell with him Pal, take the money and run!"

We were hitting on a flask of rum at the time, sitting in the Weed Bowl at the Point. I was well on the way to getting soused. As we walked to the presentation area, I was feeling waves of paranoia course through my brain as the liquor took hold. There were about a hundred fellas hanging out for the free food and party favors. As I walked to the podium area I heard a group of guys talking.

"Man, *he swam to that rock!* I seen him..."

"Well, you know how he is."

Were they talking about me? *They WERE talking about me!* Anger rose within the core of my rum soaked being.

"*Who the hell are you talkin' about?*" I said to the group of out-of-towners.

"*What's YOUR problem, asshole*"

"Hey, that's the dude that won..."

"Shhh, Paul... There are *five* of them!" Dom whispered in my ear.

"Screw that, Dom!"

"No, you fool! They're not talking about you! I heard 'em talkin' about some guy named Juan!"

"What?"

The rest of the awards ceremony was a blur. I did manage to stagger up to the podium to get my check for five hundred bucks. I also received a gift certificate for a fish mount of my choice from a Long Island taxidermist. All in all, a good haul. Dom and I left for home with a buzz and a few laughs. Life was good.

The day after the awards gig I found out the committee did indeed have that *"special meeting"* to discuss the ramifications of "Melnyk's" win and the fish I consequentially entered into the Local's Tournament. That morning, Joe handed me a sheet of paper as I came into his store for a cup of coffee.

It was then that I learned that the rules for the Local's Tournament had been amended. These new rules will forever be known as *"The*

Melnyk Clause" in my mind. Wetsuits were now forbidden. Evan's Rock, Shark Rock, Breagan's Rock, Weakfish Rock and for good measure, ALL ROCKS that you have to float, hop or dance to, at any time, during any tide, were now, and irrevocably, declared "Off Limits". Needless to say, *this irked me.*

"Joe, how could you do this to me?"

"You did it to yourself. You shoulda kept mum about that fish."

"What about my fish on the board?"

"Don't worry, it's still good. We decided you caught it before the rules changed."

I was dumbfounded that my friends would change the rules ten days into the contest.

"Look Paul, we run the tournament and we can do whatever we want with it," was how Dennis, Joe's brother and committee member, explained it.

The next day was spent at my motel with Dom. We discussed how lame we thought these new rules were. They seemed to only affect *my* fishing, since Pope had agreed to the premise. Dom and I were surprised that Pope would vote to exclude wetsuits, since he was my partner on Weakfish Rock and he was aware of the great fishing we had there. I spent the rest of the afternoon writing an essay called "The Flash of Silver" as sort of a cathartic exercise. It was a piece about my love for fishing, which I submitted to the **Long Island Fisherman**, and published the following week. Days passed and soon and there was a stack of **Fisherman** magazines next to Joe's cash register.

"Hey Paul, did you see this week's **Fisherman**?" He pointed to the magazines.

"Have I seen it? I wrote it!"

"No, not your story! The letter to the editor that *Jimmy* wrote!"

Jimmy Willburt had written a diatribe about my victory in the Montauk Classic. It was not an amiable review of my tournament win. Willburt took up a half page of the editorial section with his scathing letter, in which he called me a cheater for swimming to Weakfish Rock, *(which I didn't)* and doubly so, because I wore a wetsuit while doing it! He continued his rant, creating a manifesto stating how wetsuits should be made illegal in all future tournaments, claiming that this was akin to an uneven playing field. Swimming to rocks should be banned and Melnyk should be disqualified from the Montauk Classic for all time! Oh yes, once again he declared that I should return the prizes.

How was I to respond? What could I do to regain my good name? I do not have the type of personality that takes kindly to repeated transgressions. I tend to ignore the first offense, but quickly respond to multiple iniquities.

My retaliation started that week when I set out to put another fish on the board. One night I spent an entire tide in a neoprene surf top and waders. By first light I was soaked to the core and casting my last eel on Jones' Reef. The wind was in my face and a three foot swell threw frigid water over my head. Just as I prepared for my last cast, I got lucky once again, and happened to land a twenty five pound linesider. I was elated as I waded through the rollers back to the beach. It would be in second place if no other fish was weighed that day! Melnyk! Again in first and second place! I recognized the psychological value of this fact almost immediately.

With the formulation of a plan set within my brain, I took off, back to the motel to wake Dominique. I roused him at 6:30am and dragged him back to the beach with a camera. I had chosen a location of particular significance to shoot some special photos. There was an area of the beach that sat just below a choice piece of real estate which was, oddly enough, owned by Jimmy Willburt.

Why Aren't You Fishing?

By 8:00am I had six 8x10 prints developed at the local one hour photo which portrayed me holding my fish high and shining within a classic Montauk sunrise of pure fire. With vehemence and a bit of libation, Dom and I made the rounds to all the committee member's residences, where I promptly pinned a copy of my photograph to their respective doors. I added the caption; "Why aren't you fishing?" just for good measure. Most of the committee members thought the message was quite funny. Some even were motivated by the appearance of my new catch. Others dealt with my action with a show of contempt. By that evening I learned that Jimmy wanted to have me arrested for trespassing. He vowed to shoot me if I ever set foot on his land again.

The battle of the editorials was in full swing by week two. I had submitted a rebuttal to Willburt's rantings that was well formed and succinct. I recall stating within my counterargument; "Willburt would have us all goose stepping down the beach in our brown tops and khaki waders singing *"Deutschland, Deutschland."* The pros and cons lined up within the pages of **The Fisherman** during the next two weeks. I do not think the editors had ever gotten such response from this section of the magazine. It was apparent that my protagonists were in the majority. Jimmy was convinced that these expressions of affirmation to my cause were the ramblings of my minions. Once again Jimmy described me as less than ethical within these pages. I was vehement.

The "new and improved rules" were well known and evenly distributed among the enrollment in the following weeks. Having read them many times after the "change," I had become aware of several nuances and loopholes in the wording that I could use to my advantage. One particularly pertinent clause dealt with the filing of grievances. Any remonstrations could be presented to the committee in writing, and would be arbitrated by some "non biased" individual, such as a local lawyer or insurance adviser, without affiliation to the event.

BINGO!

So I wrote a letter of grievance to the Montauk Local's Tournament Grievance Committee. Actually, it was a rather well written letter, in which I expressed my displeasure at having had the RULES changed ten days after the tournament had already begun, and with a fish entered. I went on to state that this change was akin to having a dealer choose a wild card in a game of poker, after the hand had been dealt. I also stated that it was just possible that one day, someone may sue the committee for changing the rules, in the middle of a tournament. This letter was not well received by the tournament committee.

Back to Dominique. Dom and I are both what you would call "capricious." It is a fact that when you put two nuts together for any length of time you develop a unity of insanity. The day after delivering the letter I was feeling rather glum. Dom and I chose to cure this with another bottle of Captain Morgan. The sun was not above the mast, but hell, Dom was on vacation.

I have been a model maker of sorts and Radio Control enthusiast my whole life. I have so much RC gear that it takes up boxes in my basement. Dom, being aware of this fact, suggested that if I could not climb on my rock anymore, and that if I could not use a wetsuit either, maybe I could create a new, untried modus operandi for capturing the Morone Saxatilis? Perhaps, the use of an R/C boat could motor the eel out to the far rip? I thought this rather impractical, but not an entirely flawed concept.

"Dom, I have a giant kite that I bought for my girls to fly. Rip-stop nylon. Six feet long! I remember it picked Amber up off the ground one day. I bet I can rig it to *fly* an eel out to the rip!"

"Oh Dude! *That is Classic!*"

The bottle of rum got smaller as I rigged this new contraption. One fishing rod would be used for the kite line, and one for the fish! There would be a quick release attached to the kite that would temporarily hold the fishing line with the eel, operated by radio control. I would fly the kite, eel and fishing line over the rip and drop it into the water remotely! Within an hour, we had the completed prototype. Now we needed some flourish! We needed a theme!

Off we went to the hardware store to buy a Pirate flag that I have had my eye on since the inception of "the new rules." With a broomstick and some cord we had ourselves an authentic Jolly Roger! For a greater effect, Dom and I dressed as Buccaneers; Dom in a striped shirt and I with an eye patch, leathers and engineer boots. The topper was a sword that my wife had found while yard sale hunting. We transferred what was left of the Captain Morgan to a brown jug, and off we went, to the Point!

Montauk Point, and in particular, the Weed Bowl could be a very busy place in September when the chew was on. This day was just so, with buggies and campers climbing the dunes. The noon sun shone down on the hapless casters and gawkers, who stood in the cool breeze, trying to will a school of fish towards the beach. Boats passed by as if on parade, with tight lines pulling on umbrella rigs, full of bass.

The fish were being caught in the rip! Dom and I wheeled into the cove in my pickup, with our new flag snapping proudly, from the rear bed. We came to an abrupt stop at the bluff.

"Ahrrr Matey!" I howled as I staggered from the cab, "Hoist the colors!"

Dom ran to the back, and displayed great enthusiasm as he planted our letters of mark into the sand. All eyes turned to the two nuts with the flag dressed as pirates.

"Run out the guns for a broadside!" I cheered with the sword held high. I don't recall being very reserved in my actions at the time. Hell, I was tanked.

Such a tumult of motion had not been seen within the Weed Bowl before as we rigged for battle. Scrambling with the kite, radio control transmitter, and eel combo, we sent the whole kit and caboodle aloft. I felt jubilant as it took flight within a fair tailwind. My secret weapon was well on its way to the rip. At this point some fool decided to add to the cacophony.

"Yoo stooped mutha! Yoo are gonna hoit my brudda on da rock wit dat ding!"

Looking over at this urbanite with a glazed eye, I turned towards my antagonist, ***"What say yea?"*** I shout.

"Haaah?" says the mut.

"Ahrrr.... yea must be daft to rant at a man wearin' a sword, fool that you are!"

Dom started to shake his head. He knew what would come next. The Goog, confused to the point of inaction, stepped back and said "Well.... yoo betta watch out wat yoos do..." and then scurried away. Dom and I smiled at each other and had another pull on the little brown jug.

There, high above us, floated my eel, lofting out and over the meat of the Lighthouse rip.

"FIRE!" I shouted, and pushed a button on my controller to release the writhing snake.

All our hopes were exceeded as the eel fell from the sky a good three hundred yards from the beach. It hit the sea with a glorious splash! A fountain of spray launched skyward in its wake. Dom reeled in the kite as I reeled in the slack on the fishing line and moved to the bluff, so that my back was set in the dirt face of the escarpment, thus being as far from the water as possible. When the line came taught, I was rewarded with a firm Rap! OH my God! I was into a fish!

"Ahrr matey! Bring the gaff! T'is time for a boarding party!"

With my back still set firmly against the cliff, I reeled the unlucky fish through the surf... through the sand... and up to the base of the bluff.

"Bye Gum! She's too small!" I shouted as I tossed the poor fish back into the water. By now we had a huge audience, and I had made my subliminal statement. Dom and I quickly stowed the gear and departed the beach in a cloud of dust. The Jolly Roger snapped proudly from the bed-rail of my truck as we turned towards the highway.

Two nights later, during dinner there was a knock on my front door. I answered, and there stood one of the Local's committee members, on my porch. *He did not look happy.* Looking up into my eyes he said, "Paul, I always did like your style." With this he handed me an envelope, shook my hand and walked away.

What could this be? I was betting it was an invitation to the arbitration meeting. But I was wrong. I read the letter.

Dear Mr. Melnyk,

Several events have come to our attention which demonstrate your decision not to follow the rules of the Montauk Locals Striped Bass Tournament. It seems apparent that you are not a "team player". We therefore are refunding your entry fee. Your participation in our event is no longer desired.

Good luck,
"The Montauk Locals Tournament Committee"

There were no signatures.

There would be no grievance meeting, nor was there to be any arbitration. I was out. Just like that.

The rest of the season was a blur. I did not fish much at all, being in such a foul mood. My fishing sensibilities, however, did eventually take me to the Point one stormy morning a month after my forced retirement from the tournament.

The wind and rain had been pelting the surf for the last three days as a classic Nor'Easter hammered Montauk in mid November. I was at the motel when Dominique suggested that we go fishing,

"I don't know Dom...... I don't think I got it in me right now."

"Come on man! The fish are gonna be thick!"

Off we went. As we neared the Lighthouse, I noticed all my so called pals were driving their trucks in the opposite direction, away from the Point. This was not a good sign.

"Hey Paul! You missed it buddy! They were thick, in the bluff for a good hour." This was the chant that came through my CB radio as I passed the mooks by. "Hey, the bite may still be good, and guess what? Willburt is down there right now!"

"Good," I said half heatedly, "*I got my knife under the seat...*" This broadcast was followed by a flurry of hoots and cat calls. Dom looked at me as I drove. Dom knows me quite well.

We parked in the Weed Bowl, the point of our recent escapade with the kite, and sat in the car as the wind rocked us and sand blasted into the windshield.

"You wanna do this, Bro?"

"Shit Dom, we're here, may as well."

The beach was empty, except for Willburt's truck which sat at the edge of the bluff. "Come on, let's go."

The wind blew at us with a force that had me bent. Big dollops of rain smacked into my face. We rounded the bend under the bluff and I made my way to my favorite rock only to find it was occupied. There were two guys casting there under the cliff. Jersey Greg, and Willburt. Willburt was on my rock.

"Hey Jimmy!" I shouted through the wind, "You're on my rock!" He turned his head to look at me and his face wore a sneer. He lifted his head and cackled like a crow. He gave me the brush-off and continued to cast.

This boorish dismissal from Willburt was the last straw. I had had enough of James Willburt to last until the walls of hell crumbled. Fastening a three ounce lead bucktail to my leader, I walked a bit closer to the rock. Steam was rising from my head as I removed the hood of my jacket so I would not miss the next words that emanated from Willburt's pie hole. Closing my eyes, I took a deep breath and bellowed,

"YOU ASSHOLE! YOU GET OFF MY ROCK OR I'M GONNA MESS YOU UP!" Willburt continued to ignore me. He must have heard me because Jersey Greg turned his head upon hearing my declaration of intent and made a face like he had a belly ache.

"PAUL!" *MELLOW OUT DUDE!"* Dom tried to calm me, but I was past that point. Dom could see from the look on my face that he was staring into a shitstorm. He ducked as I let that three ounce bucktail fly, with a side arm motion that caused it to leave the tip of my rod, at a lethal velocity.

At times it seems as though there is guardian angel that follows me and diverts oncoming catastrophe because that bucktail flew straight towards Jimmy's head and then veered ever so slightly at the last instant. The missile just stung the edge of Willburt's ear, catching the lobe and causing it to snap, as the projectile continued past and hit the ocean a hundred yards ahead of him. A lucky cast all around. He twitched.

"I'M GONNA KILL YOU ASSHOLE!" I shouted at Willburt as I rapidly reeled in the line. The line looped itself across Willburt's shoulder as the wind blew a belly in it and it crossed his face. ***"I'M GONNA KILL YOU!!"*** At this point I was committed to putting out his eye with that sharp 7-0 hook! Jimmy grabbed the line and bit at it with his teeth, thoroughly expecting to part the string and drop my bucktail into the drink. Not so! I was using fifty pound braid made of carbon fiber! I pulled hard on the rod as Willburt bore down on that Power Braid with his choppers. His head snapped backwards, loosening a few teeth! At the last second before my hook took to the air and ripped a new nostril in Jimmy's wheezer, Greg snagged my line with a cross-cast and reeled the bucktail to his rock, thus defusing the bomb. I took a step back. I had no quarrel with Greg. He tossed the bucktail back towards the beach and gave me a wave.

"Paul. That's enough, let the fagot be." Dom grabbed my elbow and led me back to the truck. That was the last time I ever crossed paths with Willburt, whether by design or coincidence.

The tournament dinner that year was held as usual, in one of Montauk's better dinning establishments. Of course I was not invited to attend. But I was still bent on having the last word to my pals to express my discontent. My good friend Attila agreed to insert a photo of me into the official "Montauk Local's Striped Bass Tournament" photo album, which was to be prominently displayed in a place of honor, for all the contestants to view at the dinner. The collection of stills was essentially a photographic record of tournament highlights from years past. Attila, being fair minded and also a bit irreverent, placed my special photo on the first page of the book. It was the very same picture of that special fish that I had pinned to doors. Willburt was not amused.

Such are the trials of egos when dollars are involved. One thing is for sure, I found out who my friends were, during that fall. It took me a long time to figure this "*what are friends for*" thing out. In the process, I became notorious, taking to the water for spite; skishing in the faces of my detractors.

Eventually they started a separate wetsuit division to include some of the more extreme individuals, like myself, who just don't find it a challenge standing on the beach anymore. I would eventually be "allowed" to participate in their contest again, with the Melnyk rules withstanding. Willburt left the Tournament for good after this transgression. He never entered the tournament again after the enactment of the Wetsuit Division.

As a result of another controversy, involving, once again, the sting of innuendo, the Montauk Local's Tournament Board of Directors had a falling out with one of the original creators of the game. The entire tournament committee resigned in 2010 in protest. The "Locals" tourney has gone the way of the dinosaurs. In its stead, a new and improved competition known as "The Montauk Surf Masters" tournament, has evolved. In truth, it is the same contest, but with a different name, and a much more liberal entry policy, allowing the pot to grow exponentially. I sometimes enter the "Wader" division whenever I feel the urge. I occasionally even take some of their money.

I Am The Walrus.

After the close of the 1995 fishing season, I chose to devote my efforts to the more extreme aspects of angling. I continued to press the outer edges of the reefs and mussel shoals that inundate the Montauk coastline. The 1996 season brought great pods of bait to our area. Mullet, sand eels and herring were plentiful among the rocks of the southern side of the island. Bass cut the waves in numbers that I had not witnessed in years, igniting some of the best October blitz action, I can remember.

I had been perfecting my swim-fishing (otherwise known as skishing) technique over the summer months of that year, which gave me a great deal of confidence, when it came to utilizing this new method. I was anxious to go skishing in the cooler waters of autumn, where I could fish within the large pods of bait.

The early October sun was noticeably lower on the horizon that afternoon, as I walked down the path from the Lighthouse parking lot that leads to Turtle Cove, on the ocean side of the Montauk Point. It was a Tuesday, and I found myself relatively alone on the beach, just below the foot of the bluff that overhangs the shoreline. Gulls were cruising the surf zone. The breeze supplied them with ample lift as they soared along the cliff edge. They traveled the length of the promontory searching for the schools of bait fish. Dinner. These birds soon began to sweep the water, calling to each other, signaling the presence of food.

The air felt crisp, even through my 7mm wetsuit. I was outfitted with my flippers and equipment belt plus a small tackle bag containing live eels and a few small jigs. For this foray, I would be swimming out to a reef and drifting with the incoming tide. Off in the distance I could make out large black shadows in the clear water of the outer surf zone. The clouds undulated as they passed. The black humps of striper backs were visible within the ocean swells. An iridescent slick of fish oil extended off in every direction for miles, the telltale sign of fish, feeding on schooling bait. This was what had interested the birds. If I was lucky, the tide would place me, into the thick of this vale.

Wading out into the rocky surf, my neoprene booties skittered along the slick reef. I used my fishing rod as a staff to keep my balance in this treacherous area of the surf. When the sea reached my waist, I fastened my flippers and jumped, into the rushing whitewater. Cold water surged down my back as my head dipped into the ocean. I swam on my back with my fishing pole tucked snugly under my arm. The waves passed over my head and I arched backwards to slip below the breakers that rumbled past. Soon I was a hundred yards from the shoreline. I stopped swimming and sat in the water with a slight crouch, perfectly buoyant and balanced in my wetsuit. The exertion of the swim had warmed the water in my wetsuit leaving me quite comfortable.

It was an extraordinary feeling for me to be floating weightless in this dynamic sea, and I felt as though I had shed every pound of unwanted baggage as I rode the tide. The waves that I passed through among the breakers were just long swells out here, rising and falling with the tide. The sound of the surf murmured in the distance and I pulled an eel from my bag. I had placed each eel within a plastic (Zip-loc) bag to keep the buggers from escaping. In this way I could keep the squirmers from getting away as I fastened them to my line, by hooking them through the chin and out an eye. This was done while the eel was still in the bag as I pulled it through the plastic with a quick tug. In one motion I had the eel out of the bag and into the water, watching it writhe as it swam to the bottom, to hide among the rocks. Its movement would serve to stimulate a strike from any predator that might pass by. In no time at all, I was fighting a fish!

Fighting a substantial fish while swimming is a unique experience. A balance must be achieved between the hunter and prey. Any variation to this equilibrium causes a loss of control as the fish pulls. I was kicking hard to keep myself upright, fighting the fish while using my whole body as leverage. At the climax of the fight, I grabbed a bass of twenty pounds or more by the jaw and released the hook. I fed the striper the eel, as a reward, stuffing the unhooked bait down its throat. This would serve to bolster the striper's recovery from the trauma of the life-and-death battle it had been put through. Little harm was caused to the creature as the fish never left the water. The fish swam away with a splash and a flip of the tail.

After a short respite, I noticed the waters ahead of me began to churn with splashing life. A mass of fish bore down on me and I became concerned, realizing that the maelstrom headed in my direction, was a school of frenzied blues. Bluefish are brutish and aggressive feeders under normal conditions. Toothy smiles nosh into the prey with a zeal that is unsurpassed in ferocity. The feeding blues seem indiscriminate; they often eat everything in sight, including each other.

A swarm of splashing bodies soon surrounded me. I was surprised to see that this mass of fish avoided me completely. I was left within a circular calmness, as if these bluefish respected my space, and shunned it. All around me were splashing tails. The blue devils jumped and thrashed within the balled up bait fish. The sea around me was a churning acre of motion and sound. The splashing fishtails gave off a peculiar timbre, sounding at times like a heavy rain squall, rushing across a lake. The sky above filled with gulls diving into the cornered bait as they scooped up the wounded stragglers in their quick beaks. My eel was immediately devoured by the swarm of blues and I retrieved my hook to find only the stump of a body remaining. I pulled it from the hook and tossed it into the massed birds overhead where it was snatched by a particularly enthusiastic gull. Mesmerized by the surrounding mayhem, all I could do was stare in awe. As the school moved off, I had the time to contemplate whether or not I was lucky to still have my fingers and toes. I believe I burst into nervous laughter after the fact.

Soon after the blues passed, another body of fish arrived on the scene. They appeared more subdued in their movements, in the form of backs arching through the water. The fish were all striped bass. Splashing of tails and cries of gulls once again surrounded me. Unlike the bluefish, the stripers seemed to have little fear of me, as they careened into my body while chasing after the prey. At one point it felt as though little fists were poking into my sides as hundreds of bass pushed by. *It tickled!* I laughed. All thoughts of fishing vanished as once again I was transfixed by the unusual experience.

When the tumult passed, and I once again had the sea to myself. The fish were still present, though the blitz action had subsided, and fishing became possible once more. Within an hour I had exhausted my supply of bait as bass and blues cleaned out my stock in short order. I then switched to bucktail jigs, which also worked quite well until they were stolen by ravenous bluefish. Soon I was drifting one hundred yards off shore and rounding the Lighthouse break water. Since I had no place to land along the Point abutment and the tide was pulling me towards the north side beach anyway, I decided to stick it out and enjoy the ride around the Lighthouse. People on the jetty observing me as I floated past called out, "Hey you! Are you OK?"

I laughed and waved my flippers at them. "I'm fine! Wonderful, in fact!" I had caught at least twenty bass that afternoon. As I passed by those gawking tourists, I found myself again, surrounded by fish tails, monstrous fish tails! I had drifted into a school of giants, with nothing left in my arsenal to hook them with. Every last bait, hook, jig and plug had been expended during the previous hour of action! These bass moved me both figuratively and literally as they collided into me with force. At one point I was caught by surprise as a great tail broke the surface of the water and smacked me in the face like a wet towel. The slap caused my head to spin as the fish pushed past me and swam away. Assaulted by a striper! I laughed hysterically! I am sure that those who witnessed my reaction thought I had gone quite mad!

The blitz was a frantic wave in motion. Without the means to fish, a wild idea overcame me while one slammer after another banged into my sides. In a moment of inspiration, I stuck my rod under my arm and began to rake at the water, making grabbing motions at the fish with my free hand, as they rubbed along my flanks. Managing to snag one between my arm and chest as it splashed desperately to get away, I howled like a barbarian! "*Yee-Hah!*"

"Daddy! Daddy! Look at that crazy man out there! He caught a fish!" I had snagged a bass, with my bare hands! The fish quickly freed itself and splashed into the drink. I waved my hat, like a bronco rider, at the bewildered kid. Right then, I felt transformed into a strange aquatic mammal with whiskers and tusks. The hunt was a good one. It had been an outstanding success.

The Lighthouse retreated into the distance as I drifted into a calmer portion of the rip on the north side of the Point. I had experienced enough action for the day and I headed for the beach. I dragged my frame from the rocks at the northern bluffs and returned to my truck by way of a stroll around the Lighthouse Jetty and in doing so, I passed by the fellow with his son as I rounded the corner. "Hey! You're the guy who went swimmin' by before with the fish!"

"Yep."

"You're *nuts*!"

"You know, that all depends on your perspective, there buddy."

Spring Fish.

Montauk has always been an out of the ordinary place. There are more idiosyncratic nuts per capita here than anywhere else in the state of New York. Nestled among the hills and kettle holes of eastern Long Island, Montauk's inhabitants have long since given up on the stereotypical New York lifestyle, in favor of individualistic enthusiasm. Known as one of the most bountiful locations to pursue fish, it is not surprising that the quirks and obsessions of the residents extend to the surfcasting community.

Spring not only brings out the buds and blooms, but it also stimulates the annual migration of striped bass to the wind swept beaches of this most eastern point. As a result of the vast numbers of migrating fish and bait, the probability of scoring trophy linesiders is significant during the late spring and early summer months. I have caught many fish in the forty pound and larger class during the new moon tides of mid June. With water temperatures beginning to break the fifty five degree barrier, the larger fish swim up the southern shoreline in search of energy laden baits such as mackerel, alewife, squid and a literal smorgasbord of fry. There is a narrow window of opportunity for a trophy striper. These fish will feed in the shallow waters for only several weeks at the most, due to a warming trend. Let's not say that these bigger fish keep away from the surf during the summer, but their feeding habits and grounds are much more disbursed, and they tend to keep to the off shore regions.

It is in June when the word spreads of big fish making for the Montauk surf by way of the outer beaches and back bays of mid Long Island, and this is when the local fanatics will make their first exploratory steps into the cold surf. I fish from the reefs and shoals, wading out to a flat boulder and casting into the drop off where the surf meets the rocks. This form of fishing is not for the weakling. It is both dynamic and treacherous. A full seven millimeter wetsuit keeps the chill off and booties with cleats keep me from sliding into the drink (*most of the time*). A wetsuit also adds some cushion to the inevitable beating taken when the surf gets nasty. Preferring the calm nights for these trips, I pay special attention to the tides and weather.

Most of the guys keep to the beaches for their outings during the early season. The idea of getting soaked with cold water is irritating to the casual fisherman, and they keep to the sandy stretches of the south side where new eddies have developed behind shoals and sandbars created during the winter gales. Great cuts of flowing surf form riptides strong enough to drag a caster down to Davey Jones' locker. Caution must be taken not to succumb to bass fever; one more step into the drink may send the hapless caster off the deep ledge. These cuts and eddies often remain hidden to the untrained eye. The educated fisher will look for places where the waves fail to break. Any cut, or channel where the sea flows around a sandbar, will strand bait. This is a natural fish trap. The front edge of this bar structure is a spot where the big stripers lurk.

Sizable predators will feed on the larger baits, so the arrival of this pray signals the return of the big bass. Many of these fish are taken on bait, such as clams, worms, eels or bunker chunks. A piece of fresh bunker is irresistable to heavy linesiders. Local tackle shops vie for the limited supply of these baits, which are scooped up by the experts as soon as they are made available. Fish finder rigs and six ounce diamond sinkers keep the baits on the bottom. It is not necessary to cast far. I have seen trophy bass taken ten yards from the beach. It is luck which puts a hook in front of a cow; the skill is in knowing where to go.

The use of lures and jigs are also an effective approach for early season fish. Small bucktails and tins imitate the first natural baits to arrive. A favorite lure of mine for this time of year is a Yosuri mag darter. It will cast well for a small profile lure, and several different patterns copy natural springtime baitfish. I am also very fond of tossing bucktails dressed with a five inch pork rind. This one jig has won many a trophy for me, and is effective even in a headwind.

The 2008 season began as a quiet rumor spread through the locals in Montauk; big bass were spotted heading east. I spent the day wiping the dust of winter from my gear and psyching myself to test the cold waters of spring.

A perfect incoming tide would be pushing through one of my favorite fishing grounds that evening. I prefer sunset when on a hunt since there is still some light left to find my old perches. It is a little known fact that rocks hide during the winter. They will pull up their roots and scurry to deeper water every year, forcing me to press deeper into the surf. It is inevitable that the further out into the surf you move the closer to the breaking waves you get. The beatings have kept me on my toes, like a prize fighter who is too punch-drunk to quit.

I hit the sand just as the orange ball sank into the west. Productive grounds for me always seem to be in the less accessible locations and I scrambled along the rocky portion of the hike. One area in particular lies just past a boulder strewn section of beach where the agility of a mountain goat is needed to navigate. This area is known as the land of the giants, for obvious reasons. The hike is what keeps the riffraff away from these grounds.

In the distance I could see a cluster of terns working the water just off shore in the breaking surf, a good omen, and soon I was throwing two ounce bucktails into a hole behind a bit of structure created by several clustered boulders hidden beneath the waves. As the sky grew dark, the first stars winked into view. Venus shone bright on the horizon and cast a faint light onto the low swell. I tossed my jig at the reflection. My bucktail splashed, stirring an expanse of calm water. The swirl of a fish broke the surface and my rod bent. The fight from the rock was a one way battle for awhile, as the fish ran for deeper water. Keeping light pressure on the fish and not wanting to break it off in the rocks, I soon gained control over it. The fish fought with great skill as it wove through the shallows and ducked behind rocks, attempting to free itself. I had to hold the rod high over my head on one occasion when the striper jammed itself in a crag. Eventually the striper lay at my feet. I grabbed it by the gill and stumbled to the beach.

It is not difficult to estimate the size of a big fish. I find that there is a direct proportion to the amount of wheezing and heart palpitations caused by the mile long trek back to the truck with a slob on my back. I am sure someday this hike will kill me, as it is getting to be a bother, this hauling of the girls. This fish had me sweating and spitting, causing me to stop at several points on the way back to the truck. My estimate, by forced march, had me convinced I was dragging a forty pounder.

Arriving home, I had to jam the corpse into my refrigerator. It was a good thing that I would have it out by sunrise and on route to my "home away from home". Otherwise my lovely wife would murder me for skuzzing up the box.

One of my best friends is Paulie of **Paulie's Tackle** in Montauk. The spring is a difficult time for the local tackle shops, money being scarce, and after a long winter, hanging a big striper does much to stimulate business. This fish would also feed my family. The firm white meat seems sweeter in the early season after a long winter soaking in the cold waters.

Sunrise had me dressed and off towards town. As I turned the corner, I saw a crowd of fishermen were already hanging out by Paulie's front door. Paulie's Tackle has become a monument to fishing and is more like a club than a place of business. Paulie opens his door at seven in the morning, and the guys who have fished all night are usually waiting at the curb, each one looking to score some free coffee and hard intelligence. There was a thirty pound bass on the scale which hung front and center of the main gate to this fisherman's toy store, at least ten pair of envious eyes were coveting the fish. I sauntered around to the back of my truck and made my own slimy pull from the load bed. My catch was quite a bit larger than the beast on the scale.

"Melnyk's got one." There is no feeling in the world like shoving a cow bass up your friends' asses. Just the look on their faces is worth the long haul back from the beach. The eyes, it's all in the eyes... With "the little one" taken down, my fish pulled a decent thirty nine pounds on the needle. Not too shabby; but alas, short lived. Through the gathering crowd, the sound of a bugle was heard in the distance. "The Toad!" someone shouted, as if a celebrity had graced the stage. *Hmm...*

Sure enough, Gary Stephens turned the corner in his old beat up truck holding a bashed, bent bugle out of the driver's side window. It howled with a high metallic twang as he rounded the corner, sounding a sick rendition of "Charge" through the early morning dew. There was a plastic owl impaled upon the VHF antenna on the roof of the cab.

Gary is well known as the "Toad." He is proud of this. How he got this moniker has been somewhat obscured by time. One explanation is because Gary owns a grounds keeping business called **Integrity Landscaping.** This title seems appropriate as referenced to the amphibian that deters detrimental insects from destroying treasured flowerbeds. Other assertions refer to his masculine prowess, you know, "*horny as a toad*." Those of the genteel sex seem to qualify this statement. I myself have witnessed his affect on certain females of the species. Even though he is not much to look at, other than being a big, ruddy, hulk of a man, he seems to project a strange animal attraction that is quite inexplicable. I have seen women practically swoon in his presence. I tend to think it has something to do with an odoriferous quality, like some strange pheromone seeping from his ample, and seldom sanitized, pores. When asked, Toad will say he received the name through a bar room trick that he would often perform in order to get free drinks (*during a phase in his history when getting a libation was a priority*), which involved leaping over cars.

"***AAAAHH!..*** *Get that rat off the scale Melnyk, and let's see a real fish!*" Gary shouted at the top of his lungs as he ran to the rear of his beat up Toyota. Dressed in old shorts, he looked like a barbarian with his bedraggled hair that stood on end. His legs were covered in bass slime and it was obvious that he had just driven off the beach. Toad had to drag his fish from the street. Nobody was willing to help Mr. Toad unload his catch. They were keeping clear, since he was behaving like an escaped inmate from a nuthouse.

I will be the first to admit that it is ***not*** fun to have a fish shoved up your ass first thing in the morning. Gary's fish would weigh in at over fifty; 54.8 pounds, to be exact. This weigh-in was followed by much screaming and hoopla from the Toadster. It seemed he had won the first tournament of the year with his fish; the "Over Fifty Club Tournament," his own personal creation. Gary, knowing that his karma has no bounds, had talked the biggest braggarts in town into donating fifty bucks each to the pot. The first hoople to bag a fifty pounder would take the purse. The tourney had seen two years of such donations. The prize was indeed a grandiose one. "*Looks like I'm gettin' that new truck, after all!*"

Toad is the luckiest sonofabitch in the world. He swears it is all because of his piousness and uncompromising faith in God, whose attentions towards "the prince of frogs" seem directly proportional. Toad is crazy to boot, and constantly rubs my nose into pies of his own piscatorial prowess. He is also, alas, my pal, and I was both saddened, and happy for the guy, who had once again, out-done me. Toad raised that bugle to his lips one more time and blew a fair rendition of "Taps" as he glared into my eyes. He was having a hard time tootin' through his mischievous grin.

Next to make an appearance was old Jack Yee. Grizzled and worn, Jack stood a tall five feet in the morning light. Jack is now our resident photographer and surrogate blatherskite. Jack has had a long run in the surf and is a surfcasting legend, but too many smokes have added to his age and taken their toll. He now keeps to the sidelines giving advice, taking pictures and announcing the daily catch through his website, **jackyee.com**. It is beyond a doubt that Jack has a special skill for creating portrait images of fish. I once saw Jack make a two pound bluefish look like a gorilla. It is all in the angles.

"Move that truck! It's in the way of the shot!" Jack hollered to no one in particular as he jostled the crew into submission. "Hey! Hold that fish out in front of you, will ya! What are you, a girl? Straighten your hair! Don't show me no gills, I hate to see gills! " Click.

The Toad scored the bass at first light, using a two ounce tin with a white and red tube, casting from the sand beach. There is nobody in the world that can work a tin better than the Toad. He has the touch.

The revelation of the hot jig for the day caused a run on two ounce tins that morning. By eight o'clock Paulie was completely sold out of the precious juju. Someone had purchased twenty of them, on the spot. More donations to the fish Gods. It was a good day for Paulie. "Hey Bow! What's happenin'," was Paulie's standard greeting to the gathering patrons as the register rang with jangling change. Soon the phone began to ring off the hook, as news of a run of big fish spread. This left little time for Paul to work the cash box. "Zelco!, *(that's me)* answer the phone, This guy wants to know if he will catch a big fish next weekend. Have some fun!"

Everyone who frequents Paulie's tackle gets a nickname. There are handles such as, The Crusher, Bicycle Bob, The Eel, Bagfoot, Toad, Zelco, Shakey, the three Basskateers, Mr. Bow Tangles, Goldilocks, Crazy Al; the list goes on and on. Some individuals are wise to their monicker, but a goodly number haven't got a clue. All these gems are poignant, having "special meaning;" for instance mine.

How did I acquire the epithet Zelco? One day, many moons ago, Toad was clearing out the hovel of a dearly departed patron. In the process, Gary came across a stash of rotgut booze. No longer being one to imbibe, the Toad donated three unopened, plastic containers of hooch to "**Paulie's Tackle and Free Coffee Emporium**". One of the jugs, the one that contained either paint thinner or Vodka (*we're not sure*) was branded with the flourished hallmark "Zelco." I, not being one to ever turn down a free libation, began a month long mission to clear the shop of that evil elixir.

"Vare iz Zelco!" became my heralding declaration; Hence- the name.

Answering the phone at Paulie's can be very entertaining. I have heard callers asking some of the most ludicrous questions. "Hey Pal! Should I call in sick and fish on Wednesday?" or, "What train should I take to get me closest to the Point?" are some of the more ridiculous inquiries. When Paulie hands me the phone, anything goes. This time would be no different:

"Hello?... Feeesh?... Vat yoo vant, feeesh? *Feeesh who?...* I know, no feeesh... maybe yoo vant Feeeshka?.... yes, yes... Meeester Feeeshka iz in da john... John?.... John who? No, John not heer, *so long... Bye, bye...*" Click. This little rendition had us rolling on the floor.

Gary stood on Paulie's porch bragging and shouting up a storm for an hour. Tourists in the surrounding motels came out on their balconies, looking to see what all the ruckus was about, as it was uncertain whether there was a celebration, or a fight going on below their windows. The crowd eventually thinned to prepare for their own forays into the striper firmament. I did get my striper's picture taken along with Toad's. Mine looked bigger. It is all in the angles.

Look. To show I am a true gentleman and an "up n' up" kinda guy, I will now tell you where to go to hook a slob in Montauk. It is a fact that the local saloons have their share of fat slobs sitting at the bar after 1am on a Friday night. Or you could stand next to Gary about a mile south of town on the sand beach around mid June. Look for that truck with the owl on the roof. Gary loves company. He is a natural teacher and will more than likely show you some pointers. Make sure to cast in front of the Toad. This is where the big fish are.

Fingers.

The Pope once told me, "All fishermen are LIARS and ASSHOLES and you are the biggest one, YOU LYIN' ASSHOLE!" This was of course, the infamous Livingston Pope Noel III, not the Prince of Peace, and I believe we were in a heated discussion about who had managed the greater catch one night on Weakfish Rock. With that said, I will now relate an interesting ditty about my lost body parts..

As many of you know, I am a cabinet maker of some renown, to the rich and famous out here in the "*Hamptons.*" Loosing my fingers, (*in fact, it was three of them*) took all of about a millisecond, during an argument I was having with a Delta Unisaw, which is an industrial sized table saw with a 10 inch blade. The saw won. Anybody who has hacked off a body part will tell you that it does not hurt, 'just feels kinda weird... As I watched the piece of hard oak I was cutting fly past my gut one morning, I experienced that weirdness. ZZZIPP! Bye-bye.

At once, I cupped my hands together and swore at the friggin' machine. I then hurt my big toe by kicking in the front dust port with my boot. Damn, that toe hurt... Looking down at my closed right hand, I could just see a small drop of blood dribble from my closed fist. No big deal, but dammit, I was sure I was gonna need stitches! There goes the day. Well, let's see the damage.

Opening my palm, I watched as three fingers flopped off the ends of knuckles, each kept attached by a bit of sinew. Not good. I wrapped the mess in a rag I had on standby, just for such an occasion, and called 911. This is when I figured I was gonna have a tough couple of days, you see, it is hard to use a telephone with missing fingers.

Thank God for modern medicine! I didn't feel much of anything (for the sixteen hours it took to get from the emergency room to the operating room), but *REALLY GOOD....* Sister morphine was at her best that day. It was just my good luck when I was relegated to the end of the queue. Another poor schlep had hacked his hand in half and beat me to the ward. It was ok though. Time flies when you're havin' fun!

Through an opium induced haze, I realized I might be in trouble when my orderly finally came to get me around midnight. (*Did I mention I waited sixteen hours?*) My "escort" had that wide faced gaze and quivering curled lip of a somewhat less than normal human being. In fact, I was quite sure he had Down's Syndrome. My orderly didn't say much as he wheeled me down a warren of corridors. I do recall banging off the walls of the elevator as he wheeled me into pre-op. This is where I met the anesthesiologist, who of course was Polish.

"I'm just going to give you a shot to help you to relax," he said... With that, I was out like a stinkin' bag of trash.

After a *twelve hour operation*, in which I was reassembled, I found myself in the recovery room surrounded by nurses who were intent on finding out if I knew where I was. I did, in fact know. I was in the hospital. I also knew that I hurt. Bad. Like I had been in a fight, and lost. The hurt was not from my fingers alone, but the pain centered on the back of my head and my left shoulder. This I found confusing as all the sawing was done to the other arm. After I related this bit of information to the staff, things became sorta frantic around my gurney. They wheeled in an EKG machine and trussed me up within its tentacles. All of a sudden they started asking me all kinds of questions, such as, "what's your name" and "who is the president." I think they thought that I either had a stroke or a heart attack. They kept asking me if I was sure that my left arm hurt and not my right.

"No, it is my left arm and it hurts like a *bitch*. It hurts like *Gigantor* lifted me off the ground by that arm and *shook me*! Oh and by the way, don't forget that the back of my head feels like it was hit with a BAT!!" This is when I began my two week stint with pain meds.

The following day, (after they determined that I did not, in fact, have a heart attack, or stroke), I was givin' a Cortisone injection in my shoulder and I finally could move my left arm. The first thing I did was reach for the back of my aching head and palpated a lump about the size of an egg on my scull. It then dawned on me that I had somehow had my head smacked while I was unconscious. I was willing to bet those bastards had dropped me!

The anesthesiologist came in to see me and I confronted him about this. "What did you do, call for Dr. Moe, Dr. Larry and Dr. Curly to administer a special form of anesthetic on me?" I said none to politely, as I fingered the lump on my noggin. He nervously looked way, and promptly left the room.

My surgeon, (*who, by the way, skillfully saved two and a half of those hacked off fingers and has my everlasting gratitude*), brought in a neurologist, just to make sure I truly hadn't stroked out. The two doctors finally came to a consensus. Yes, I had been injured somewhere between the O. R. and the recovery room, but no, there was no one who would fess up to this little 'maldito.' My wife wanted us to sue the hospital. I said what the hell; I had been hit on the head quite a few times in my life... No big deal, *but I would inflict my own sweet form of revenge upon the staff of that joint!*

Within three days I was out of the I.C.U. and in a private room. Free TV. Lotsa' food. Nice view. No roommate. Someone was worried. Throughout the boredom of this extended stay, I formulated my retaliatory strike.

I had visitors. For some reason, unknown to me, there were people out there who seemed to care about me. I made a request of one of my friends and asked him to bring a special treat from home.

"You know what Don, I have a urge for Vienna sausages. Could you bring me some, please?"

"Vienna Sausages? Ah... sure, if you want, pal."

"I want."

That afternoon, Don arrived with a can of those sweet little treats. I popped the can and swallowed all but one of the stubby little morsels. For this one, I had a plan. Squeezing out a packet of ketchup that I had saved from lunch, I rolled the little bugger around in the mess. I took my bandaged hand (*which was wrapped up like King Tut's*) and set the gooey glob of meat in the top of my bandage and held it over my head.

"Paul, what the hell are you doin'?"

"Shhh... Don, take me by the waist and walk me out to the nurses station."

"Are you kiddin?" No, *I was not kidding*.

With my best pain face and moaning ever so lightly with each step, Don walked me out to the receiving desk, an I.V. rack in tow. As we approached, all eyes were turned towards us. "Nurse," says I.

"Somethin' dreadful has happened!" Looks of concern followed. "I fell outa bed and now my fingers feel awful.... *LOOK.*"

The nurse jumps up to my aid as I lowered my arm slowly. The sausage slipped out of the top of my dressing.... *Splat*! It hit the floor with a splash of red gore. The seated secretary turned green. A candy-stripper gave a startled gasp as she covered her young lips with her palm and began to moan. A passerby leaned up against the wall with weak knees. The head nurse (*I lovingly called her Nurse Rachette, from this day on*) looked up at me from her desk, as Don and I started to giggle. "*Paul*... You gotta be kidding me! I've seen *BRAINS* splattered on the floor in this joint! You think a stupid *hotdog* and some *tomato sauce* is gonna *fluster me? GET BACK IN BED!*"

She was a tough old bird, I gotta give her that. She never even lost her stride as she shooed us back to the room. Don and I laughed our asses off! *It was hysterical!*

About an hour later, wouldn't you know it, my pain meds were wearing off, and things were once again starting to hurt. I pressed the call button. In walked Nurse Rachette, the bull nurse from hell.

"Can I help you, *Mr. Melnyk?*" she said with a demure smile.

"Why yes," said I. "I'm kinda in some pain right now and I could use another shot."

"*HAH!*" She said, as she quickly turned around and walked out of my room. I had to wait for the night shift before I got that shot. But that was OK; I was the talk of the hospital. My doctor even heard about my little skit. Payback is a bitch.

Crazy Al, Revisited.

OK, it had been about two months since I had hacked my fingers off. As a form of therapy I decided to make several mementos of this event by molding copies of one of my fingers and painting them to look as gross as possible; then turning them into fishing lures, *poppers* to be exact. As I found out later, these little demons turned out to be quite effective as their intended goal, which was to catch fish, of course.

I had received one of those cryptic calls from Crazy Al sometime in September, "There are fish in your area, Bub. Big fish..... and I'm comin' out your way tonight. You wanna come?"

"Al, I'd love to go, but my fingers are still bloody stumps."

"Aw, come on, the trip will do you good, and you should start fishin' again. We will just be chunkin' and I've got fresh bunker."

Fresh bunker... Everyone who knows anything about bottom fishing with bait knows how much a striper loves to glom fresh menhaden. This is the equivalent of fillet mignon to a hungry lunker.

"Well, In that case, I'll come along, just for the halibit."

"Good, I'll see you at midnight; we'll meet up at the IGA"

Done deal. All that was left was for me to prepare a special gift for my pal. I don't know, but I am very generous and I like to give my buddies some stuff when I see them if I can.... A trip to the "old, out of service tackle bag" usually does the trick. I also think this is another reason why Al fishes with me. He can't pass up a free plug.

I was still working in my cabinetry shop, doin' what I do by building pretty boxes. You have to get back on the horse, so I fashioned a little coffin out of a piece of teak that I had laying around, being very careful with the few digits I had left. It was quite a nice piece, as I shaped it with a router table, (*I only nicked my thumb once*), fitting hinges and a latch to it. I even created little handles out of brass wire. It was a little coffin, detailed enough to be accepted as the center of attraction, at Mickey Mouse's wake.

Midnight. The IGA. I met up with Alberto and his entourage. They were a nice bunch of fellows, Jud, a mutual friend with whom I had fished in the past, Mattie from up Island and Simon, who was visiting from England. What a merry band! Al stuck his nose up in the air and sniffed like some blue point hound on the scent of a raccoon. "They're here Bub!"

Yes, those of us who have been at it long enough can smell the fish, though what we are usually sensing, is the aroma of chewed up bait; same difference.

At this point, I removed my gloves and showed Al and the boys my stumpy, bloody fingers. Al had not seen me since the accident and he winced at the sight. Needless to say my fingers were not functioning very well at the time. Tying knots would be a bitch with just a working thumb and pinky.

A presentation was in order, so I gave a little speech and handed Al the miniature coffin. He opened it and freaked! I thought he was gonna drop it and run! I had done a very realistic job of painting that special lure. It was dressed with tan, green and blue paint, with some blood red at the stump end where the leader is tied. I explained to him that it was actually a plastic casting and he could truly fish with it. The evening was rather dark out there under the sodium streetlight and I am sure this added to the general effect of a severed finger in a box with hooks sticking out of it. I thought the black teaser at the fingernail end was an especially interesting detail.

"You are not well, Melnyk!" Al said with a giggle in his voice. I love making people laugh! He seemed quite delighted after the initial shock and passed the memento around for all to admire.

As I had expected, Al had brought along a big cooler filled with bunker and beer. Ah, the combination had a beautiful bouquet, which allowed the beer to have a smooth earthy finish with just a delightful aquatic afterglow to press upon the pallet!

Now I am not a chunker at heart and I am sure that there are some of you who have strong opinions about the method. I do, however, retain a meat-stick, a remnant of my tournament days when fighting fair was not part of the equation. This device is an eleven foot Lamiglas, that I once slammed on a rock under the light, and lost six inches (*don't worry girls, I have another seven to spare*). Johnny Kronich from **Johny's Tackle** re-wrapped it as a baitcaster and I had it equipped with Penn Squidder on the business end. It is a nice outfit. I was fishing with a Castaway rig on the terminal end of this setup. This casting gizmo holds the weight and bait together until it hits the water, and it is a great way to get another ten yards out of a cast.

So off we went this motley, winsome crew on a grand expedition. I cannot tell you which direction we chose or even how far down the sandy shore we went, as this is the case when fishing with Alberto; spies are punished with banishment. Let's just say we drove along the beach, in time to arrive at the proper stage of the tide. It was a grand tour, and just how phantasmagorical; (*Yes dear editor, I made up another word*) this trek was going to be is something that will burn in my noodle forever.

Our drive along the beach was like a cavalcade, with our four vehicles flying down the sand. We would stop and peer at the water every quarter mile or so to look for cuts, bars and structure where we could expect to find fish. The best way to judge a good hole is to find a cut where the surf washes way up the beach past the tide line. This is a good sign of a passage in a bar where the waves have scooped out a channel. Another good tell is to look for a spot where the waves are *not* breaking. This will prove to be a deeper hole, as the waves do not break in deep water.

The new moon sky was very dark, with an onshore breeze of about 15 to 20mph blowing in our faces. The tide was rising, with slack water being about an hour away. I would stop every so often to pick up a nice piece of driftwood, filling the bed of my truck along the way. A fire is an inevitability when Al and I are together.

Our team stopped at a great scalloped cove on the beach where we saw piles of driftwood and debris distributed along the dunes. The ocean had washed most of the sand away at high water, leaving a big hole and a sandbar in its wake.

"This is it, Bubba!" Alberto spoke with that clipped tone of his that expresses excitement.

First things, first. I pulled a plank out of my truck and we cut the bunker into two inch steaks. Of course (*and only because they were in the way of the bait*) I took a bottle of beer. Al was the first one in the water so as to insure his prime spot to fish. I was next; moving off to Al's left.

I proceeded to make my first cast in fifteen months. A fingerless cast. It was awful! My hand slipped off of the butt and the rod-tip hit the water as damaged digits refused to perform. A big backlash was the result. I spent the next ten minutes pulling loops out of the reel. When finished, I retrieved my line to find my bait had been stolen. Back to the truck. I met Al there. He had also had his bait taken.

"*Shhh. They're here Bubba.*" Alberto said to me under his breath as he grabbed a hunk of bunker. I don't know why he was so possessive of these fish, as we were all there to catch. I can only suppose it was from a sense of competitiveness.

The other guys were fishing further to the east. We meandered back to the surf and made our casts. I finally had a good one and backed up to where the previous tide had pulled five feet of sand out to sea. This bit of beach was undermined by the waves and there was a drop off where the tide threw a flood of water against the sand after every braking wave. I watched as Alberto also began to back up. He was into a fish, too! He brought it in with little effort. He did not turn on his light, but I could plainly see a flash of silver in the dark. Yes, there were fish here.

I found it hard to reel with just a thumb and pinky. I missed my next strike, dickering and trying to adjust to my mauled hand. Al had another fish soon after the first. I lost my bait once again. We met at the truck and I grabbed a new piece of bait. I kept the guts and wrapped them around the hook, skewering the stomach on the barb in hopes of developing a nice slick.

"About 20 pounds, Bub. They are thick." Al said.

Nothin' like havin' your pal tell you that the fish are thick to screw up your luck. Jud saw us making trips back to the truck and moved into our area. Matt and the Brit were still off to our left. Al hooked another fish which dragged him down the beach. "Screw him!" said Jud, as he moved into Alberto's hole. He was greeted with a run and a spit. "Shit!"

The tide climbed steadily until we were pressed up against the drop off. I finally hooked up and was rewarded with a twenty pound dogfish.... Jud had caught a few skates. The tide was over. Time for a fire and some refreshment.

It was not long before we had a blaze burning brightly in the dark.

The flames danced, flaring ten feet into the sky, while illuminating a hundred yards of the beach. 2am: Al saw a commotion in the surf as Simon hollered that he had a fish. Al and I ran over to see what he was doing.

"Ease up Simon! You'll pull the hook!" Simon fought the fish with flair as would be expected of a proper British gentleman, and had his fish in the wash directly.

"Holy shit! Look at that!" Alberto exclaimed as the fish washed onto the shore. What we saw was a three foot long, thirty pound Tiger shark! The jaws of the shark snapped; choppers clicking fiercely, threatening to remove fingers. I swear I had never seen so many teeth in my life! With twice as many dentures as a Mako's, the critter's jaw was full of white razors, like a monster from some Steven King nightmare. Figuring since I had little to lose, I reached down, and took hold of the fish by the ears.

"Watch those teeth, Bub!"

"Ahh... What's another finger or two!"

The creature's flanks were covered in brown dots. The beast twisted within my hands. It was a solid hunk of muscle.

"It looks more like a leopard, than a tiger."

"Yeah... Don't ask me why they are called tiger sharks." Al bravely cut the leader as the demon snapped at his hand. Back into the water it went. Simon was very impressed. We all went back to the fire for a rest.

Another hour went by without a bite. We left our rods staked into the beach and warmed ourselves by the fire. I remember going back to the surf with my gear, casting, then walking back to the sand to repose and passing out with the rod propped in my hand with the butt half-buried into the sand. Al, of course, waited for me to nod off before sneaking over to me and plucking on my line to roust me, having a chuckle.

"Come on Bubba, the tide has started to move again. Time for that big fish!"

"I've had enough of catchin' skates and watchin' you reel in fish Al." Jud said, "I am gonna go sleep in the truck for a while. Wake me if somethin' comes up."

"Jud, the bite is about to happen! You should stick it out, man." This Alberto said with a very serious expression. I knew the look well *and I know that he knows what I should know.* I was tired and cold, but I *would* make a few more casts.

Five more tosses and I had figured out why Al had caught so many fish (*nine to this point*). The SOB was just flicking his bait out into the current, no more than twenty yards off the beach. I had been casting as far as I could and I was missing the honey hole. As Al hooked another fish, I moved into his spot and made a weak toss.

Bang! I was into a fish!

"What you got there, Bubba?" Al remarked as he heard the drag singing. I looked at him with moon sized eyes.

"Holy cow! That's a nice fish!"

I was dragged down tide by the fish as I tried to keep the pressure on. My busted fingers kept slipping off the handle of my reel. Thumb and pinky. Not good... Al followed me down the beach. I fought the fish for twenty minutes before I had it coming towards me. The problem was that I was bringing the fish into a part of the beach with a big shore break and a steep bank. My biggest mistake was thinking about how good it was gonna be to shove this fish up Al's ass.

I had the fish on the sand! It was a slob! As I went to grab the fish the waves took it back into the sea as the water dragged it back down that steep sand slope! Two more minutes and I had it on the sand again. I could hear Alberto screaming something to me but I was transfixed. Once more, the waves took the fish back within the shore break.

My stump fingers hurt from the cold. They felt like they were on fire. That's it, I said to myself, third time's the charm. This fish is not going back into the water the next time I get its belly on the sand! With a big pull, I heaved the fish within the breaking wave which brought it further up the steep embankment than it had before. Once again, as the water receded so did the fish. I was tired and hurting and I didn't want to get my raw meat claw of a hand wet. The damned fish was going to stay on the sand this time! I held the spool with my thumb and the fish's retreat into the surf slowed. The fish was mine!

The ocean had a different idea.

"YOU GOOOOGAAAN!" Alberto screamed at me from about ten yards away. "I TOLD YOU TO GO IN THE WATER AND GET IT!"

But it was too late.

"You Goog! THAT WAS YOUR FISH-OF-A-LIFETIME!! I SAW IT! *Do you know how big it was?"*

Yes, I knew how big it was. I also knew that it had gotten away. I also knew that I would never live it down. But most of all, I knew that fingers or no fingers I was never going to give up surfcasting.

"You GOOGAN!!!"

Never.

On a lighter note, I also knew that I was not in my truck, and asleep when the biggest fish of the night was hooked.

Jack and Eddie.

One of the perks of living in Montauk is having a world class tackle shop in town. I am, of course, referring to **Paulie's Tackle,** and Free Coffee Emporium. Paulie's has taken on a pivotal role in my life. During the fishing season, I feel as though the place is practically my second home. I eat, drink and live in there for days on end, arriving at the crack of dawn, and often hanging around until dusk. I have been introduced to some of my closest friends within the walls of this shop, and I am sure that there will be many new friendships developed in the future.

Paulie's shop is a focal point for the fishing fraternity in our town. Any fisherman with curiosity and a brain will stop in during their stay to say hello and grab a free cup of coffee. The novice is especially welcome at Paulie's Tackle, and will find a visit informative. All that is necessary is to grab a chair at the front of the shop and digest the jabberwocky that permeates the air. Gossip, intelligence reports, and advice accentuate these conversations. New entrants join these bull sessions on a daily basis, making the cast of characters a fluid composite.

I have come across some unique cats while warming a chair at the shop. Quite a few of them have found themselves within this book. I know good copy when I hear it and besides, I feel my lot in life at this point is as a collector of peerless souls. I am a mind picker. I absorb the memories and ideas of others and use them to my own fruition. I turn them through my mind and separate pearls of vivacity. I am well versed at recognizing potentially intriguing scuttlebutt. I love a good story.

I met Jack and Eddie while immersed in the development of another one of my wacky schemes. I had been tweaking the details of a new creation, a floating fishing chair, which would have the primary function of enhancing my ability to provoke my pals. This contraption was, essentially, a resort pool chair, with a gimbled rod holder in the center of the seat and incorporating a safety belt with a quick release to keep me from falling off. The gizmo also sported a beverage holder (*standard issue for a resort pool cushion*) and a customized socket to hold my beloved emblem, the Jolly Roger. With the addition of my skishin' flippers, this plastic coated pool seat was set to make its debut. Once again, Dominique and I departed for the Point to try the thingamajig out.

Arriving at the False Bar, Dom and I gathered the doohickey and took it to the water's edge. We happened to be near a group of campers as we primed my nerve for the first voyage of the SS Mel-Minnow; its pirate flag snapping proudly in the breeze.

"*You're a sick dude, Dude!*" I heard from over my shoulder, and I turned to see two fellows walking over to us, wearing big smiles. Their campsite, featuring an old Winnebago, was just off to the west, nestled within the shelter of the sand dunes. The guys looked like two characters from an early seventies underground comic book.

"You're Melnyk, ain't yah?" the one, who stepped out of a Fabulous Freak Brothers cartoon, said. "I hearda' you, you're supposed to be crazy!" That was Eddie. He was a thin man of about 5'9", with long blonde hair tied in a pony tail that he kept tucked under a bandana. Sporting a big handlebar 'stash, I swore I was looking at the personification of Freewheelin' Franklin. The other fellow (Jack) on the other hand, was a huge man. I will politely state that he carried over two hundred and ninety pounds on his six foot frame. The two characters were brandishing more tattoos than a heavy metal rock band, mostly renditions of skeletons and fish. I knew I liked them, right away.

"What you gonna do with that thing?" Jack growled in a deep baritone as he pointed at my twisted yacht. I then explained my intentions to kick out to the rip and troll for bass. And did they laugh!

As things would unfold, that stupid contraption actually worked, and I managed to hook and release several fish from about two hundred yards out while my impromptu glee club cheered merrily every time I flung a striper through the air towards their general direction.

Later that day I met Abstract Al, who finished off the trio as an aging eccentric whose lifestyle is defiantly moored within the confines of the nineteen sixties stereotype. During an evening of bullshit, cocktails, and more roasted pig meat than I had ever eaten in my life, I was happy to call this band of fellow travelers my pals. It is a gratifying relationship, as these three have supplied me with some of the best yarns to be told.

****

Dropping in on Paulie's one summer afternoon, I encountered Paul immersed in telephone intercourse. A big smile was plastered across his face.. "Holy shit! *Get outta here*! You're kiddin'? Nah, nah, I can't leave, the shop is full... *Here, talk to Melnyk*." Paulie handed me the telephone, shaking his head. I put the phone to my ear.

"Wazzup?"

"Melnyk, you gotta help us out." I recognized Eddie's voice on the other end.

"What?"

"Me and Jack are at the Sportsman's Dock, off East Lake. We need a lift..."

"No problem."

"Bring your pickup; we got a kayak with us..."

"A kayak? How did you get over to the lake with a *kayak*?"

"Don't ask, just get over here before the Coastguard gets here."

"OK, but you owe me one."

Thoroughly intrigued at this point, I took off to rescue my pals anticipating an interesting turn of events. I entered the marina and came across Jack and Eddie, looking like a couple of half drowned rats! At their feet was a two man kayak. I got out and helped lift the contraption onto the load bed along with some oars and fishing rods. About five gallons of water poured out of the upturned boat as it stuck half out of the back.

"You gotta towel?" Eddie said. Jack just shook his head, looking at his feet, seemingly dejected. I threw them each a towel, which is standard equipment in the skish-mobile, and started the truck as they dried off. They shook with a chill, waterlogged as they were.

"OK, what's up with the kayak, guys?" Jack and Eddie don't own a kayak. As a matter of fact, I wasn't sure if either of them could swim.

"Melnyk, you ain't gonna believe this one!"

"Try me..."

Eddie's soliloquy:

Well..... it all started when we saw two of our pals screwin' around on a kayak. They were in the process of havin' a sword fight with the paddles, you know, like Punch and Judy, about a stone's through from the beach. They're battin' at each other, knockin' themselves silly, havin' a grand ol' time, tryin' to knock each other off the thing, ya know?

I says to Jack, "Hey, that looks like a pisser!" I figure, if they can stay afloat while fightin', we can stay afloat fishin', so I say to Jack, "Come on Jack, let's grab it from 'em an' take a ride!"

"*Oh nooo, not me!*" says Jack, shakin' his head, wearin' that big eye look of his.

When they get back to the beach, I go over and ask them if we can borrow the thing, thinkin' we could try and get some bass or somethin' from the rip.

Again, Jack says to me, "*I'm not goin' out there,*" but I was bettin' I could convince him. I figure he don't wanna go 'cause his knees are bad, you know, so I say, "Come on, just walk down there and sit on it and I'll push us off." Again, he says "I'm not goin'!"

"Well alright, then, I'll go by myself!" I said. He looks at me sayin', "OK, I'll go, but we ain't taken no stinkin' life preservers, they're just gonna get in the way." We get our rods and grab the kayak. Jack gets on the front and I give us a push, jump on the back yellin' "Ship ahoy!" and off we go!

We tried zig zaggin' in the cove for a while. Nothin' happens, so we start to row out a bit, almost to the buoy, about a quarter mile off. We're just sittin' there, I swear to God Paul, we weren't screwin' around or nothin'! Low and behold, *Ker-splash!*, The freakin' thing flips over on us! Jack went flyin', you shoulda' seen his face!

There we were, treadin' water, hangin' onto the overturned kayak. We're afraid to right the thing 'cause it's full of water, we got hands full of fishin' stuff, and anyway, Jack is so big, he could never pull himself back on the thing. On the beach we see Al wavin' to us, holdin' up the two life jackets, sayin' "Hey you guys, you forgot these!" So now Al thinks he's gonna save us, right? He swims out with his rod, dressed in a wetsuit and flippers, just like you do, you know, skishin'. By that point we're too far out and he can't swim to us, so he puts a tin on the end of his leader and tries to cast it to us, but we were just to far gone by then.

Now we're driftin' with the tide. The winds blowin' us off, too. I say, "Jack, kick, kick harder!" So we're kickin' but ain't goin' nowhere. As a matter of fact, we're driftin' further out! Now the fog starts rollin' by. I figure we're goners, we're freezin' and getting' socked in! I'm in the process of prayin' for my life, when a 25 foot Grady White with three guys on it, pops outa' the mist and pulls up next to us.

"Hey, take it easy!" the captain says, "We're gonna help ya out." One of the guys reaches down and pulls the kayak out of the water and into the boat while we're still hangin' on, leavin' Jack and me thrashin' around in the drink! "Don't panic," he says, "the water's only *sixteen feet deep!*" Like that makes a difference. I still don't get how they was more worried about the freakin' kayak than me or Jack. "What do you want me to do pal?" Jack says, "*Stand on the tippy toes?*" It took all three of 'em to get Jack into the boat. He flopped around in the cockpit like a beached whale.

With that, my rod slips from my hands just as I'm gettin' ready to climb aboard, and it's sinkin'! I dive down to get it and the freakin' line gets wrapped all around my neck and my legs! I was startin' to go down when I feel a hand grab' me by the ponytail and I got hauled in! My rod came in too, since it was wrapped all around me... (*Eddie winks.*)

So now we're on the boat. The captain introduces himself as doctor so-and-so. He informs us that the other guy is an EMT, who starts takin' our pulse and shit. That's when the third guy says to me, "What can I do? I'm just the asshole they brought along to pay for bait." I says, "That's good 'cause we get along good with assholes, we're hangin' with you pal!" That's when the doctor gets all nervous and starts to call the freakin' Coastguard! I say, "Jesus H. Christ, their gonna site us for not havin' life jackets, buddy hold off, will yah?" I donno, I think maybe they was scared of us or somethin', 'cause the free bait guy never took his eye off us. Next thing ya know, were pullin' up to the dock. Now I don't know if he got through to the cops or what, but let's not take no chances, OK? Let's get outa' here.

Charlie.

Intent on meeting up with the Murderer's Row gang one afternoon, I made my way to the Point, driving down the rocky coastline towards the False Bar. It was one of those doldrums days of August, when a fish is a hard thing to hook. Even still, I brought along a rod, figuring I would give it a go. Around the corner, I came across a collection of RV's, and noticing that they belonged to my friends, I decided to stop for the while and shoot the shit. I pulled up to the dune and jumped out of the cab, and walked over to Eddie and Jack, who make it a habit to drive out to Montauk on a Thursday night for a long weekend of fishing, eating and carrying on.

The sand was warm even though the sun was low in the sky, bringing a cool south west breeze onto the beach. As I approached the guys, I noticed a pile of lobster shells at their feet. It appeared that my buds had a feast of sorts, noshing on an exceptionally fine crustacean.

At first glance, the pile of red exoskeleton remains did not seem out of place, as Jack and Eddie make a habit of pigging out for the entire duration of their visits. It was not unusual to see my pals surrounded by a crowd of freeloaders, chewing on a slab of cow. You see, Jack is the portly sort, and he is not at all shy about cooking for a mob, whether or not there is a mob available. As I came closer to the pile of crusty remains I was struck by the awesome size of the empty claw shells. These mitts were the size and girth of a littoral monster, taking on the appearance of crimson baseball gloves. With closer inspection of the corps, I saw the carcass of an armored tail which was almost two feet long!

"Holly shit! Did you eat that sucker all by yourselves?"

"Yep," Jack said, with a sly twinkle in his eye, the sheen of butter glimmering upon his chin.

"That thing musta weighed ten pounds!"

"**Fifteen pounds**, to be exact, Eddie weighed 'im on his Boga Grip!"

"Was some good, too!" Eddie chimed in as he rubbed his belly in mock satiation. "I'm still pickin' lobster meat outa my cavities..." The two old boys laughed heartily at that gem of a remark.

"Damn, that lobster musta cost a fortune!"

"Paulie, you ain't gonna believe how we got it."

"Try me."

What unfolded was a tale of questionable validity, but being intrigued; I sat down next to my friends and absorbed this dubious yarn.

"Me and Jack was out near the Lighthouse, makin' a couple of casts, just to see if we could scare up a bass or blue, when all of a sudden like, I feel somethin' thumpin' against my waders. I look down and I see this monster lobster just kinda floatin' by, not makin' tracks, mind you, but just barely swimmin'."

"Get outa here!"

"No shit! I thought at first, this freakin' thing's gonna take my foot off, but to tell ya the truth, it was half dead, so's I reach down and grab it by the back! Can you believe it? The bastard was like some kinda mutant! Me an' Jack stare at each other and freaked out! We threw that sucker in the pot and *voila, Lobsterfest!"*

"Come on! You expect me to believe you plucked a fifteen pound lobster from the surf?" With that, the two fella's start giggling. "I swear to yah, it happened just like that!"

"Boy oh boy, either you two are full of shit, or the luckiest suckers in Montauk!"

"Better to be lucky than good!" Eddie said, giving me a wink and lighting up a smoke.

Now the thought of a lobster or two, found walking in the sand, is not as far fetched as you may think. I myself have reaped the crusty fruits of the sea on occasion. I recall how some friends and I went for a walk on the beach at Oyster Pond in the lee of Hurricane Gloria a few years ago. Along with buckets of mussels, we scavenged *thirteen lobsters* just strolling along the tide line, their shells bright and shiny, their claws going click, click, click... I must say, the largest was no more than a pound and a half, but we did make lobster salad sandwiches all weekend. But a *fifteen pounder*... Hmmmm.... I don't know.

Later that very weekend, for some unknown reason I had the hankering for the taste of lobster. I decided to make the trip to Duryea's lobster house so I could grab a three pounder as a special treat for myself.

Perry B. Duryea and Son is one of Montauk's oldest establishments, as old as the town itself. It is nestled within the bluffs and kettleholes along Fort Pond Bay. The old red and white buildings are kept in immaculate condition, having been in the Duryea family for almost a hundred years. These buildings contain neatly stacked tiers of green salt water tanks along the interior walls. The tanks are filled with thousands of dollars of New England Lobsters, which are packed, and shipped to the market. The sound of the water as it circulates throughout the place is hypnotic, and I used to love to go in there when I was a kid, just to hear it and visit with those giant grasshopper-lookin' things. Chip Duryea, the proprietor, is not opposed to selling a lobster or two for the retail market, if the price is right.

"Hey Chip, you got any big ones back there?" I said as I peered over the counter into the back of the lobster house.

"I've got a tank full of jumbos, up to five pounds, out back."

"Wow, five pounds huh? Well grab me a three pounder from back there, will ya." I followed Chip into the back and watched him scoop a nice one from a tank full of chubby crustaceans. "Hey Chip, you ever get anything really big in?"

"Yeah, I had a fifteen pounder up until a couple a days ago. We had him in here so long he was like the shop's mascot. Then, the other day, some fellow comes in here with his family, and starts poking his nose around. He starts lecturing to his children about how inhumane it is to keep the poor lobsters caged up like that. When they looked into my tank of jumbo's and saw ol' Charlie, they just about had a fit."

"Charlie?"

"Yeah, Charlie, the fifteen pounder. That old claw had been here for so long, the girls out back gave it a name. It's kind of hard to sell a fifteen pound Lobster at eighteen dollars a pound, now-a-days."

"Hmm..."

"So the fellow says to me, "You should be ashamed to keep a beautiful animal like that in a tank. Ashamed!" (*He laughs*). Can you believe it? I always thought they are just big bugs myself. Tasty bugs. *Then he tried to shame me out of the thing to let it go!"*

"Are you serious!"

"Yeah, no kidding! He starts giving me a lesson on lobsters; how old they have to be to get that big and all, like I need a lesson... I told him, if he was so concerned about the thing, he could buy it and do whatever he wanted with it. "Well that's a great idea!" he said, "We're gonna let this poor creature go, right kids!" and he throws down a cool 200 bucks like it was nothing. Then he picked it off the counter and took off with his clan. One of the kids was carrying it like a babe in arms. The last thing I heard was that they were all headed to the Lighthouse with it. *I'm willing to bet they were gonna have a little ceremony out there, and let it go."*

The Plug.

It seems that I spend a lot of time talking to Jack and Eddie lately. This will usually bring out a good story from one of the boys. On another occasion, fueled by several fried turkeys and a few beers, my pal Eddie's lips were loosened up enough to tell me this tale:

"Hey Melnyk, you know how I like to go scarfin' plugs while I'm here, right? Well this is a story that very few people know about, although I bet after you hear it, that's gonna change."

Well one mornin' I'm out huntin' the rocks for plugs. I'm doin' good, 'cause the tide is way out. By the time I get from the False Bar to the Point, I had about ten plugs in my pouch, some real good ones, too, Musso's, Gibbs, even a Beachmaster. It was the best score for me all summer!

I was feelin' real lucky, you know, so's I go off to look around the rocks under the Lighthouse. The water is real low, like I ain't never seen it before. I'm in the drink, walkin' under the Lighthouse and it's not even up to my knees! I'm searchin' around in the rocks when I see a brandy-dandy new Afterhours bottle-darter, just sittin' there under the surface, sayin' *here I am, come an' get me!* So I reach down and grab the thing. I'm pullin' on the freakin' thing, but it's stuck! The leader was jammed between two rocks and wouldn't budge. I'm tryin' to yank it outa there when a wave blind-sides me and I go down in the rocks! The next thing I know I see a big ol' hook buried in my finger!

It ain't commin' out, see, stuck through, all the way as it was. OK, no big deal, I reach in with the other hand to undo the snap. What the hell? The freakin' thing is crimped onto a wire leader and it ain't breakin' off, no way! Why the guy used a crimp instead of a snap, I'll never know. Anyway, I pull and pull but the thing ain't comin' out of my finger, or the rocks! I'm stuck real good, see? I start hollerin' to the tourists that are walkin' around the Light, hey, how about a little help here! Those bastards wouldn't even look at me! It was like I was invisible! "Hey Asshole!" I says *nice and sweet like* to the next dude that passes by, "I could use a hand here!" Nothin'. I couldn't believe it.

Now the water is risin' and the next thing I know, I'm gettin' bashed into the rocks by the waves! The tide is comin' in fast and my head's bouncin' into the jetty like piece of driftwood. At this point there's blood pourin' down my face, I can taste it, yah know?

"HEY YOU!" I say to this cat who was just watchin' the whole thing from about fifty feet away, holdin' a rod in his hand. ***"YOU WANNA HELP ME OUT HERE, OR WHAT?"***

The Goog looks at me and says, *"I ain't goin' down there, I'll get killed!"*

"Well then you're gonna have my dead corps on your conscience, moron! I'm dyin' here!"

"I'm not goin' down there, you just hold on, I'll get some help!"

"Look stupid," I say, "By the time the cops get here, I'll be crab bait, for cryin' out loud! Just put your pliers on the end of your line and send 'em down to me, will yah?" So he clips a pair of pliers to his leader and drops them down to me. I got bashed a few more times before I could cut that damned thing off.

Now that I'm outa the rocks, everybody wants to help out, see? "*Gee, that looks like it hurts,*" some chick says to me. I thought she was gonna pass out. With the plug still hangin' from my finger, I hobble back to the camper and had Jack drive me to the hospital forty miles away. You know, that freakin' plug wound up costin' me *five hundred bucks!*

Melnyk's First Fish.

I guess most of you guys can remember your first "bona fide" fish caught from the surf. Of course for a few of you, this might not have been very long ago, but my first fish was caught quite a bit further back, when the act of shaving was considered a goal instead of a chore.

My passion for this sport took seed when I was about five or six years old and my Pop took the whole clan (*I'm sure it was Mom's idea*) to the Hanger Dock off Navy Road, to do some fishing. At that time it was an old abandoned naval base where they tested torpedoes during WWII. The place was like a ghost town, with abandoned aircraft hangars and rusting Quonset huts everywhere. There was a wide concrete launching ramp that led into the bay which was used to launch Navy PBY sea planes. A long dock was the focal point of the place. This was where the subs would pull in to load up with experimental torpedoes.

I was handed a rod and a worm to drop off the end of that long dock sometime in the summer of 1962. I can still remember the feel of my first hook-up. Of course, Dad helped reel it in. It was a blowfish, which promptly expanded to four times its normal size as I brought it over the railing. We caught a slew of 'em that afternoon! Let's not call this my first fish 'cause honestly, Pop brought it in.

My pursuit of the piscatorial (*again?*) delights continued. Within a few years, I had advanced to sunnys and the occasional perch, hooked from Fort Pond with worms that I would dig out of my Aunt Helen's garden. But the real motivator was seeing Grandpa and Uncle Frankie come home with huge stripers which they had caught on Teddy Steven's charter boat, the "Storm King." The sight of those monsters was enough to make my heart skip! Heck, I couldn't even lift one up at the time! We all stood around and took pictures of a back yard full of those shinning silver bullets. In those photos, my ears stand out about six inches from my head, making me look like a little mouse with a crew cut! *Ahhh, the Sixties!*

That was it. In that moment, standing among the scales and blood, I just knew that I had to catch a *big* fish! But I was too little to go on the darn boat! (*I think this had more to do with the bawdy stories and a bottle of Scotch than my size*). What was I to do? I pleaded and pleaded to go fishing, but my father would have none of it. He did not have any interest in fishing and preferred to lounge on the beach. Finally my Aunt Helen suggested one afternoon that I take my big sister Vicky to the jetty at the end of West Lake Drive. We could ride our bikes there, getting some sun and exercise for our efforts. There were plenty of people there and we would be looked after. Remember, these were the sixties when every adult watched over us kids, whether you were theirs or not.

By God, what a cool idea! I had to formulate a plan! This would not be some impromptu outing, but an expedition! I spent all that afternoon with Grandpa in the back yard as he taught me how to make an underhand cast without a bird's nest. He must have had "the Rheumatism" that morning because he stayed off the boat that day, teaching me the finer points of the craft.

Near the end of my lesson, Grandpa looked around to see if anybody was looking and then slipped his hand into his back pocket. He handed me a shiny pocket knife. It was a new Uncle Henry made by the Kabar Company. They made bayonets in WWII! "Don't yoo dare tell Momma!" You know, I still have that old knife. It is one of my most prized possessions.

At 10 am the next morning, (*late by my standards, but my sis would not shake a leg)* I scooped a handful of quarters out of my junk drawer, and grabbed one of Grandpa's old rods. Vicky was already telling our Mom how she didn't wanna baby sit for her bro.

With dreams of glory, I grabbed my Schwinn "Black Phantom" and took off for the jetty; my sister, was way behind. She had a creepy "girls bike." With youthful determination and a bucket slipped onto the handlebars, I had to negotiate the sandy roads single handedly because the rod was jammed into my other fist.

Grandpa had told me to get some real bait if I wanted to catch a nice sized fish. "Blood voims. Make sure yoo get da blood voims, Pavel. Sand voims no verk too good."

I stopped at Tuma's Dock to get the worms and give sis a chance to catch up. With my box of worms and Vicky in tow, we headed for the jetty at the inlet to Montauk Harbor. This formation of rocks is one of a pair of breakwaters that guard the entrance to the harbor. It is a long affair, of maybe 200 yards with a light tower at the end. Back in the sixties, there were places where the rocks had washed out and large gaps separated the monolithic blocks in certain areas. You had to jump across these slippery hazards.

"I'm not jumpin' over that Paul."

"You better, or I'll leave you here."

"If I get hurt, I'm tellin'!" We leapt across the canyons of craggy crap to reach the very tip of the west jetty. I recall Vicky had tears in her eyes by the time we reached the light tower on the very tip.

"I'm not stayin' more than an hour!" she said as the warm June sun shown down from within a deep blue sky. "I'm not wasting my day so you can stare at the stupid water!"

Sure.

I especially enjoyed showing my sis the teeth the blood worms have. I let one fasten to the callus on my fingertip and chased her across the rocks with that wiggling leggy monster hanging down, while yelling "Help me! *Help Meee!"*

Rocks... I fell in love with the rocks while shimmying down to the water's edge to fish. The rocks were covered in slimy green seaweed that glistened in the sun. The smell of salt air and old bait was like a balm to my senses.

"Where are you going? You'll get killed down there!"

"Awww, shut up, will yah?"

"I'm tellin'!"

That hour went by for me as if it was only a second. I watched jealously as the guy fishing about twenty feet away from me pulled up a burgal. I was psyched! Vicky seemed a bit more docile when she watched that fish come up right next to me.

"Do you think you can catch one of those Paul?" she said.

My cast had improved. I was soon able to get the sinker fifty feet from the rocks. It splashed into the clear aquamarine water and sank to the bottom. Grandpa had told me to reel in the line slowly.

"Valk da voim along da bottom, Pavel. You get da feesh, for sure!"

Sure enough I got a strike! The fish started to take line and my sister began to scream!

"Oooh...Oooh!"

"You got one! You got one! Keep his head up kid!" the guy next to me hollered. Keep his head up? What the heck does that mean! I reeled and reeled as I watched the drag spin. I had no idea how to slow the fish down, but soon enough it was coming! I looked down and there was that fish attached to my forty pound test mono! *"Vicky! Help meeeeeee!"*

"Oooh.... Oooh!" was her retort.

I dragged that fish out of the water and up the face of the jetty. It had swallowed the hook and I took great pleasure in using my new Kay-Bar to cut the line.

"Where did you get that knife? I'm tellin Mommy!" sis howled with a sly look in her eye.

I was amazed! I had never caught a fish so big in my life! It must have been ten pounds!

"Hey kid, look at that! You got a codfish!"

Sure enough, it was a cod! I tenderly tickled the fat little whisker under the cod's chin and reverently placed the fish in my pail. Its tail hung out.

"You're not gonna kill the poor thing?" Vicky said with a mush-face.

"Kill it? Hell, *I'm gonna eat it!"*

With that said, the fish promptly jumped out of the bucket... The scene that followed was so comical, it was like a speeded up view of an old "Keystone Cops" movie. I chased that fish all over the top of the jetty as it flopped and slipped and wiggled.

"Vicky! Gimme a rock, I gotta sock it in the head!"

"Oooh...Oooh! Your gonna hurt the poor thing!"

Just so. The fish slipped into a chasm between the rocks, far out of reach, but not far enough. It mocked me as I tried everything to get it back. No good. It was crab food.

We rode home after that, the silence of the dead drifted between us. I was so mad at my sister! It was she that I wanted to hit in the head with a rock!

I went right to Grandpa to tell my tale with tears in my eyes. I was sure he would be disappointed, but to my surprise, *he was proud of me!*

He asked me over and over again that day just how big that fish was as I relived the event for my aunts and uncles. Each time I told the story I showed him the size of the fish with my arms stretched out, and each time, those outstretched arms would get further and further apart. Grandpa laughed and laughed! He spent all afternoon praising my feat to all who would listen.

"Don' vorry Pavel, next time you get 'em... for sure!"

A Fluke.

During the '80's, I was the owner of Ann Breyer's Cottages as you know by now. I enjoyed chatting with the clients and making new friends, and I eventually realized that the way to get return guests was to relate to them, and make them like us personally. It was right up my alley. I was always interested in meeting interesting people.

One summer afternoon, I was checking in my guests when I welcomed a new family to my place. The father of the brood was sort of a gawk, a nerdy kind of fellow, but I figured I would go over and introduce myself. I watched him carry in some fishing tackle while he squared his stuff away. We got to talking, and I asked about his gear. It seemed that the fellow knew very little about angling and was rather low key about it, but he was intent on giving it a try. He asked me if I knew of a place where he could "catch a fish" from the beach. I had to contemplate this for a moment. It was August and I was not very confident that he could handle the places that I personally frequented. Finally, I came up with a suggestion. "You know, there is a place called Gin Beach at the end of West Lake Drive where there may be a bluefish or two. Your wife and kids will love the beach there and you can go swimming if the fish don't bite. Why don't you grab some sinkers and sand eels and cast them from the beach about a quarter mile east of the parking lot? I have caught fish there in the past." The guy thanked me for the advice and said he would go and make a cast or two with his sons. I was sure he would get skunked, but the sand and sea there was so nice in August, I was sure he would have a good time anyway. As I left for home, I saw him pack up his stuff and take his family for their first Montauk fishing trip.

I arrived to work the following morning and in a short time I saw the fellow sitting on his porch. I went over for some friendly conversation.

"How was your first day in town?" I said.

"Well, it was OK," was all he said. He was either very shy or just one of those people who have little to say.

"So how was your fishing trip?" I had learned that in this business, the best way to create return clients was to be amiable.

"You know, it was pretty good." I had to prod him further for more information.

"Well... how did you do?"

"We had some flounders in that spot you sent us to. It was fun."

Now this peeked my interest. "Really? How many did you catch?"

"Well, we filled a garbage can with fish in about an hour."

A garbage can? *Yeah right.*

"It was funny how it happened," he said, "The fish were jumpin' out of the water." This was said as an aside, like maybe this sort of thing happens every day.

"Really?" I said. I was not very convinced but this was an interesting story nonetheless.

Later that afternoon my friend Mark came by for a visit. We got to throwing back a few beers and I discussed this conversation with him. What the heck, we were a bit loaded and we decided to bring along my family to give it a go (*by this time we were in need of a designated driver*).

Sooo... We grabbed some fluke rigs and a big bag of sand eels from the tackle store. We made it home and I asked my wife Dawn, my sister Vicky, and brother-in-law Don if they would like to join us. Off we went on a merry chase to watch the sunset. Now my wife and sister were no fisher-women, and my brother-in-law, Don, was a drop a sinker sorta guy, but with the whole gang in my truck we were headed for some fun on Gin Beach.

"Yo Bro!" Mark said to me with a wink, *"Let's bring a garbage can, so we can fill it up!"*

I relayed the story to my family and we all had a good chuckle. We threw a thirty gallon can into the back of the truck just for shits and giggles. My wife had never driven on the beach before so this was great excitement for her. With Don driving, and Mark and myself in the bed of the pickup, we bumped along the beach havin' a grand ol' time.

"This looks like the place!" said I, when we reached a goodly spot past the tourists and blankets. Out we jumped and into the water we went. No waders, just bare feet and fishing poles. Before long we were picking a few fluke here and there. Most were in the one to two pound class.

Now all you busybodies, remember, there was no limit on fluke in the 80's and the legal size was just sixteen inches. These were nice fish for the times. The girls were having very little luck, but the guys and I had about three fish each within an hour. We watched the sun set onto the still water as a cool summer breeze settled on shore, gently stirring the top of the sea.

No sooner had the sun touched the ocean, when the water erupted in a rolling boil. There were eight inch sand eels flinging themselves out of the sea, jumping for dear life! As this was occurring, we all began to hook up, even the ladies! Soon the water was full of fluke jumping right out of the surf chasing the bait. There must have been an acre of 'em! They looked like Frisbees as they sailed through the air. Their bodies undulated, as if they had wings. The fish were now coming in with every cast and they had gotten bigger. Quite a few three and four pounders were dragged in.

The girls were a bit of a pain in the butt since they were scared of the teeth; feminine beauties that they were. They gave up and relinquished their rods, to take on the task of picking up the fish we threw behind us (*of course they waited till they stopped moving*). It became like one of those old Cowboy and Indian movies from the fifties, where the actions of the "women-folk" takes on a frantic pace as they re-load the guns, and hand them to the "men-folk," one redskin after another biting the dust! (*Oh God... Am I being politically incorrect?*) Soon it was not even necessary to throw out a hook; the stupid fluke were beaching themselves as they chased the biggest sand eels I had ever seen right out of the water! Now the girls kicked them towards the tide line, giggling like young co-eds.

No sooner had the sun set below the horizon and twilight took hold, the fish disappeared. The whole event was over. None the less, we had thirty minutes of phenomenal fishing. *We FILLED that garbage can!*

It took the rest of the night to clean all the fluke. We all stank to high heaven from the gore and carnage. My back yard was full of blood and guts, our pet cats happily purring away, gorging themselves on the offal. We filled the upright freezer with fillets. We gave away so much fluke that week, I felt like a delivery man. In all my life I had never seen such a thing as that day of the flying fluke.

Free Willy.

Anyone who has been fishing under the Lighthouse in Montauk on a stormy fall morning knows how treacherous it can be. With ten foot waves slamming into the jetty and salt spray penetrating to the soul, this place can take on an almost surreal atmosphere. Watching the casters vie for a perfect rock, hovering over the perfect hole, there is little doubt that mornings such as these will yield a slob of a bass, and on rare occasions, will provide a fat striper to every fisherman who braves the tempest.

This gathering of surfcasters becomes even more intense as the season progresses to the point at which the fall run of big fish is overdue, usually when all of the associated tournaments enter into the equation. There are times when every rock under and around the Point is occupied and all present are taking a beating by the surf. I have been witness to scenes such as these when the "Locals" monopolize the front of this breakwater and cast with relentless abandon into the strong rip of a flooding storm tide. Under such circumstances, a relay of fishermen may be seen fighting one fish after another, their rods held high above the audience as they weave between the rocks and fellow casters to land great fish in Scott's Cove.

I can recall an occasion when all the big shots were under the Light during a Nor'Easter. They stood at the top of the jetty with their backs against the fence that surrounds the Lighthouse bluff. The sea had been particularly deceptive that day as long periods of deceivingly smooth white water rolled into the jetty. A person could get the idea that the lower rocks were fishable that morning. Time and tide, however, would prove this to be a dangerous assumption as great waves would sweep the abutment every so often with enough force to send a tremor along the rock face.

Watching my pals, I noticed a fellow stumble along the jetty and climb down to the water's edge. It was clear that the man was not in a rational state and that he may have imbibed a nip or two for courage before he had the nerve to attempt a storm tide. The sorry fellow was drastically under equipped, wearing only foul weather gear and rubber boots.

"Hey Pal! You may wanna keep to the top of the rocks, you're gonna get killed down there. Those waves are fierce!"

He looked up at me with glazed eyes and gave me the "mind your own business" stare. *(I don't know, is it me? I often get these weird looks when I insert my two cents).* I suppose the fact that he was alone in his quest for that lower position on the face of the jetty had not occured to his addled mind. He faced the sea and made an effort at his first cast. As he lifted his rod, he was slammed in the chest by a great wave which tore the rod from his hand and slammed him into the rocks.

Someone yelled, "Hey pal! Are you OK?" The dazed fellow looked up at us with a frightful expression. At that exact moment, a following wave of much greater ferocity slammed into the listing caster and swallowed him whole within the tidal surge of wet hell. As the wave receded, the rock where he had once been was swept clean. He was gone.

"Where the hell did he go?" Joe Gav said to me with a look of panic on his face.

"Did you see that?" I said. "He just up and disappeared!"

We scanned the water hoping that the guy had not been killed. There he was! He stumbled up the rock face almost twenty yards from where the sea had gobbled him up within its great white maw. He scurried for the top of the rocks and shook himself off like a wet mongrel. His rod and tackle were gone. As we watched to see if he was alright, we saw him slink off into the storm, apparently to his car and home.

****

On another occasion when the sea only pretended calm, I was to finally prove to the gathered anglers at the Point the benefit of wearing a wet suit. For the first few seconds of sunrise the sun took on the appearance of an orange mushroom within the morning haze. A thermo cline caused the light to shimmer within this silvery mirage. The ocean rolled toward the lighthouse abutment with a five foot swell as huge swells on the horizon would occasionally bring a powerful wave to the rocks. Once again there were distinctive lulls between these breakers, and succumbing to tournament fever, the hardcore of our group decided to risk it and cast into the perfect whitewater that rolled below. We stood among the second tier of rocks, halfway to the water's edge.

The sun brightened; its new light had a warming effect, displacing the morning chill. Great streams of purple and gold clouds passed overhead, in stark contrast to the white caps of the choppy sea a quarter mile off the Point. There were fish. Bass and bluefish cued up to gulp at the first sign of movement set before them. If you missed a fish as your bucktail hit the water, two more cranks would inevitably bring a strike. Their size was an enjoyable treat as the ocean had been baron of life for the last four days. All of us were in a cheerful mood and we basked in the joy of it. I was singing the theme song from that old TV show of the 1960's "Rawhide" hoping that this chant would bring in the cow bass for us.

Rollin', rollin', rollin,
Keep those doggies rollin',
Keep them doggies movin',
Raw hide!
YEE HAAH!

To my left stood an older guy with a green hooded slicker, cinched tightly under his chin, hiding his face. He was also enjoying the excitement of the "hot bite." The two of us were casting into a hole that was holding fish. Attila was off to my right on the next rock, getting frustrated, even though he was casting right next to us. Sometimes it just works out that way.

As I landed another fish in the rocks below, the crest of a wave worked its way towards my perch. I saw it coming and jumped into a hollow, ducking for cover as the wash flew over my head and crashed along the jetty. As I climbed up the rocks I gave a hoot of joy; the cold water was invigorating and I had escaped fate with the help of that lucky hollow in the rocks. I glanced to my left to see what havoc the wave had set within my fellow casters as it rolled along the front.

The fellow next to me had taken a direct hit and was floundering in the rocks! "Holly Shit!! Attila! Hold my rod! That guy is in trouble!" I scrambled across the boulders and reached the fellow. It was no less than the legendary Willy Young, the aging surfcaster extraordinaire.

Willy's foot was jammed between the rocks! I could see that one of his Korkers was firmly stuck in a crevice. He was frantically trying to free himself by pulling at his leg. Another wave was fast approaching. I jumped to his left and leaned into him as the wave rolled over both of us. It took all of my weight (*I am a bit more massive than Willy*) to hold us firmly in place. I tasted the salty white fingers of foam flowing through my sinuses. With adrenaline pumping, I managed to keep us standing. I looked into Willy's wide eyes. He had the appearance of a frightened rabbit. More waves were on the way. "Keep Still!" I shouted into his ear as I tried to free his jammed foot. I could see his leg bending sideways in a most unnatural position. I hoped it wasn't broken. I had to forcefully pull his foot down below the ensnaring boulders to get it released from this trap. I am sure he got a good bruise from this maneuver, but what the heck. It worked.

Throughout all the turmoil and panic that I witnessed within Willy's face, I realized that he had never dropped his rod. He clung to his juju as though it was his life's blood. Once freed, the old mountain goat, scrambled up the sheer face of the jetty, like an athlete.

"Boy that was a close one! Thanks Buddy. Thanks a lot."

"Piece of cake."

Willy fished for the rest of the tide even though he must have been soaked to the bone. Later, I watched him limping away. He was gonna need a good smear of Bengay that evening.

Mr. Blasko's First Southside Skish.

I never experienced someone so tenacious about learning how to skish before. Frank Blasko was determined to learn how to do it, and that was all there was to it. There was no convincing him otherwise. I think he corresponded with me about five times through Email before I relented and, finally, simply agreed to take him on a rock hopping trip. Forget about skishing. He would need to be tested to see if he met the requirements. The exercise would be the 'Vito Orlando March.' Now Vito has been a surfrat forever. There are few that can keep up with his stamina and amazing willpower when it comes to finding big pods of bass and Vito is famous for his little ten mile fishing hikes.

So I met Blasko at the Montauk IGA one evening in July. The first thing I noticed was the man's massive physique. Bald, tattooed to the max, and weighing in at around 250, he was a monster. I knew he was my kinda guy from the get-go, and I told him so. You see, we could have been twins. He looked at me like I was a nut, so I had to explain myself. Men of grand anatomy have an advantage when it comes to skishing. First off, they float better. Secondly, all the muscle that it takes to carry a heavyweight is an advantage when you are weightless in the surf. The most important benefit, however, is the ability to retain body core heat; the "*Elephant Seal*" effect.

Off we went to Ditch Plains for a *short trip* in wetsuits and korkers. We stopped at every point between the trailer park and The Teahouse; about a seven mile expedition. He didn't wheeze once. No complaints. Best of all, he was quiet and pretended to listen to my bullshit. I think I caught one fish and gave it to him as a boobie prize. If I recall correctly, he got skunked.

I won't go into much detail about the first sissy attempts at skishing we took on the north side, which was the next exercise to see if he had the spirit. Let's just say he did well. Like a duck to water. I do remember Frank catching a fish or two.

So it was decided, this Blasco character had potential to be a good swim fisher. The big day had come and I had Frank bring the eels. I always made him bring the eels. We took his truck to the place known to hold big stripers and parked about a half mile from the beach. On the walk in, I gave him the lecture about how it is much different to swim the south side. Bigger water and rocks make the swim out a bit more of a challenge. We would also be situating ourselves in twenty feet of water about 200 yards from the beach.

The first thing I noticed that was out of place was a humongous fence, newly placed, in the middle of the road, just passed an area I knew to be a county nature preserve. The damned thing was fabricated out of 8x8 timbers and steel mesh. Frank and I decided not to trespass and instead, backtracked a few yards and took the nature trail where we were eaten alive by deer flies. These little bastards were chasing us down as we passed through the swampy portion of the path. The little suckers don't just bite (*like some fiery be-Jesus*), they will chase your ass until you kill them, and the only way to kill them is to let them bite you first!

Well, we crossed through this no-man's-land and made for the beach trail. The next surprise was when we passed a butler and maid on the trail. Hmmmm.... Now this is a nature trail, not the path to Versailles, so I suspected things might get interesting. There was a small clearing just before the low bluff that leads to the beach access. We blundered into the a narrow meadow where there was a table set up with fine linens supporting rounds of brie, brochettes and of course, silver buckets of Don Perignon. Off to the side, was a set of stairs that led to the beach. There was a circle of chairs, on which sat two women and a gent, sipping from fluted glasses. We two bald, bare breasted and tattooed bastards had crashed Thurston Howell the Third's little private sunset soiree for little old ladies!

"Hello!" says I. "Do you mind if we play through?" The ladies seemed shocked but also somewhat intrigued by our burly masculine forms which were naked from the waist up; the evening being warm, we sported wetsuits with the tops tied at the waist. They started up a pleasant conversation about fishing until Thurston, apparently feeling left out of the conversation, broke in. "How did you get here? *Did you climb my fence?"*

"Oh no sir, I happen to be a member of the Nature Conservancy, and we took the nature trail." (*I, being a fisherman, lied*).

"Ahemm, well... This is quite irregular... quite irregular indeed..."

We continued to flirt with the old broads. We understood who ruled this roost. I asked for a canapé, and was quite perturbed when I did not receive one from the attendant.

"Well good evening to you ladies. If we are lucky, you will see us on the way home with some world class striped bass on our shoulders." As we were shooed down the stairway by the butler, the ladies wished us luck and Mr. Howell looked on with searing eyes. (*I now understand there is a guard posted at this gate to the Manor. Even the nature trail patrons are required to make an appointment to travel along their path.*)

We double-timed two points east to beat the setting sun and entered the water. Frank broke into hysterical laughter when the first wave lifted him five feet into the air and washed over his body. We kicked through the surf on our backs to a point where the waves just began to grow from the deep. By the time the sun hit the horizon we were swimming into the rip and drifting east, with eels at the ready.

I explained to Frank how the fish will not bite unless I tell a story or two. Frank seemed to question this remark but humored me anyway. I started one of my many yarns about sharks and sea monsters. No sooner had I spewed a few paragraphs when Frank's rod bent in half.

This was followed by hoots of delight from Mr. Blasko. Frank was pulled several hundred feet and I did my best to supply encouragement and advice.

Fighting a fish while you are swimming takes quite a bit of exertion. You have to balance your body so that you don't get pulled onto your face. You have to kick like hell to keep the right amount of pressure on the thing. If the drag is too tight, the fish will spit the hook. The closer the fish gets to you, the more you must loosen the drag. Frank was a natural and in no time I had his striper in my grasp. It was a fine specimen of an animal, which was evident by the way my fist was dwarfed within its mouth! I handed it off to Frank and he tied the beast to a long stringer that was attached to his belt. This allowed the fish to stay alive and swim a bit away from us.

"Holy shit! I think this is the largest bass I have taken yet! What do you think it weighs?"

"Jeez Frank, that bastard looks like a forty, for sure!" The fish would weigh in at 38 pounds, three hours later.

As the sun set, we were flowing within a lightly rolling sea. The tide had taken hold of us and we had just about drifted back to the place where we had originally stepped onto the beach. The night had become essentially lightless, with just the residual glow from the lights of town illuminating the tall spires of the cliffs as they passed by. With the darkness, Frank's excitement seemed to increase and we were soon both fighting nice sized stripers, a double header. "You ever come across a shark out here, Paul?" Frank said in passing as he played his fish. "I mean, I am swimming with a forty pounder tied to my waist, and another one splashin' around in front of me."

"Nah, nothin' to speak of Frank. Maybe a seven footer or so, but he was not interested in eating me at the time." Frank looked at me quizzically, wondering if I had been serious. His eyes shown like a cat's within the glare of my dive light as he released his fish, which slowly sunk into the sea and disappeared.

Frank got stabbed in the ass by his fish's dorsal spike as the beast swam around him, tied to his lanyard. They will do that, you know, just to let you know that they are not quite finished yet. I did manage to hook a 33 pounder, and I think we had three other fish over 25 pounds between the two of us, which we released, that night.

We walked the trail back to the truck with those two slobs on our shoulders. Too bad, the old biddies and Howell were nowhere to be found. We did climb that gate on the return trip, just for spite.

Lights.

I love to fish during the small hours of the night. It seems these are the times that God has reserved for those of us with the determination and perseverance to grasp at that elusive trophy fish. These beasts are on the prowl in the darkness, in search of some tasty morsel left behind by the frantic, gorging young. Odds are odds, and the vig is a lot shorter during those dim hours.

It is amazing what can be seen through the darkness once you have cleared your night vision. The stars pop into a three dimensional panorama of infinite depth. On a clear, moonless night the Milky Way paints a band of cool radiance across the sky. Old friends, in the form of familiar constellations rise to greet you. Shooting stars pass fleetingly in the corners of your vision, leaving green streaks. On exceptional nights, the Aurora Borealis may be seen shimmering like a purple, magenta and green curtain in the northern heavens. The ocean itself will speak in tongues reserved for those of us who are willing to listen. Sheets of surf roll into the rocks, creating a haunting resonance of white noise. Through the clear depths, incandescent microorganisms pass in blue-green moats. A calm, humid night will cause a strange parallax in which the terminator of sky and sea becomes obscured. The stars morph within the blue phosphorescence, and the krill become the stars. Often in the distance, you can see the bright lights of cities and towns across Long Island Sound, which take on a glow that radiates like a halo above them. Blinking lights of towers and navigational beacons pulse unfailingly through the darkness.

The Montauk Lighthouse is a favorite haunt of mine during these dark nights. Time is measured through the pulse of that sweeping beam, its radiance passes in what seems an endless white ray, out to sea. Those of us who can remember know of a time when that brightness rivaled the moon. When the Coast Guard gave up on the old sentinel, the light lessened from five thousand candle power to what now appears to us old timers as the dim glimmer of a twenty watt light bulb. In a way, it is just not the same, and we miss it, along with that craggy breakwater that once stood guard over the foot of the Lighthouse bluff. Those rocks were also different then. Twisted and pummeled by the surging wakes of great storms, they brought schools of bait into their crevasses with much more regularity than today. The great fish would follow, hiding in ambush, among the broken rubble below. It was a time of plenty, but then we were young, and we could scoot among those boulders to take possession of our favorite perches, hopping like toadies within the gloom.

So now I must seek the far rocks to reach that productive shoal of the Point rip which once simply lay below my feet. In order to get there I must swim. In the dark, the journey out is analogous to some clandestine mission. To swim to a place, unseen in the night, with just the knowledge of dead reckoning and a visual bearing, then to find it, is quite an achievement. No lights out there, unless some lucky bastard, has beaten me to the punch.

On just such a night, I got myself situated on my favorite platform which sits in ten feet of water, seventy five yards from the shore. I was casting into a light rain, the kind that tickles your face. A tropical squall, a slight breeze, cooled me in the warm September mist and I was comforted by the drizzle. My wetsuit was feeling heavy on my frame and this shower was refreshing.

Off in the distance I noticed the lights on the horizon, and as I often do, I stood transfixed; a moment of semi-consciousness. Soon things would change.

It was not long before I noticed a peculiar light in the distance. It was changing color. Red, yellow, green, yellow, red. This was not done in an orderly fashion, as would a strobe, but was done with quite irregular intervals. I watched as this light grew brighter and higher in the night sky. My first thought was that this was one of those Air National Guard C-130 refueling planes on station and waiting for her little parasite helicopters, which were sure to show up at any moment, but there was no sound, even as the changing lights grew in intensity and height. Red, yellow, green, yellow, red, no change to this pattern, even though there was a constant change in the duration of each color. The fascination was that it grew on the horizon, climbing into the sky.

I began to see a strange white shape below this light. It was illuminated with each sweep of that dim glow from the Lighthouse. *What the devil is that?* I struggled to discern some meaning to the object. The mind plays tricks and after a while, I was convinced that I was watching a U.F.O. Another pass from the Lighthouse beam left a silver streak descending from this light high in the sky. *What the?* The dead giveaway was the appearance of a wake. *It was a sailboat!* The bow had finally come into focus. The yacht was under motor power in the still air, and it was headed straight at me! "SHIP AHOY!" I yelled at the top of my voice! There was no response.

"**HEY! SHIP AHOY! YOU ARE HEADED FOR A SHOAL!**"

"What... dude?" was the response issuing from the mist.

I turned on my ever present flashlight and now could see the entire boat within its arc. It was about fifty yards out and on a collision course with my rock!

"TURN THE FRIGGIN' WHEEL! TURN THE FRIGGIN' WHEEL, YOU MORON!! YOU ARE ABOUT TO RUN AGROUND!!!" My light had targeted on the captain at the helm of the craft. He was so close at this point that I could see his long brown hair in the circle of my flashlight. His eyes seemed to glow red within the beam like a mongrel's in the dark. A bikini clad babe of about twenty stood, eyes agape, at the bow of the vessel. With one hand on the rail she was frantically waving her other hand towards port side.

"WHOAH.... *DUDE*!" I heard this refrain from the thirty footer, as it swung to port and motored past my rock, at a distance of no more than fifteen yards; so close that I could hear the mast stays lashing as they snapped against the rigging.

"*WHOAH!... WHAT A RUSH!*" The sound of hysterical giggling could be heard chortling from the pretty first mate.

There was that distinct odor of marijuana drifting on the breeze. No wonder, I also got a rush.

The Flash of Silver.

I've been fishing the beaches and coves out in Montauk all my life. During that time, I have advanced in skill from bumbling beach bum to fully wet suited hotshot. I have seen days of ecstasy as well as pain. This day's experience would contain both.

The reports I had gathered from my various spies were all positive. If the intelligence was true, the bass had been thick for the past few days in the remote portion of Montauk's rocky southern shoreline. That afternoon I would be walking to the cliff which overlooked Caswell's Reef, an isolated spit of serious striper territory on Montauk's Atlantic coast.

The sun shown brightly, with only the hint of a chill in the fresh October air, as I arrived at the only parking spot on the old highway. I put on my wet suit, gathered up my gear, and set off for the cove. The entry point for this beach access was hidden down a twisting dirt trail that seemed to go on forever. I slipped between the overhanging grape vines and bittersweet, forming a natural tunnel through the scrub oaks, bayberries and beach plumbs. The sun cascaded through the overhanging bows, settling on the path ahead of me. The hike was nine hundred paces, or about a thousand yards from the road. I know, because I counted them. The mind does strange things. After the ten minute hike, I finally broke free of the woods, and peered down over the edge of a steep bluff, the fresh sea breeze filled my nostrils. The ocean had taken on a dull sheen, no doubt a result of the wind and tide rousing the sea into a medium roll. The water looked promising. Descending the cliff, I waded into the surf, working my way out to a distant rock, but after an hour of casting and having no luck at all, I began to doubt the productivity of this piece of real estate and my confidence waned. Doubt is the great conqueror of the angling spirit. For the fisherman, it is the harbinger of fate that may cause him to make rash decisions, often leading to a skunking - or worse - causing him to move away from the fish, usually, only moments before the big chew.

After thirty minutes, my live eel bait had basically drowned. A sensation of uncertainty came over me to where I began a frantic search for any signs of life. In the distance I could see what appeared to be a darkening cloud gathering about a quarter mile away, just east of Kings Point. This cloud took on a brownish, boiling nature as if some puff of smoke was hovering on the horizon. I could almost swear it looked alive. *Birds*?

Gulls are the great forecasters of bait just below the surface of the sea, and as a consequence, those great scaly beasties that chase after them. The awful truth though (*about spotting gulls*) is that with the effects of temperature, and humidity, a person can never be exactly sure where the damned things are situated! It is an unwritten law that if you go off chasing birds, you will undoubtedly find them a mile out to sea, by the time you get there. Soon after spotting this distant mirage, I noticed a man, rod in hand, walking the beach from that distant point, and into my sphere of influence.

All in all, the best way to put yourself onto fish is to have someone tell you where they are. This technique also has its drawbacks. You may never be totally sure of the integrity, or timeliness of this form of information. Your best fishing buddies may send you off on some wild goose chase and then have a good laugh at your expense later! God forbid you should go seeking advice from a stranger, for you never know whether he is a pro, a rank amateur, or comedian. With this thought in mind, I found myself wading back to the beach to have a talk with this kindred spirit. "What's going on at the other point, over there?" I asked after we exchange pleasantries.

"Well, I saw a few fish a while back, but they just kept movin' in and out, took a couple a rats, though." My ears perked up with this report. Could it be that my new friend had committed the first sin of fishing by walking away from the fish?

"It sure looks like there is some bunch of birds over that way," I said, as I nodded nonchalantly toward the far Point.

"Yeah, well . . . that's the problem. There were so many freakin' birds flying around that they were gettin' in the way. I even got one caught up in my line! Took me ten minutes to untangle the damned thing."

Hearing those words, I hitched my eel to a guide on my rod and took off on a mad dash through the rocky badlands of Driftwood Cove. I didn't even say goodbye. The guy must have thought I was nuts to go charging off across that treacherous terrain.

The environment at Driftwood Cove is one of the most boulder strewn beaches in Montauk, there is not a bit of open sand to be seen for a quarter mile, with enough stones, rocks and pebbles along the way to satisfy a homesick mountain goat.

The afternoon sun pressed down on me like a weight upon my chest. After a quarter mile I was gasping for air, but I continued to stumble along through the boulder field, passing by great driftwood trees and broken lobster traps. *All I wanted was to get over to those birds*. Reaching the halfway point, I had to stop to catch a few breaths; my wetsuit clinging to me like a hungry python. I could smell ozone in the air caused by the sparking cleats of my spiked soles. Taking deep breaths, I looked out to see... *Yes, those birds were still there!*

Delirious from the exertion, I rounded the bend to reach King's Reef. There in the surf I saw the backs of striped bass as they humped above the water like miniature dolphins! The fish were a ways out past the tide line. I dragged myself wheezing and stumbling through the surf. Three other guys were already there, fishing the rocks, each with a bent rod! The sight was like spurs to my sides.

Patches of thick kelp caught at my feet as I made for the center of the reef and I stumbled into the surf. It was refreshing! The sky had darkened with the canopy of hundreds of gulls. Their screams added to the scene of pure pandemonium, as they picked at an acre of churning bait, which I soon realized was mullet. I slowed my approach, not wanting to spook any fish and waded towards an elevated rock about forty yards from the sand, swimming for the last few feet. Finally reaching the boulder, I ducked behind it as the waves crashed into the front and swept around the sides, and in the process, splashed great plumes of suds in my face. During the next lull, I hoisted myself up onto the platform. Setting myself to make a cast, I noticed that my eel had died in the heat during my long trek. It now was a dried sausage. I pulled it free, of the hook, tossing it into the surf and fastened a fresh snake to the rig. The wilted piece of rancid meat drifted within a cloud of mullet. Immediately a group of competing gulls swooped toward the treat. As they fought over the bait, it sank slowly within the current. A great shadow erupted from the bottom and with a flash, that shrunken piece of flesh vanished. I swallowed hard and made my first cast into the wall of frantic birds.

The most important aspect of fishing with an eel is not to rush the process. The eel should work along the bottom, and in order to achieve this, you must reel slowly, allowing it to sink. The water was teaming with life, infecting me with a strong case of "bass fever." With each crank, I had to remind myself, to take it easy. I could sense the eel becoming agitated; the line vibrated with frantic gyrations. With all its darts and feints, the unlucky eel secured its fate. I felt the distinctive tug of a strike but I lifted the tip too early and missed!

At this point I had reeled the bait halfway in. The fish were all around me again, meandering around my rock. I steadied myself, as a swell rolled over the reef, slapping at my knees. Two more slow cranks. The tip was pulled down toward the water by another strike! Wait. This time, out went the drag! Now I could feel the fish's tail hitting my line and I knew that I had her in the perfect striking position. Tightening the drag, I jerked the rod back.

The fight was on! Out went my line in a series of long rips that stripped fifty feet from the reel. I saw the line cutting laterally through the water, leaving a little wake as it tore through the surf. A nice fish! The line began to sing with tension as it quivered in the wind. My drag began to skip and I palmed the spool to try to gain some control. The fish thrashed in the vain attempt to free itself from the torment of the hook. It doubled back on the line and I quickly cranked in the slack. As the fish moved closer, the gulls went wild; hollering at each other. They jockeyed for space over the fish anticipating what they thought would be a free meal. One gull flew into the line! "*Get outa here*!" I shouted at the critter.

Time slowed at the end. The fish rolled in an attempt at freedom. Its great tail breached the water like some upturned broom sweeping the sea. There it was, big and beautiful, under my feet. Jumping off the rock and into the churning surf, I grabbed it by the jaw, as a wave broke over us. I had it! My hand seemed small as I fought for control. Then, just like that, it went limp. A huge belly signaled the presence of a million eggs. I carefully contemplated my next move as I pulled the hook and slipped her gently back into the water. Off she swam splashing me with an indignant flip of her tail. I smiled and waved goodbye. "Hey, nice buddy!" my neighbor yelled as he, also, leaned into good fish. It had been about ten minutes since that first cast, and I took a moment to climb back onto the rock, relishing the memory of the fight. As I gazed off I took in the world around me.

Dynamic and in motion, the water and the sky animated me more than ever, as I revisited some repressed primordial instinct; the irresistible compulsion of the hunt.

Each cast brought another challenger. As I fought one striper after the other, I was absorbed in the moment, my senses sharpened like a thousand razors. The green water was crystal clear in back of the breakers. The smell of chewed bait drifted in the breeze. I watched as mullet swam passed. The wind and surf had little effect on their course. Like a sea bound flock of swallows, this body of fish darted from one direction to another, sending an intense flash of silver through the water. Every so often a clearing would appear within the school of bait. It was inside this cavity that huge bass swam, gliding along like animated vacuum machines, inhaling the unlucky stragglers, who wandered into their path. These great stripers showed no haste as they cruised past my rock. They began to congregate in groups, three and four abreast, as though they were on parade.

As the sun sank lower, a peculiar image shone before me. Held by the wind, the great, green, curved, transparent wall of a wave shimmered with a beast of at least fifty pounds, chasing a succulent morsel within the curl. Backed by the setting sun, I was witness to the silhouette of God's great aquarium; the wave, the bait, the fish.

Joey "Bag-A-Donuts" rigs an eel.

"Rule of thumb number one if you wanna consistently catch big bass, if you are lookin' for that trophy slamma to put on the (*ahem...*) "Social Club" wall... you should be fishin' wit the bait." Rigged eels are the oldest trick in the inventory. Guys have been sewin' these slimy bastards up since the turn of the last century. There are many different methods to riggin' the eel. All have their merits, but the method I have learned is one that has served me well in the past. I hope it will nail you that ever elusive fiddy.

Meat, such as the hunka bunka, the clam, the eel, the woim or even the calamari will have ya into the fish even under conditions that would leave "*pluggers*" (*Hey! I ain't talkin' about "Lefty-The Gatt", ya know?*) stinky. I will fish with live eels whenever I get the chance, see? 'cause it woiks, but quite often these "eel trips" leave me with a baga deaders. At $2.00 a pop, I find it difficult to toss these sausages away, jus' 'cause of the small technicality of their sudden death, ya know? Sooo, the big bastards, I will bring back to my, *ahem*, "safe place" to rig for silent runnin'. Or (*should you be the impatient type*), ya can kill 'em in advance! This can be good sport! I find throwin' 'em up against a concrete wall is very effective. (*It makes a sweet sound, yah know?*) A pin in the chin and out the toppa the head to put 'em out of their misery, woiks too. It sorta scrambles their noodle (*He He He...*) To be humane, ya could put 'em in the freezer for a while, ya know, nice, nice, go to sleep little eelsey weelsey, (*but hey! What's fun in that?*) Ya want big eels to rig, see? But, not too big. Three or four ounces are good, say the size of a nice pepperoni. This way ya will not break your rod right off the bat.

To start off, you'll need some specialty tools. Most important is a set of upholstererin' needles and a stiff sail maker's spike. For you who don't have a clue of what the frick I'm talkin' about, an upholstery needle is one of them big suckers with an eye you could drive a truck tru. This can be substituted with any large eye needle, ya know? You should be able to find one of these in your ol' ladies sewin' box. ("*Hey babe, how should I know where your stoopid needle went!*") As for the sail-maker's needle, it's kinda hard to come by one of these now-a-days. You know, as luck would have it, you can make one!

This big-ass-pig-sticker-needle needs to be at least sixteen inches long, with an eye on one end and a point on the other. (*Duh!*) Let's start our scavenger hunt in the closet where *she* hangs her frillies. Toss that rag on the floor and confiscate the wire hanger. (*She got 'em for free at the cleaners, see?*) Now run down to the cellar with it and cut a straight piece from the bottom of that hangar which will be 16" long. (*Just like "Benny the Stud's" schlong, He, he, he...*) Take it ova to your grinder/sander/ pencil sharpener, (*whateva*) and hone a point on one end of the thing. (*You guy's from Brooklyn could use the sidewalk for this operation.*) The point should be real sharp (*'cause ya gonna shove it up the eel's ass, see?*) Now take a hamma and flatten the other end of the wire for a quarter inch or so. Now ya gotta drill a hole about a sixteenth of an inch into this now flat spot, see? (*Hey Brooklyn, no drill? Use the ice pick!*) Okay! Now that ya have made a new tool, we are ready to rig some snakes!

Go into your old lady's nick nack drawer and steal a roll of dental floss. You can get waxed riggin' thread if ya wanna get fancy. Now it is time to spend some money. Go get some 8-0 or 9-0 straight shanked (*siwash*) hooks from ya friendly neighborhood tackle shop. You should also get some eighty pound test leader string, or substitute wire leader stock where there are lotsa choppers around. (*Bluefish stoopid, not Harleys!*) Tie one end of the leader to the eye of a hook. This leader should be about three inches longer than the dearly departed eel. The other end will be tied to that special sail maker's needle which ya just made, but not till afta the next step.

Now ya shove that special needle up the eel's keister until it comes outa his face. Be careful how ya shove or you'll find out what it felt like to be Jesus Christ. Tread the leader tru the hole end of your home made impaling device.

Now ya gotta pull the leader tru that poor dead bastard. This is the tricky part. You must twist the eel into an "S" shape so's as to *facilitate* (*a big word! The Don's gonna be so proud!*) Ahem... You gotta *facilitate* the fastening of the second hook to the first one, in such a way as to make this contraption an *integrated* (*oh boy!*) unit. A lota the old timers enjoy breakin' the vertebra of their snakes to make that bend easier. This makes them feel important, ya know?, just like "*Tony Soprano*", see? If ya don't care for my high class explanation, then lemme put it to ya this way. They say the squirmin' bastard swims betta after ya break his back a buncha times.

Now pull tight on the leader so that the hook just sticks outa the eel's bung hole. There's a bit of thinkin' needed at this point, see, 'cause you'll have to figure out how much of the leader to cut off, whilst allowing enough room to tie on the second hook. The second hook has to be stuck tru the eels face and come out somewhere around his lungs (*as if an eel should have lungs!*). Soo, ya gotta cut the leader just right, see? Before ya perform the stab-tru-the-troat, ya must fasten your leader to the eye of the second fishing hook, see? *Get it right!* This will be the weakest point should the slammer take that back hook and run!

It is often useful to add weight to the eels head. A lead drail/hook combo may be used for the front snagger if ya like. This will make the eel swim a bit more realistic like, 'cause the weighty thing is spoon shaped, see? A piece a soldering lead can be slipped down his throat as a cheap-out way to add weight. (*Hell, you are jus' gonna lose the freakin' thing anyway...*) and this will also make the rig sink to the bottom where the fat bass chew. So now, go ahead and shove that piece of lead into the eels face, right along with the second hook.

Now get out the riggin' twine once again. Ya gotta tie the hooks into the eel's flesh so they stay in place, see? Hopefully, ya got the length of the tail hook leader right, or else the hook will pull outa his ass and the eel won't swim too good. So tie the rear hook into the eel's guts. Try to get the tread tru the eye o' the fishing hook, then tru his groin. Don't mind the oozin' blood and guts too much; unless of course, they're yours (*He, he, he...*) The head hook is the one which must be tied to the bastard eel the best. You're gonna put all the castin' force on this hook, see? So, tru the chin, out the eye, with the tread; about 4 times should do to keep that bastard's mouth shut, but good. Don't forget to tie that piece of lead in there, too. The tread should pass around it too or else the eel will spit it out with the first cast! Look, it ain't too pretty, but it should smell and taste likes an eel to the stupid fish.

Now take it to ya favorite rock and give it a toss. Power cast? *Fagetaboutit... You'll* bust your rod unless your tip is as tick as your dick (*He, he, he...*).

Oh, by the way... A live eel on a hook woiks a lot better than a rigged contraption that cost ya five bucks and an hour a time when ya should be oilin' your hardware, but what the hell. Be traditional!

Things That Go Bump in the Night.

Montauk has a curious past. Shipwrecks, murder and monsters are said to have graced our history, making our folklore rich with spooky tales. One of the oldest yarns is a story of a giant serpent. This snake was supposed to be a giant anaconda which was the pet of the Montauk Indian shaman who lived on Star Island in the nineteenth century. The wizard was said to have traded a magic love elixir to a sailor from the Sag Harbor whaling fleet in trade for, the then, four foot snake. The beast apparently grew to unimaginable proportions, and one night devoured the witch doctor while he slept. Satiated, the creature was said to have slithered away into the woods. When a local preacher reported running over a log on the highway on a dark harvest night, after stopping to see what damage was done to his undercarriage, the reverend saw this supposed tree trunk "slither away" into Hither Woods.

The hullabaloo concerning the fabled Montauk Experiment is another myth that is often recalled. According to the legend, during World War II, there was a secret laboratory at Camp Hero where experiments with time travel, teleportation, and temporal manipulation caused a group of soldiers to disappear into the ether from within one of the many bunkers that existed on the army base. A great generator was built to supply the energy for this device. I have personally seen this power station, which is still there. High voltage cables run from the plant to those bunkers, now overgrown with thorns and sealed with concrete like crypts. Odd capacitors and insulators can be seen to this day, hanging from thick wires, like wounded birds.

Then there is the Devil's Footprint. This icon had been on display at the Second House Museum for many years. Legend has it that the great chief of the Montauketts had a fierce contest of will and strength with Beelzebub on the beach north of Hither Woods. Having lost the rencontre, the beast from hell furiously kicked a boulder with his fiery foot, imbedding the likeness of his stride for all eternity, like a fresh, bare, footprint in mud, only this mud is solid stone.

Giant fish, mermaids and all sorts of denizens of the deep are whispered about in our little fishing community during cold winter nights. Many of these sightings can be verified, such as the monster Great White shark that is hanging on the wall in Salivar's Restaurant. Giant sturgeon have been taken from Fort Pond Bay during the winter season. Wild screaming voices are often heard in Hither Woods during the dead of the night. There have also been reports of a two hundred pound snapping turtle living in the deep watery hole of Fort Pond.

Ghostly hauntings also abound in our town, due to the age of the community and it's nefarious past. One of the old Carl Fisher homes now vacant is reported to be inhabited by the souls of game which were shot, mounted and hung upon the walls of the great room. The creatures stare into eternity from the gabled chamber. Ferocious and moldering, these disembodied heads have been heard roaring into the darkness from their hooks on the dank tobacco stained walls.

The Manor is said to have a haunted room that is often in high demand at the end of October by those intrigued with the paranormal. Filled with eerie squeaks and squeals, the room is perpetually chilled and incapable of heating. Strange shadows appear in the corners. This chamber is thought to be inhabited by the ghost of a slaughtered Indian chief. The land that the Manor is built upon was once the scene of a great battle between the Montaukett and the Narragansett Indians. Many artifacts and skeletons have been unearthed in the vicinity. The Fort Hill Cemetery was the final resting place for the fallen braves of this battle, long before the round eyes were interred there. This is exactly why the area is known as "Fort Hill." Remnants of this Indian fortress may be seen surrounding the Manor grounds, among tangled briars and hidden kettlehole swamps.

There are regular reports of sightings of the Phantom of the Light. This creature has been spotted standing under the bluff at the base of the Lighthouse. The apparition is said to be that of a man-shaped entity dressed within a black cape. It stares with a longing gaze, while plaintively moaning at the surfcasters who ply those waters under the late October moon.

Of all the strange occurrences that have been part of the folklore of Montauk, there is a tale which I will use, in justification of this little detour, into macabre trivia.

****

Montauk was in the grip of the first big gale of the season. The windswept dunes drew long shadows on the rocky shoreline surrounding Murderers Row. The heavy overcast crowded the wave-tops as the storm wound its way up the eastern seaboard. The shoreline was particularly deserted and lonely. The beaches and bluffs took on an eerie aura during this cold night.

The dreariness of the area surrounding the north side of the Point seemed exceptionally bleak as I drove through the rain squalls which left rivers of mud at the base of the cliff. I thought back to the many shipwrecks and strandings that must have occurred in times past. Before the construction of the Montauk Lighthouse there must have been an abundance of souls lost to these waters. Some of the more notorious deaths have been those of the careless fishermen who were just too aggressive; lost to the reef. I hoped that my own crusade for that trophy bass would not place me within the ranks of these poor devils one day. I have often pondered on the chances that I may depart this world in some freak fishing mishap.

This late October Eve, I made the choice to fish the waters at Jones' Reef. I found myself wading out to one of the rocks that lay submerged in the wash. It is usually easy to get to this perch. A bit precarious maybe, but not difficult. This time though, the Nor'easter had made the dynamics of the place change. As I climbed a good rock a wave toppled me into the surf. While I thrashed around trying to regain my footing, the clasp to my flashlight must have come undone. I watched as the light dropped into the water and sank into the foaming surf below me. Try as I might, I could not bend to retrieve it, without filling my waders with water.

Frustrated, I left to dry out and maybe make a few casts from under the Lighthouse. Standing above me, the light shone down like an ancient sentinel, flashing off into the distance. As I approached the base of the tower, the sea below the rock walkway was furious. The clamor of wind and surf seemed enhanced by the repeating blasts of the fog horn on the bluff above me. I made several casts into the wind and began to feel more at ease as I found my rhythm.

Suddenly, as I tossed my plug again into the night, from behind me, came the most horrific screaming! This howling gave me such a fright that it took several minutes to compose myself. The harrowing din was coming from the rocks below me. I stood quietly, listening to the blood, coursing through my eardrums. I could only surmise that the howling was the machinations of some local wildlife. On occasions, while fishing these rocks in the darkness, I have seen raccoons the size of dogs steal fish right out from under my feet, then disappear within this craggy sea wall.

Unnerved by the shrieking, I decided to move on. I headed for my truck and a nice hot thermos of coffee. As I rounded the cove, I came upon two excited fishermen. I was just able to catch the gist of their conversation;

"I tell ya, there is someone in the water!"

"Poor fool musta hit his head or somethin'."

"Hey guys, what's going on?" I said as I was drawn in by their eerie dialogue.

"I think there is a body in the water, near the get-on!"

"Come on, let's go take a look." Off we went, stumbling down the rock strewn cove that ends near the service road. As we rounded the bend, one of the guys began to point. In a hush, he whispered, "*Look, there he is! Down there below that rock!*"

We all stood there, glaring into the night. I strained my eyes trying to make out any man-like form, below.

"I don't see nothin' Sam," his buddy said as he swept the water with his flashlight.

"Turn your light away from the rock for a minute and you'll see him, just below the surface!" Switching our lights off, we waited for our night vision to return. "Jesus Christ... *there he is!*" As we watched, we could see a green glow radiate from below the surface. This caused the bottom to shimmer and dance with strange motion. The illusion was swaying slowly, back and forth... and blinking... on and off.

"Holy Mother of God! What *is* that?" As a swell passed the rock the green vision suddenly disappeared.

"What the .....?" Another swell passed and the spectral light returned. A strong case of the heebie-jeebies passed among us.

"***Did you see that!***"

"Well, don't just stand there... go see what it is!"

"*You go and see what it is!....... I'm stayin' right here!*"

The brave one waded out to the rock to duck under the surface. We waited for the fateful moment when the would-be rescuer surfaced with the poor drowned fool. Again, he dove.

"Well... what's doin'?" Another wave passed, and the ghostly light faded.

"I can't see nothin' down there. There's nobody here, fellas, just that awful green glow. I don't know about you, but ... I'm outa-here..."

Turning to flee the scene, the three of us had convinced ourselves that this was some frightful apparition. But,then...... I began to understand the truth to the matter...

"Man... I'm not gonna fish down here no more..." one of the fishermen said, as they both jumped into their jeep and took off down the beach, sand and rocks flying.

As I climb into my own cab, I looked over towards the phantom rock. Damned if I didn't see that green glow under there again. I didn't have the heart to tell them about my lost flashlight ... If you twist a Mag-lite just so, any bump will cause it to blink on and off... Nothin' like a good ghost story to keep the competition away from my rock.

Further down towards the North Bar, the place had become even more deserted. The passing storm and the associated high seas had sent all but the most steadfast home to their beds. I could not, however, shake the thought that the strongest ebb tide in weeks would push some quality stripers onto the beach up at Shagwong Point, a mile and a half to my west. I drove across the beach, stopping for a cast here and there and picking a few rats, ending up at the Wong for the 4a.m. tide.

The trip west had been slow and tricky. The storm swell had brought the water to within a few yards of the bluff in a few of the tighter places. Several times, my wheels splashed through the tidewater, my truck tipping precariously towards the surf. It appeared as though the storm was finally breaking. Long columns of clouds raced by overhead, as the wind drove steadily on. This low deck was riven with the most brilliantly crisp air and breaks in the cloud cover were appearing. When the moon shone through, it burned with the intensity of a spotlight. The temperature had dropped even more in the aftermath of the gale. I was beginning to get sleepy and here, at Shagwong Point, the sky took on a surreal quality. This combination of cold and fatigue must have caused my mind to play tricks, for at times, the air was so bright it almost seemed to be midday, rather than midnight, then, quite suddenly, the sky would dim as though a switch was thrown and the moon would passed behind the sweeping clouds. Tired as I was, I grabbed my pole and made for the beach at the water's edge.

I was immersed in my cocoon of gear. I wore a fully hooded neoprene top, gloves and my heavy winter waders. I was bundled up like a nervous toddler. The only sensations I had were the numbing cold on my face and at the tips of my damp fingers and toes. It is funny how a tired mind can play tricks... "*Don't get wet! ...And stay out of the puddles!*" I heard my mother's voice, from a distant memory.

What a strange thought. Hmm... My mom had passed away years ago.

Casting into the 20 knot wind was a challenge in the dark wrapped up in a womb of gear. Running towards the retreating wash, I would cast hard and then turn to race the incoming waves back to the high water mark. I was using a bailess reel and, being new to it at the time, my line had a tendency to jump the roller in a head-wind cast. The riptide was so powerful, it seemed to pull my legs sideways, digging deep ruts under my boots. As the moon broke through the clouds once more, I threw my favorite cow catcher, a bottle plug, into the surf. I began the retrieve and in a few moments I noticed that I had been reeling nothing at all. I missed the roller with my pickup. Damn! My line was steadily drifting down-wind creating the "mother of all tangles." Boy was I glad that I was alone at that moment because it was a sure thing that my buddies would have given me the ribbing of a lifetime for this faux pas. Squinting in the dim light, I slipped the line back on the roller and as I turned the crank, I realized that I must have let 100 yds. free in the wind... Just then, in the shadow cast below me, I saw the form of my pal Joe coming up from behind. The brim of his distinctive fishing hat stood out like a duckbill. Somehow that brimmed cap seemed exaggerated in the dimness, almost like a long snout. Keeping my eyes on the line, I greeted my buddy, "Hey Joe, what brings you out on a night like this!"

Nothing.

I mean no answering remarks... no laughter.

Nothing.

I turn to see what's up with Joe... and... no one was there... I was surrounded by solitude except for a bit of kelp blown in the wind; my only companion. The shadows blinking in and out, danced around me. I was truly alone, out there.

Desolation.

Another unnerving event to quicken my heart was all I needed to send my thoughts racing. I could not figure out what I had just seen from the corner of my eye. I was sure it was Joe... I began to reel, in earnest this time, quickly returning line to the spool.

Easy boy... You've spooked yourself... I felt the line finally come taught. My wrist was sore from the cold damp air. I was losing interest in this fishing trip rapidly. There was a strong tug at my shoulder and I just about jumped out of my skin! "Jesus Christ Joe, don't you have any sense! *You nearly scared the shit out of me... you....*"

I turn to confront my prankster pal, but no one was there. The wind drifted the shifting sands at my feet, and there I was with my shoulder in the grasp of some loathsome, yet invisible, monster! *I could still feel it pulling on me!* I tried to flinch away the grasp upon my arm but it was relentless! With bile in my throat, I reached behind to free myself from that clutching, tugging horror...and found my bottle plug stuck securely into the back of my jacket... *How could this have happened?* I had cast far into the surf just moments before.

Thoroughly freaked out now, I packed my gear and hit the road, for good this time. The trip home was alive with shadows. The radio was filled with strange static. A truly weird scene appeared before me as a doe and buck thrashed through the underbrush in a mad dash to escape my headlights, flashing into my peripheral vision as I rounded the corner into my driveway. Taking a deep breath, I cursed myself for getting spooked on the night that was sure to bring in that trophy striper. Returning to the warmth of my bed, my wife stirred as I slipped between the covers. Sleepily she asked, "How did it go honey... any luck?"

"Same old story," I remarked, "*Nothin' worth shaking a stick at.*"

The Montauk Sea Turkey.

There's something about fishing during the Thanksgiving holiday that appeals to me. I am convinced that it is a lucky time. If you remember, even Jimmy Willburt caught two fifties to win the Montauk Locals Surfcasting Tournament on Turkey Day. No doubt about it, the kickoff to the holiday season can be a fortunate time for the steadfast few who will brave the elements, along with the chastisements of their loved ones for fishing during a holiday.

This one particular Thanksgiving, I awoke early and arrived at the Point in the dark. The predictions of a perfect dropping tide had me convinced that the chew would be on at the Montauk Lighthouse that morning. This was the day I hoped to win the Local's Tournament and I was mentally cued up. The lead fish that year was a puny thirty six pounder, not very large for a winner. Not being able to sleep well, I scrambled out of bed and was rigged and behind the wheel by five a.m.

Dressed in my waders and a neoprene dry top when I hopped down to the flat rocks at the water line, I was set for action, quite sure that the Point would produce a money fish. Whitewater washed into the boulders and with the help of an east wind blowing at between fifteen and twenty miles an hour, the conditions seemed perfect. Best of all, I was absolutely alone when I arrived, allowing me to have the first pick of the rocks, which can often be the difference between a slammer and a skunk. I fastened a Musso darter to my leader and after making my first cast, I was rewarded with a small bass of about ten pounds. The waves were hitting the jetty with force enough to throw sheets of water at me every now and then, but I didn't care. Getting a bit wet seemed a good trade off when my follow up cast brought another bass.

As I reeled in my fish, I saw movement above me and looking up, I saw another fellow strolling along the jetty. The guy seemed to be an occasional fisherman. He was seriously under equipped for fishing in this location, being dressed only in a yellow raincoat. He carried a little blue tackle box and an eight foot spinning setup. He stopped right above me and began to cast.

"Wow, you're catchin' fish! What you usin' buddy?"

He had something crazy attached to the end of his line. I could make out a small propeller at the front, like some sort of fresh water plug a guy would use to catch pike.

"Hey fella, yah think you could move over a bit, *you're castin' right over my head."*

"Oh... Sorry." He scooted over a bit.

Three more casts brought me three more fish. They were getting bigger. My new pal remained fishless, yet he still kept casting frantically at the moving water.

"I just can't seem to catch nothin'. What am I doin' wrong?"

"Try usin' a different plug. That one's not gonna work here.

He opened his pretty little tackle box and took out another freshwater plug. It flew about ten feet into the wind and got lost it in the rocks below my feet. Now, I was sorry to see, he was getting in the way.

"Darn it!"

"Look,my friend, the sun's commin' up... It's time for you to use a bucktail." I responded, not wanting to wear his next hook in my face, and giving him a little bit of solid advice, super sharpie that I am.

"Bucktail? What's a *bucktail?"*

I held up a 3 ounce Jetty-Caster and showed it to the dude.

"Oh boy. I don't have one of those. You think I can use something else?"

"You could, but you would cross my line with every cast. When someone under the Light is usin' a bucktail, everybody has to throw them, or it will be a mess." My patience was starting to wear thin. I was not in the mood to give fishing lessons this morning.

"Aw hell... I came out all the way from the city to fish. *This stinks..."*

This plaintiff whine touched my cold heart and I felt sorry for the guy. What could I do? I took out the most beat up bucktail I had from my bag and tossed it to my new friend. On the business end it had an old, dried up pork-rind cemented to a rusty hook.

"Here! Now you have a bucktail. Cast it into the wash and do what I do!"

"You sure this is gonna work?"

Please!

In unison, I cast. He cast. The two bucktails landed in the sweeping current no more than ten feet apart. I reeled in the slack and my line immediately tightened up on a nice fish! I must have hit it on the head!

"Hey! I think got one!" I heard from over my shoulder. Sure enough, the guy had a fish on, too! His rod was bent in half and his drag was screaming.

"You've got your drag too tight! Your gonna loose 'im!"

"Whah?"

I scurried down the face of the jetty to land my fish, twenty yards from my perch. It was a low thirty pounder; not big enough to place in the tournament so I tossed her and scrambled back to my rock. My pal was still fighting his fish when I returned. He was trying to horse it in, pumping on the rod like he was lifting bricks in a bucket.

"Hey! Take it easy! You've got a nice fish on there fella!"

"Whah?"

Putting his back into the rod, I watched his face turn red from the strain. He dragged that fish straight into the base of the jetty and it disappeared between the rocks below my feet. Now he began pulling on it, trying to drag the fish up the rock face, but it wouldn't budge. I saw the tail slapping in the wash and my eyes bugged. "OH MY GOD! Take it easy, will yah! You're gonna break your pole! Here, grab my rod and I'll go down and get the fish before you bust it off. Just relax and ease up on your drag a bit."

I jumped down to the water. The fish was now deep in a hole and I couldn't see it. A wave broke over my head as I grabbed his line. Easy! The line was only twenty pound test, and he was not using a leader. I couldn't believe he hadn't broken the line already. I reached into the whitewater and put my hand into a big hole, which turned out to be the fishey's maw! It was as if I had put my hand into a stew pot! I grabbed her mouth and heaved, just as his line broke with a twang. He almost fell over as he lost his footing. **"Holy SHIT!! *It's a slob*!"** I said. I pulled the beast from the surf and held it next to my body. The thing was over four feet long.

As I dragged the fish to the top of the rocks, Dennis, one of my Tournament rivals, just happened to be walking up the Jetty. He saw the slammer in my arms and did a double take. "Jesus, you got a winner, Melnyk!" Obviously, he thought that I had caught it!

We put the fish on my scale. Dennis was sweating as I weighed the cow. The fish was forty eight pounds. Denny looked so dejected that I finally told him it wasn't really my fish. "Whatda ya mean?" I explained, and he smiled with relief. My new best friend was right there at my heels to take the striper out of my grasp. I think he thought I was gonna steal it! That old bucktail was still swinging from an inch long hole in the fish's face.

"Wow, you know, it was my uncle who told me to go fishing today! I didn't even wanna go, but he put the sign of the cross on my forehead and said he would pray for me! He's a priest at St. Patrick's Cathedral, yah know? You don't turn your back on that kinda blessing! But I couldn't a done it without you. *Thanks pal, thanks a lot!*" His smile was infectious. Then he ran off with that forty eight pound fish, as if his ass was on fire. I stood there, rubbing my hands, glaring at his back while my temples twitched, contemplating evil ruminations, (*There goes my precious.... My precious!!!*) I did not get my forty pounder that morning. I did not win the tourney either. All for the dumb luck of ten stinkin' feet and a ratty old bucktail! *Damn! I didn't even get my stinkin' bucktail back!*

By 6:30am the rocks were crowded with my fellow contestants. Not another slob was caught that morning. Lots of twenties though... I would have to wait for another day, maybe tomorrow.

So, it was the following day and once again, I arrived early. Would you believe it? *My new best friend was there waiting for me!*

"The sun's coming up! Time to use a bucktail!" he shouted down to me. He still wore the yellow jammies from the previous day and my piece-o'-shit bucktail was securely tied to his line. Once again, he was fishing without a shock leader.

We both cast at the same instant. This time our lines crossed in mid air. *I would be damned if he got his bucktail behind mine again!* The two jigs landed ten feet apart. I tighten up, *on a fish. So did he.* My fish was a high twenty pounder. Being the good Samaritan that I am, I made one more trip to the water and grabbed his fish. We weighed it. His striper was thirty seven pounds. Good enough for third place had he been in the contest.

"Wow! Another slammer!" (*He was learning the vernacular.*) "Damn, I owe you big-time buddy! What's your address, I'm gonna send you a case of beer! What would ya like?"

"Heineken"

You know, *I'm still waiting for that case of beer.*

The Christmas Goose.

As long as I have been with my lovely wife Dawn we have had a customary Christmas Eve dinner. Usually, we have roasted a domestic goose for this ritual. There is nothing like the taste of this bird. The closest thing I can compare it to is roast beef flavored chicken (*everything different seems to taste like chicken!*). We would buy our bird freshly butchered from the **Iacono Poultry Farm** on Long Lane in East Hampton. It has been a regular traditional journey for me on a glorious Christmas Eve morning. I would leave early in the day to pick up the goose and finish up my shopping with stocking stuffers and candy for my daughters.

As I reminisce, I recall that I once was given a wild goose that was taken by a hunter-friend of mine. We prepared this bird with all the trimmings and I found it delicious, but my wife, on the other hand, did not enjoy it because someone (*that bastard, as she called him*) had shot the poor thing. I will never understand this twisted form of logic. In my mind, it would seem to be more humane to be killed in the wild as a free spirit, as apposed to being penned up for six months and then have your head whacked off!

God love all the women of the world! I know that I would have been dead a long time ago without my darling's even keel to keep me on course. She is my converse, an opposite opinion in almost every situation. I am sure this has kept me from diving head first, into the shallow end of the pool, on many occasions. Without her form of logic to balance the equation, my life would be far less interesting, and probably fall apart.

Before my children were born, wet and screaming into the world (*this was another one of her swell ideas*) my wife and I would take long walks on the beach each Christmas Eve to enjoy nature, while beach combing the flotsam, jetsam and believe it or not, to search for beach coal.

Coal on the beach you say? Well, it seems that some time in the early sixties, a coal barge sank off shore at Ditch Plains. Consequentially, and usually after a storm, chunks of coal would wash up along the surf. These hunks of pure energy would range from an inch to ten inches in diameter. As with most young couples, we had a tough time making ends meet. We could pinch every penny dry. I don't need to tell all you old timers how expensive oil was back in the seventies. So, to supplement our fuel expenses, we picked these smooth black gems from the sand to burn in our wood stove. These black ovaloids would sparkle in the afternoon sun as we walked along the beach. We would gather these oblong treasures, weathered by the surf, in buckets as we kept a loose eye on our dog Quill, who romped along, looking for dead things to roll in. A good haul could yield a garbage can full. On a good day, we could pick a peck within a half mile of the car. This coal would burn like Kryptonite, and could heat our humble shack for a week for free!

On one cold winter solstice day, we found ourselves particularly wanting on the income scale of life. We were so poor during this particular Christmas that we were substituting our goose with a big chicken. So down-and-out were we that we had to go into the woods and cut our own Christmas tree from the wild. You might think that I would feel self conscious about being broke, and not want to think about it, but I truly enjoy this memory. The smell of that fresh pinewood will always be with me.

Our Christmas idol was a scrub white pine which we brought from the depths of Hither Woods. I remember how the mid morning sun beamed through the overhanging trees, causing shimmering light to form broad patches between the low and twisted branches. That special pine was revealed to us in the middle of a low glen, surrounded by a cranberry bog. The freshly cut tree swept the path clear of the dark debris as we dragged it along that wooded trail, back to the car. I can remember the clouds of vapor our breath sent streaming.

That afternoon, after trimming the little tree (*bush?*) we went to the beach to take a nativity constitutional and hunt for free fuel. At the time we were childless except for my surrogate son, that 160 pound black Great Dane, Quill. Quill lived to run the beach. He would bolt from one rock or log to another, leaping about on his long legs and depositing as much scat as his metabolism could muster. His bowels seemed bottomless. Dawn and I walked hand in hand, bundled up like Eskimos, daydreaming. That day, the thermometer had dropped well to below zero, and Quill, who was short haired, wore one of my sweatshirts to keep him warm. You know, he looked better than I did in it, with a rope tied around his waist, to act as an impromptu belt.

There was no wind on this frigid afternoon. Any breeze at all would have made it impossible to walk through the arctic blast that had sat on the East End for days. The ocean was steaming, like a soup pot, with long tendrils of wispy white vapor drifting above the surf, giving it the appearance of a boiling sea.

We rounded the bend with our bucket of coal and saw Quill barking and hopping around a peculiar downy lump huddled next to the bluff. As we moved in to investigate, I saw that Quill had cornered a wild goose! It was an enormous bird which flapped its wings and hissed at our dog. As I neared it I noticed that the creature could not move on its feet. It lay there, snapping at the air in front of Quill's face with its black beak.

"Look Dawn! A goose!"

"Oh Paul, don't let the dog hurt the poor thing!"

Poor thing? I was waiting for Quill to snap its neck! (*By God, this would be our Christmas dinner!)*

"Oh Paul, the poor thing is sick! What do yah think we should do?"

"Do? Why, we're gonna eat it! (*Good dog, Quill, Good Dog*!)"

"Don't you dare! Quill get away from that bird!" The dog backed

away from my dinner, more attuned to my wife's commands than mine, traitor that he was.

"Oh Paul, we have to do something about the poor beast. You go and grab it. We'll take it home and I'll call the vet."

Take it home? Yeah! It was sure to die on the way! *I would be that much closer to my roast.*

Have you ever tried to grab a goose? The creature, even though it was lame, was biting and snapping at me like a cornered lobster! It grabbed a hold of my glove and I thought my finger was in caught in a vise!

"Gimme the shirt off the dog. I'll throw it over its head." Sure enough, that did the trick and I had the beastie covered up and docile. I swear that goose had blue feet, ice-cold and clammy. We got back to the car and I sat with the goose on my lap. Quill sniffed at it from between the seats and moaned like a lost child.

"Shut up you bad dog."

The goose perched on my legs with its frozen tootsies chilling my thighs on the trip back. They seemed to warm up a bit by the time we brought it into the house. Wouldn't you know it, there were no veterinarians open at 5pm on Christmas Eve. There would be no vet at all until December twenty sixth. The bird went into our shower stall with a dish of water and an open can of corn. We ate that stupid chicken for dinner, although I have to admit that it was delicious, surrounded by yams, sausages and cheese stuffing with gravy. *(Though not as good as that freakin' goose would have been, I bet).*

The goose was silent all evening. This was worrisome because geese are prone to honk, well, like a goose, so I got up to look at the poor thing a couple of times during the night. When I would open the shower door, it would flap its wings at me. Its feet were now a nice shade of gray and it was hopping around.

Along with the a meager pile of gifts under our decorated scrub pine, Christmas morning brought with it, a vast change in the weather, The temperature had risen to a balmy 36 degrees during night and the sky had opened with rain. We had a happy time opening our simple presents.

You know, that goose seemed to have recovered during the night. I swear it had even eaten some of the corn! It was now honking and prancing around in the stall. I began to take a fancy to the stupid thing, Good Samaritan that I am. Dawn named it "Honker". That was that.

Have you ever given a name to a farm animal? There would definitely not be a wild goose dinner in our future. By noon I was thinking:

"Dawn, let's put him outside and see what happens."

"Ya think?"

Yeah, I think. You ever hear the expression "Like shit through a goose"? Well you should have seen the shower. The goosie's feet were now covered in green offal! I took the beast out the door, wrapped in a towel. Dawn followed. I put it on the ground and removed the towel. The goose took off in a run and hit the air like a B-52. It circled the house once and made for due south, making that low honk that geese will do as they fly.

"*Oh Paul, how wonderful! This is a Christmas we'll never forget...*" I got a big kiss.

You know, it *was* a wonderful Christmas after all, even without the goose dinner.

A Night to Remember.

The fall is considered to be the high point for surfcasting in Montauk and I would often indulge my obsessive need for large bass by swimming to the far rocks at the Lighthouse rip. It was another one of those magnificent days here in Montauk when all the ducks are lined up in a row. Warm October breezes played along the bluffs as fish-signs, in the way of milling gulls and bait slicks, dressed the water. The moon would be new tonight and the sky would sparkle with the light from a million stars. I was confident that this evening's tide would bring fish to the reef. Lately I had been noticing that the beach was collecting the bony remains of some huge fish which I suspected were discarded carcasses of past battles won. The freshness of the remains was evident. There were still trace elements of blood and flesh on the bones that appeared to be recently butchered. The sight of these bones had me psyched.

The word was mum among the hotshots who kept vigil at the beach under the Lighthouse. Not a note of success played in the wind, but the signs, however, were present. My plan was to be at the bluff near the Point early enough to have my pick of the most productive rocks. I had my heart set on fishing Weakfish Rock, which was always in demand by those "in the know." I had arrived early enough that no other fishermen were around but I suspected other wetsuiters would be making a play for this special spot tonight and I had no intention of being boxed out of my first choice.

Because of my early arrival, Weakfish Rock would be under water, and could not be seen in the usual way, as a rip curl forms over the rock when the tide begins to pull out. I used a technique that I had perfected to find this rock at high tide, in the dark. I set up Cyolume light-sticks, (glow sticks) on the beach at pre-determined locations to create lit markers to get a visual baring on my rock. I swam to the spot where these four points of light paired in a way that two near and two far aligned with each other to indicate that I had arrived at a set point in the water. When all the points were in their proper places, I searched the bottom with my toes and soon felt the rock with my flippers. Once again my technique worked like a charm. I stood on the rock and prepared myself for a night of casting live eels.

I spent the next two hours wondering what ever convinced me to arrive so early. *Oh you are sick,* I said to myself, when, occasionally, a swell would roll into me and I found myself swimming, just able to keep stationed as the tips of my spike soled flippers clung to the edge of the boulder. It was a rather precarious perch for a while.

About an hour into this test of balance and patience, I heard two guys arguing on the beach. They seemed rather upset to find that I had beaten them to the rock. Being denied their prized post, they set off, swimming for the less productive rocks which were situated towards the west.

It was an eternity waiting for the tide to turn. I had become very tired, almost sleep-fishing you might say. I had my first hook up around 2 am, which was a dog fish, a bothersome by-catch that will often foretell a night of bad luck. I was disappointed, you see, everything was just right; perfect in fact. I contemplated swimming back to the beach but decided to give it another hour and make another hundred casts. Finally, the tide had turned and I hooked a decent bass.

Well, I guess I'll just have to make a few more casts, I said to myself as I picked a fresh eel from my pouch and tossed it into the rip which was now beginning to leave a "V" shaped wake around my thighs. I slowly retrieved my line and watched as the current swept my bait downstream. The telltale smack of a good fish startled me out of my daze. I set the hook and was rewarded with a bass in the thirty pound class. *Oh yeah, the big fish had arrived*! As the striper swam away, I reached into my bag to grab the biggest eel I had. It was time for the special talisman I was saving. It was a snake of an eel, about eighteen inches long that was still quite lively. After several drifts with this bait I heard a big splash in the darkness. The line began to peel from my reel.

I was momentarily stunned by the ferocity of the strike. *What should I do? Should I tighten the drag? Should I give a heave and try to stop it?* I chose to just hold on. I watched as the spool spun; my line running out in long rushes. After five minutes of this one sided fight, my rod went limp. Just like that, nothing, the fish was gone.

As I reeled in my gear I was talking to myself. *You fool! I can't believe you lost another slob!* I was heartbroken. What could I have done wrong? As I brought my gear to the surface I noticed the leader had a peculiar look to it. The eel was slipped all the way up past the swivel. I turn on my light and saw that my 7/0 hook had been *straightened!* Another lost slammer! I began praying, *Please, just once more.*

It took quite a while to redo the rig with my trembling fingers. Starlight darted in and out of the clouds, making it even harder to tie the knots. I put the same eel that had been retrieved fishless back on the new hook as I invoked a new prayer for luck. A cast. Nothing. Another cast, another benediction. Nothing. With one more cast the eel swung down tide and I began a slow, agonizing retrieve. *Jeeze - You blew it - You blew your only chance at a........* Something felt funny..... Was that a soft bump at the hook? I stopped reeling and concentrated on the line. *Ah, there it is; a pickup!* The feeble bite had me thinking this was just another mediocre fish. Even so, I set the hook; the rod felt instantly heavy, as if it was fastened to an immovable object. *Then the fish awoke.* ZOOM! A big run. It swam past my rock, making a big arch in front of me then took off towards the rocks behind me! As it passed my rock it spun me around. With a big splash, the beast moved away towards the in-shore reef. I tried to slow the fish down but it was no use, the fish was in control.

The fight was now within the rocks; a formula for disaster. I could feel the line catch an obstruction, skipping across the reef's jagged structure. "*OH GOD-please-not again!*" Its head shook; the rod tip thrashing. I held my breath. The line began to drag against something. It was near the breaking point. "Oh God, Please don't let me loose this fish! If you would only allow me to land this fish, *I'll... I'll.. I'LL LET IT GO! I PROMISE!!* I began to sweat and a chill passed through me. Throwing down my last card, I slipped the line off the roller on my reel and left it to free spool. Several long seconds went bye before I saw the line start to move. First one loop slipped past the guides, then two. Then the line was moving steadily, without any resistance and I picked it up and placed it back onto the roller. As it came taut, I applied pressure steadily to the fish. It had turned out of the snag! The weight of this linesider once again had my rod doubled. Within a few more short runs, I felt its strength waning. I coaxed the fish to my rock. Please line, don't break- Please line, don't break. *OH PLEASE... OH PLEASE... OH PLEASE DON'T BREAK!* My flashlight illuminated a huge swirl in the water and I couldn't believe my eyes! This fish was almost five feet long! I reached down and grabbed her huge lower jaw. It was over.

It was the whopper! The head was a great shining thing, slick and glistening in the light of my lamp. Its mouth was big enough to insert a grapefruit with room to spare. For a second, I actually thought about slipping the fish onto my stringer but then I remembered my plaintive prayer shouted in desperation. *What would I do with fifty pounds of fishmeat anyway?* My wife would surely never let me hang it on the wall, it would dwarf the room. I looked within its golden eye as I supported the massive frame under my arm. I was barley able to lift the fish from the water. The swollen body was draped over my sleeve. Her belly was full of eggs, the gift of a million small fry for next year. With a sigh, I kissed her on the lip and push her off into the night. She righted herself and moved away. With a splash and a swirl she was gone. No one would believe that I released this fish; my fish of a lifetime.

The night continued on with action for another hour. The guys to my left kept jabbering among themselves every time I turned on my light.

"I don't believe this..."

"Jeeze, he's got another one!"

Eventually the tide was done and I kicked off my lucky throne and swam back to the beach.

Back in the shallows, I met my two companions as they stumbled out of the wash. "Hey! It looked like you were doin' pretty good, for a while there," said one fella, with his flashlight panning the water beside me. "You got anything to show for it?"

"Ah... You know...I did okay."

The Mermaid.

Spear fishing was a natural progression for me. In my teens, I acquired my first spear gun and would hunt for flounders in Lake Montauk. I soon advanced to the calm surf of Long Island Sound. The rocks of the north side surf were as big as Volkswagens and covered with seaweed, snails, and barnacles, a natural habitat for fluke, tog and an occasional bluefish. I soon learned to hold my breath by hyperventilating, a dangerous method where it is possible to inhale too much oxygen and pass out as the air compresses with depth and saturates the body. I must say though, the tingle of brain cells was a particularly unique experience. By the end of the summer I could stay under for up to three minutes at a time.

I would often go diving on reconnaissance trips, spending the early part of the season searching the surf to find where the fish were hanging out, so that later in the year, I would know where to find the big fish. Occasionally I would take a smallish bass to eat, but I didn't make a habit of it, preferring to hook the beasts on a rod and reel.

These exploratory trips allowed me to stumble upon a shipwreck or two. One notable find for me was the wreck of the Culloden, an eighteenth century brig, that sunk off the coast during the

Revolutionary War. The cannons and keel timbers were all that were left of this ship, which set in about 40 feet of water. The best wreck I had located was not a wreck, as much as debris left behind after the grounding of the USS Baldwin, which floundered in 1961 off the south side of Montauk Point. I stumbled upon the superstructure of a deck crane which was tossed overboard to lighten the ship as she was grounded in the rocks. I came across the crane in about twenty feet of water. It is quite dramatic in appearance, covered in rust, barnacles and green seaweed.

I have been face to face with many strange things while pursuing my passion for diving and swim fishing. Sharks, rays and strange bumps into my legs in the depths of the night have often given me the willies, although to be truthful, I have found these experiences to be quite exhilarating! This is what my style of fishing is all about.

One occurrence took place back in the '90's when my friend Attila and I had discovered that the middle of Driftwood Cove was holding fish. On our first dive on this reef, Attila and I stumbled into the largest striper we had ever seen! This old girl had to be more than 70 pounds. One look and you could see that it was timeworn. Its scales were the size of quarters and the tail was split in several places. The fish sat there and looked at me for a good 10 seconds as I came upon her, while other fish in the school (thirty and forty pounders) swam past. Attila and I had seen this distinctive animal on several occasions and it was evident that this shoal was holding the same school of large fish for much of the summer. Bass are creatures of habit and will often make a daily trip to certain rock formations to feed.

Attila and I set out in a quest to hook this beast. We caught many fish on that reef, but never did hook Granny. She was a smart one. On occasion, Attila would spear fish the reef in hope of sticking her. I remained the purest, and would swim on the surface with rod and reel, but I held no grudge towards my friend. In my opinion, it is just as hard to spear a big bass as to hook one. Anyone who has tried spear fishing will tell you that a big fish will sound with your line when stuck and it becomes a test of wills to see who will drown first.

One evening we both swam out to the reef. I had my rod and Attila brought his spear gun. We were hovering above the reef when I saw Attila breach the surface of the water like a nuclear submarine. His eyes were huge as he swam to me.

"Holy Shit! You won't believe what I saw down there!"

"Tell me it was Granny!"

"No, it isn't Granny!"

I became concerned when I could see the veins in his forehead beating a blue tattoo. "Don't tell me it was a SHARK! I'm not in the mood for a sprint to the beach!"

"No, I saw a manatee!"

"You're so full of shit. You saw a seal."

"It's a MANATEE, I TELL YOU!"

"Yeah, right..." At this point I could see a big shadow flow below us.

"IT'S A MANATEE!"

"Attila, there are no manatees in Montauk."

"Paulie, do you know what a dog looks like?"

This question had me a bit confused. "Yes, *I know what a dog looks like*," I said trying to follow his train of thought.

"WELL I KNOW WHAT A MANATEE LOOKS LIKE AND THAT IS A FREAKIN' MANATEE, DAMN IT!"

Well, needless to say, we argued like a couple of old women for a while, until I finally relented. I think I got him quite hot having a good laugh at his expense, but there was no doubt that a huge shape had drifted under us that evening.

So, never one to hold back on a good sea yarn, I went about spreading the word to all our friends. None would bite. I was told that I was the world's biggest bull shitter (*Me?*) It became a running joke as to how Melnyk and Attila had lost their minds from too much water on the brain. Some people even kidded that we had actually seen a mermaid; skishin' fools that we were.

A week later, much to the surprise of the entire town and the news media, our little imaginary manatee turned up swimming in the lake! This beautiful creature took to Montauk like a tourist. He would visit the West Lake Fishing Lodge every evening to be hand fed lettuce and gulp fresh water from a garden hose at the dockside. The Marine Science Lab estimated his weight to be over 600 pounds. It made quite a splash (*sorry*) and the restaurant there had a substantially more profitable year than normal, hosting a resident celebrity. He stayed until the fall sun grew low on the horizon and then one day he just up and disappeared. Just another Montauk Snow Bird.

The Gut.

I had a short fling at cold water diving, descending to over forty feet within the murky waters of the north east Atlantic. How does one describe the feelings involved with a deep dive? The first time I attempted it was quite by accident. I was in the Caribbean with my family, snorkeling with a resort crew in the blue waters off Grand Turk. These waters are magnificent in their clarity. Reefs and sea life abound in this tropical paradise. We left the pier and sailed off a mile or so from the resort to a spot on the reef where a protected marine sanctuary was located. As we tied off on a marker buoy, I noticed a shining object on the ocean floor off our port side. I had visions of Rolexes, expensive dive knives and gold doubloons. *Booty*! I jumped into the water as if I was shot from a catapult! Down I dove, launching myself like an errant torpedo. One minute later, I found myself at sixty feet or so, starring at an old dive mask, the glass of which had caught the light. I recall the return trip, feeling my lungs expand as the pressure decreased in the assent. I broke the surface to great gasps of air, vowing not to impetuously sink into those ever so blue waters again. You see, I had imagined the depth to be only twenty feet or so. Not so. The rest of the afternoon was spent on the shallows of the reef where I found that the tingling sting of a sea slug could cure the arthritis in my fingers for several hours!

It was in search of free diving in Montauk when I happened to make the acquaintance of Augie Brown. Augie was in his early seventies when we were introduced. I soon found that Augie was a notorious free diver whose exploits had given him a modicum of fame within the ranks of this special breed of divers. I explained to Augie my unique approach to fishing called Skishing, and he seemed impressed. I was invited to join Augie and his friends on a dive the next weekend which would be a world wind trip around Montauk, and nearby locales, in search of giant stripers.

"If we are lucky, we could catch the tide at the Race and dive the Rock," Augie said.

He informed me of this fact as we pulled away from the public launching ramp in a fifteen foot Boston Whaler. Along with Augie, we were joined by Gene, another world famous free diver, who was Augie's regular dive partner and also getting on in age; being in his early sixties. John made up the last member of the expedition. John was a burly man of my age and stature, soft spoken and reserved in nature. At our feet was the most remarkable assembly of dive gear I had yet to see. There were a number of weight belts containing at least twenty five pounds of lead a piece. It was explained to me that the trick to deep diving is neutral buoyancy, which turns into negative buoyancy after twenty feet of seawater crushes your lungs and tissue, making the body quite sinkable. Seven millimeter wetsuits were used to keep the cold of the deep water from chilling the blood. The flippers these guys used were specialized, with long length and a supple spine. Slow kicks of great power were created without expenditure of energy with these oversized duck feet. Most impressive of all were their spear guns. These were the pneumatic type, with energy released by a piston within a cylindrical body. With a bull pup design, (handle and trigger centered in the middle of the contraption) these weapons were compact and deadly. Each gun was equipped with a reel of Kevlar line of 100 pound test, 100 feet in length. This allows powerful fish to run after being darted, so as not to drown the hunter, by pulling him to Davey Jones' Locker.

"These babies are from Italy. We got them in the seventies when the design was borrowed from the Russian Spitznatz divers," Augie told me with a grin. These guns were prized possessions and were very rare, indeed. Knives were in inventory. Big knives. "To keep the sharks and hooks at bay." *Hooks?*

As we passed the Montauk Inlet, we headed east for the Point and an area known as "the Elbow" where the bottom of the ocean rises from eighty feet to forty feet forming a reef. This is the favorite feeding ground for big stripers. Twenty minutes later, we were drifting among the charter fleet with our dive flag flying. "The trick is to find the edge of the reef, drop your man off and drift along with him as he swims with the current." *The current. Hmm.*

Gene went into the water as soon as the sonar showed the bottom rising. My new friends had been diving this locale for so long that they could find their bearings through dead reckoning by lining up the landmarks of the Lighthouse and the radar tower which overlook the bluff at Caswell's. Within moments, Gene turned to descend, his fins breaking the water like the flippers of a seal. Gene remained under water for almost four minutes and I began to worry. "Jeeze, he seems to be down for a while."

"Don't worry, Gene has the lungs of a whale," Augie said as he kept the skiff pointed into the wind. Sure enough, Gene appeared a few yards from the boat, not even breathing hard. He had been submerged for over five minutes! "Lots of bass down there.... Let's make another pass." Gene said, as he hiked himself over the rail, using the wave action to give himself an upward boost. We circled the reef and Gene made another dive. Five minutes later, Gene surfaced and raised his gun over his head, the universal sign of a speared fish on the line. As we approached, Gene fought the fish on the surface like an angler with a very short rod. I noticed that the fish was taking line in a good run. In a few more minutes, Gene was handing his gear to John at the stern. The fish that came over the gunwale was very fat.

"Look at that!" Augie hollered, "He got himself another fifty!" So there, we were on station for fifteen minutes and we already had a fifty pounder on board. Just like that! Easy as all! "OK, Paul, it's your turn."

No sweat, I have been diving for thirty years. Pump up the lungs, dive to the bottom, spear fish. Piece "o" cake! So in I went. The water was very cold a mile off shore. My 'nads shrunk to the size of grapes. The first thing I noticed was that there was no sign of a bottom to this sea on the trip down. As I descended the water got colder and darker and I found myself kicking through a layer of green soup. I could feel the pressure squeezing me as thirty feet went by, without so much as a hint that the ocean floor was below me. Where is the bottom? I began to kick harder now, after all there had to be at least a twenty pounder down there for me, right? What seemed like an eternity passed when I broke through the murk into a clearing, and finally reached what must have been the forty foot mark. Gloomy green light defused around me as I set myself into a drift, facing down tide. There was a slight hitch to the whole scenario. I was on the bottom for less than a second and I was already running out of air.

Where were the fish? That peculiar lump in my throat that signals the need to breathe triggered the thought that most deaths occur on the return trip. Miscalculating oxygen supply and passing out before surfacing can and does happen. There had to be at least one fish. I would have speared a dogfish at this point!

Rocks. Big ass rocks, the size of houses, were drifting by me now, passing like buildings along the roadside as I sailed by, within the swift current. Long ribbons of kelp clung to the sides of the rocks, waving to me like sirens through the defused green haze. I was being swept through this maze like a leaf in a whirlwind. As I passed close to one monolith, I saw the snags of a senseless death pass before me. *Hooks!* Big ass hooks! These were umbrella rigs, with their four hooked fingers, reaching for me. An occasional remnant of a fishing net seemingly dragged me closer as the current drew me on. With my eyeballs just about hitting the glass on my mask, I reasoned that it was time to go, fish or no fish!

The turn to the surface was at first a relief, but then that green cloud enveloped me once again, like a funeral shroud. I was out of breath and my lungs felt as though they were on fire. *I was gonna die!* I dry swallowed to keep from exhaling. Just then the slim tendrils of sunlight drifted towards me, spurring me on. I broke the surface in full kick; half flying. To my embarrassment, I had surfaced five feet from the boat, breathing like a racehorse. I had been down for a minute-thirty, or so said my dive watch, I was sure it had malfunctioned.

"Anything?"

"Na, all gone for now."

Those fifteen seconds on the bottom were the longest fifteen seconds of my life.

We secured the gear and left for the harbor. Back at the dock Gene's fish weighed in at 51 pounds. I was invited to next weekend's dive to "Race Rock." *It would be great!*

The following weekend I was on my way to free dive one more time, I jumped in my truck and took off for a meet up with Augie at his house. Augie's home was nestled into the side of a hilly knoll up in the area known as Shepard's Neck in Montauk. I had to navigate three different dirt roads to reach his hidden sanctuary, with tall oaks and wild cherry trees turning these private roads into natural tunnels through the woods. Song birds flickered past my vision, singing happily in the ever present breeze which rippled the foliage. I passed the little Boston Whaler on its trailer as I pulled up to the front of Augie's. I was struck by the beauty of his place, the view was fantastic and it was one I had never seen before in Montauk. It's funny how a person could spend a lifetime in a place and not know every nook and cranny, for sheer lack of finding access. The view from the back yard was one that overlooked Fort Pond Bay from the summit of a high hill covered in azaleas and shad trees. I could see Gardener's Island in the distance, through a peculiar aperture of cool air that made the isle seem very close. Augie met me at the door and introduced me to his lovely wife.

"Today we will dive Race Rock, my boy!" announced Augie who then proceeded to tell the tale of how he and his cohorts found this mound in the sixties, while looking for fertile grounds to explore.

"Race Rock is located off the south west side of Fisher's Island in Long Island Sound; about an hour's sail from the inlet. It's a lump in the sea floor, situated at a place where the bottom rises from eighty feet to form a small ridge. At its shallowest spot, it is about forty feet down. The east end of the mound is where we dive, son. An eddy forms there, where the colder water brought into the Sound from the Plum Gut sweeps down the slope of the ridge and descends to over one hundred forty feet! You don't want to get caught in that current, Paul."

Augie also told me how he had lost several dive buddies on Race Rock over the past few decades, all highly skilled divers, with hours of experience at the Race. Augie explained that the proper time to fish is when the tide is barely moving and will take a diver to a plateau on the east side of the structure.

"The tide descends at this point and you must slip into an eddy formed by a bunch of rocks situated on the flank of Race Rock. It's like an elevator ride to hell," Augie said, with a sly smile on his face. OK, this sounded a bit "*iffy*" to me. I was not so sure I was in the mood, or if I even had the stones for this type of extreme activity.

"The bass are all monsters there! They circle the rocks, looking for bait to swallow. The difficult part will be the assent. You're fighting the current, so make sure you save enough air to make it back! By the way, this is where Gene speared a world record bass."

With the gear in place in the back of the boat, we drove off to the launching ramp where we met the rest of the crew, and were soon under way. The morning sun was cool in the breeze which is ever present from the southwest during summer. There was a small chop and our craft hopped the crests, skimming across the tide, as we headed west.

"We're gonna be early," Gene said. "We should kill some time..... What do ya think Aug? Maybe the Ruins?"

Actually, the Ruins are the relic of an old Army base built in the nineteenth century. This small isle on the way to the North Fork of Long Island was used as a target for experimental torpedoes and bombs during WWII. Of course, it is listed as 'off limits' on the charts, as it is surrounded by unexploded ordinance. The patch of sand and brush was also the site of a fort that blocked the entrance to Orient Point from the east. The fort has long since been blown to smithereens by a century of munitions tests; thus the name. We pulled up to the shoreline where the sandy bottom extended about twenty yards from the beach and then dropped off into an abyss.

"You should dive to about thirty feet on the side of this sand wall and let the tide drag you around the corner."

I donned my gear and dove over the side. Immediately struck with the beauty of the rippling sands that slipped steeply into the deep, I cruised the edge of a huge undersea sand dune. The bottom disappeared into the crystal green glass of a yawning declination. I swam along the edge, taking my time, you might say, *"killing"* it. You see, I was not in the mood to even think about this Race Rock "thing" today, with the memory of "the elbow" and its clutching fingers of lost tackle fresh in my mind. Yet these slow passes into the tide had me shivering. I could occasionally sample cold waters which descended into the depths feeling... fear... not something I was used to. It was both stimulating and disquieting to me. What would become of this day?

"Nothin' around here today," Gene related after the tide slowed to a crawl and the water became quiet.

"Well, we have an hour or two of slack water," Augie said.

"Let's try the rocks around Plum Island, it's on the way."

Plum Island is situated at the north end of Orient Point where these cold waters flow with a great rushing, through a channel of shallows that creates a natural funnel. Great shoals of fish collect in the turbulent water that passes by this ridge. We, however, would be diving the shoreline of the Island, where we would find Tatog, Striped Bass and Seabass lurking in the rocks along its craggy coast. Plum Island is another restricted area, which is used as a biological laboratory for infectious diseases. It has long been rumored to be a bio-weapons research facility and the beaches there are littered with off limits signs, threatening the use of deadly force. It appears for all the world to see, deserted. Nothing moves across the surface of this sandy isle.

We arrived at a place where the shoreline was reinforced with a long stone breakwater. The water here was no more than twenty feet deep and John and I dove in. I was very glad to be able to see the bottom as I kicked towards the rocks. I saw little in the way of life here. Several more dives had us fishless and Gene suggested we try the west end of the Island.

"Are you sure? The tide is about to run, and we don't wanna get caught up in that rip," Augie wondered.

I had seen this rip from the CROSS SOUND FERRY on occasions when I would take the boat to New London, Connecticut. From the deck of a ship, these waters take on a harrowing appearance. It is an area of disturbed, turbulent water at least a mile in length and often one hundred yards wide. The rip is usually full of drifting boats, searching for the fish that love to feed in these unruly waters.

"Let's do it," John said.

Soon we were on our way, cutting through the now deceptively quiet waters of this beautiful summer afternoon. I could just make out the movement from the new tide forming as we rounded Plum Island. We headed towards a dive site, very close to the beach on the northern side of the isle, and upon our arrival, John jumped in first. I soon followed after the boat had drifted about fifty yards down tide from his entry point; the water was warm and calm. The visibility was a good fifty feet in this uncharacteristically clear water. Expending little energy, I began to drift over the bottom. The clear water was a welcome complement to this part of the dive and I was pleased when the fish began to show themselves.

Tatog, otherwise known as blackfish, were all over the place, their dark bodies gliding through the current. The 'tog' seemed to be protecting their territory as I drifted by; their vigilant eyes watching me. These rocks were monolithic giants that formed long rows, their sides littered with bait and life. I also noticed the delicate fins of several large sea bass. Taking aim, yet misjudging the speed of the drift, my shot went wide. Surfacing, I looked at my watch and saw that I had been underwater for a good two minutes. Back into the grove of diving, the clear water and abundant fish helped to relieve my fears. I pulled in several deep breaths at the surface and once again descended into the rocks.

As I sank below the surface I felt the grip of a strong tide envelope me. Once again, I was zooming past the flanks of huge undersea boulders. The tide created odd eddies within the water column and I was intrigued by the way the sea swung me past the rocks. A sudden current turned me, mere moments before crashing headlong, into a massive stone block.

Things were developing rapidly. The tide swung me towards a big 'tog' which was set to ambush his dinner as I flew past. I pulled the trigger and was rewarded with a clean strike! The fish was stopped by a kill shot. *Augie would be proud of me!* I surfaced and reeled in my catch which turned out to be a fish about two feet long. Struck by the unusual appearance of this fish, it was indeed black with a white bottom that was highlighted, by its orange patches. The face of this Tatog was a study in bad dentistry with protruding buck teeth and fat lips which it used to suck up the crabs and mollusks that line the rocks. When I raised my speargun over my head to signal a successful dive, it was then that I noticed the little boat was nowhere to be seen. I made another visual sweep of the horizon and could just barely make out the whaler about a quarter of a mile away from me.

What were they doing so far away? When I last slipped below the surface the boat was not even fifty yards from me. Now I could just make out the whaler, as a silhouette in the distance, *heading away from me.* The small craft was well into the heart of the Plum Gut. Keeping it within view, it seemed to rise and fall within the whitecaps of a tormented sea. Obviously my pals had sailed into a particularly nasty piece of water. I could just make out John as one of the guys struggled to pull him from the drink. How had he managed to drift so far into the rip?

No doubt about it, I felt the grip of an unseen force, as if I had passed into a raging river. I began to pick up speed and was swept into the racing current with the sea churning into a violent torrent of crashing waves, none of which flowed in the same direction. They collided with each other, rumbling and splashing around me. I could feel the impact of each breaker as the water seethed the surrounding air into a fine mist. I was once thrown up into the sky at the top of the turbulence then dropped back into a trough below. There was no let up; I began to struggle within the tidal surge.

Fear and the uncanny exhilaration of a burst of adrenalin brought my mind into stark focus. This was a life threatening situation. Dropping my weight belt, which at the time, was doing its best to drown me, helped keep me on the surface like a bobbing cork. I tried to relax and enjoy the ride. Moments later I noticed the guys motoring at speed in my direction. The small boat scaled the crests of the waves and skidded into the trough of sea that surrounded me. Things got complicated, as one minute the boat was five feet over my head and the next, five feet under me. Then, just by chance, I was able to hand Gene my gun with the fish still attached to the spear, which hung in the water below me. And moments later I grabbed the railing of the boat. The sea dragged me upward, nearly dislocating my shoulder as the skiff shot skyward at an unusual angle. As it dropped into a flume, I landed on the deck and found myself lying in a boat full of water! We were sinking in a torrent of roiling motion. Gene gunned the engine as a wave broke into the stern and swamped the cockpit.

"We're going under!"

"Hang on!"

With little warning and as if in slow motion, the whaler capsized, throwing us overboard. Bubbles besieged me as I clawed my way through the pounding surf and managed to surface next to the hull. My diving mask was evidently torn from my head. I was also missing a flipper. Searching for the others, I soon was greeted with the gaping stares of my three, now very old looking, partners.

It was amazing how fast that current moved us through the Gut. We were free of the tumult in five minutes and quickly surrounded by rescuers. Other boats had followed us into the calmer waters and threw us life lines. It was soon after that when a Sea Tow boat appeared at our side, tying a line to the bow rail, and motored us towards the shores of Plum Island. Hanging on, we rode the overturned Boston Whaler as the towboat brought us in.

"I told you that it was too late in the tide to dive here!" Augie cried at Gene and John. "Look! All our gear is gone! My favorite speargun is somewhere on the bottom! You're a bunch of reckless jerks!"

"Augie, we are all safe and sound. Let's just concentrate on that for now," I said, trying to console the waterlogged crew. Gene just shook his head in disgust. "Gear can be replaced, Augie." John sat on the stern with his feet over the side, like a kid dipping his toes.

"*Well, I must admit, this was all very exiting!*" I said. "I don't think I ever had such an eventful day!" And I meant it. It dawned on me, at that moment, that I was a hopeless thrill junky.

On the beach at Plum Island we got out of the water and the four of us managed to flip the whaler over. A half hour of bailing had the boat pretty much emptied of water. It was obvious that the engine was water logged and wouldn't run until some proper attention was paid, so we were towed to Orient Point by the Sea Tow guy. Eventually, a mechanic came to the dock and fiddled with the motor, paying special consideration to the carburetors. After two hours of piddling, the motor was once again ticking along.

"Augie, I've got a friend in Southold that I am sure will drive us back to Montauk, if I ask him," I offered.

"I think we can make it back. The engine seems to be running pretty good."

"Sounds like a bad idea, Aug" Gene commented. "I think we better not bet on the thing gettin' us home."

"No, I have called my friend Ben. He says he will follow us back to Montauk with his boat and be ready to give us a tow if we should need it."

We sat at the dock in Orient Point for two hours waiting for Augies friend, Ben. When he finally arrived, I could not believe the vessel which was expected to shadow us back to Montauk. It was like some sad hulk from the fifties, an eighteen foot cabin cruiser that looked to me as though it should be in the scrap heap or nestled snuggly on the bottom of the sea, with pretty little fishies dancing through its scuppers. There was a ring of green algae surrounding the little craft where the waterline should have been painted.

"Aw gee Augie, I don't like the looks of this..."

"Nonsense! We're gonna be fine. In an hour, we will be back home."

With that, Augie revved the motor which coughed throwing a puff of black smoke into the warm afternoon and off we sailed with the little canoe following in our wake. Just west of Gardener's Island, the engine began to sputter.

"Oh shit!" The revs cut and the little engine that could, just couldn't.

Augie waved down his pal and within a few minutes, we were tied to Ben's stern, and once again, headed east. As we passed the tip of Cartwright Shoal we heard a snap and the tow rope flew past the bow of the whaler and splashed into the sea behind us. The tie-down on Ben's boat had pulled free of the gunwhale and shot past our heads like an arrow, released.

"Oh shit."

A bit of maneuvering had us once again tied up and under the tow of that ancient weekend lake cruiser, this time fastened to the starboard cleat. The little putt-putt was definitely struggling with the whaler fastened behind.

"Augie, I don't like the way Ben's motor sounds."

"You know Gene, you worry too much."

John, being the silent type, just sat on the rail and shook his head. Our little flotilla muddled through the waters of Long Island Sound at the staggering velocity of three knots, with the towboat oscillating back and forth like a drunk. There was a pronounced list to the little rescue craft towards the side that was fastened to our bow. Without warning, our convoy began to circle in a most alarming way, then, we were dead in the water.

"What the hell?"

"Aug, this doesn't look good...."

"Aw... *can* it Gene!"

Frantic hand signals from Ben had us scratching our collective craniums until we drifted closer to the now derelict towboat.

"I have lost steerage!"

"Your kiddin', right?" Ben was not kidding. His "long passed the junk heap" cabin cruiser had parted ways with its rudder cable, leaving our two aging hulks adrift in the sea.

"*What the blazes is next...*" Gene mumbled under his breath.

"Well, get on your VHS and call Sea Tow again."

"Hate to tell yah, but it's been down since we flipped."

"Cell?"

"Drowned"

A chat with Ben brought us to the conclusion we were screwed. No cell signal. *Can you hear me now?*

"Look guys, I know a bit about small motors. You got any tools? Lemme give it a go, I think it's just water in the carbs," I said, even though I was not quite as sure of my abilities as I professed to be.

2:00pm crept relentlessly forward to 3:00pm by the time I had removed the float valves from three carbs and drained the water from them. I labored under the constant threat of dropping a screw overboard as I hung over the stern precariously with my feet dipping into the drink. As the Lord would have it, after cranking the motor several times, the little bastard sputtered to life. We were once again under way! This time with the *towboat* in tow.

"Augie, we're wallowing. I don't think this is gonna work."

"*Can* it, Gene..." Up the lazy swells we chugged, just making enough headway to keep a course. The revs began to drop as black smoke bubbled from our feeble wake. After a mile, we found ourselves stranded once again.

"This can't be happenin'. It's all just too bizarre!"

"I know...I know..."

4:30 pm. We drifted. The engine casing was open; again I drained the water from the carburetors. It was now evident that water had managed to get into the fuel tank. You would have thought we would have been passed by a boat or two. Not today. 5:00pm, the motor sputters to life, and we struggle to make two knots as the revs once again proceeded to the point of diminishing returns. Another mile behind us and back we were to floating aimlessly.

"Hey look! I see a boat!" Sure enough, a seventy five foot yacht was on a direct course towards our position. We all began to wave frantically, all the while screaming for help. As the yacht came within 200 yards of our starboard side, she advanced the throttle and turned away, flying past us at no less than 30 knots! We all stood agape with disbelieving eyes. A two foot wake plowed into our port side, threatening to overturn us while the glisteningly white yacht sped in the distance. *The bastard had blown us off*!

"I don't believe this!"

"This is like the Twilight Zone!" Augie said.

Déjà vu.... yours truly sat over the rail, draining the carbs. I don't know what poor Ben was thinking throughout this ordeal, all alone aboard his craft, not wanting to desert the old scow. By 7:00pm, the sun sat low on the horizon, making mechanical manipulation a trial in frustration and patience.

"What's that?" Gene pointed off towards the east as we spied a wake on the horizon. I continued to labor with the carburetors while the boys stood waving at a potential rescue craft. It was the Coast

Guard! Mr. Trump had not deserted us after all, but had called the cops, presumably taking our little flotilla for a collection of Somali pirates! Within ten minutes we were alongside the cutter with a boarding party preparing to search us for contraband.

In the long run, we made it back to the dock by sunset, comfortably in tow by the Coast Guard Cutter. We looked like a procession of circus elephants, holding each others tails, as we passed in between the jetties of the Montauk Harbor Inlet. Augie and the boys received a citation for not having the required safety devices aboard, those having floated away when we overturned at the Plum Gut. I never did get to free dive on Race Rock. Too bad.

Montauk's Fishing Holes.

This chapter is to be considered "Sub Rosa", meaning that if you divulge any of this information to anybody, without me receiving my royalty vig, I will personally *haunt you*! (*My spies are everywhere...*) The only reason I have added this section into the book is so that the less sophisticated among my readers may find something which they believe is worth the twenty bucks to buy the damned thing! (*Ahem... Should this be you, your purchase pleases me to no end and I personally thank you for your good judgment, dear reader!*) There is no doubt that some critics will find this passage despicable, but then again, I am a graceless shit stirrer.

Montauk is an enigma. In order to be able to thrive in this place, a person needs to live it, (*or know someone who does*) like a wild animal that wanders the glades and woods of the land. I have roamed these secluded vales my entire life, most often in search of solitude and solace, but occasionally with a mentor or fellow searcher, and as a result, I have discovered many productive grounds for hunting fish. All these locales are tried and true. I am not a person who covets rocks. (*Well, not always...*) For one thing, at any given time, there will be fish at *any* location (*it's a crap shoot*) and for fish to hold on these perches for any length of time is somewhat rare, indeed. This list will be in order of volume of fish to be had. The best are the first on the list. Some are dangerous, some are crowded, some are even secrets....

The most productive location in Montauk for the sheer quantity and quality of the fish it harbors is, undeniably, under the Montauk Lighthouse. I have seen many huge stripers taken from this spot over the years. The best time to fish here is during the flood tide with a northeast wind in your face. Bucktails and lures are prevalent. THIS LOCATION IS EXTREME! You will need to be equipped with cleats, waterproof jackets and waders. It will be crowded at the Lighthouse (*Up-front*) during a chew; newcomers to the Montauk should not attempt to fish here. To fish under the candle, it is wise to use a bucktail, or to match the lure of the others who will be fishing along side you. This is the only way to keep from crossing your fellow fishermen (*in more ways than one!*) Also included in this area are Scott's Cove, Jones' Reef, the Weed Bowl and the Bluffs. These places are within walking distance of the Lighthouse on the northern side. Hardcore rocks, such as Evans', Weakfish, Shark and Blackfish are located in the deeper waters within the confines of the Point.

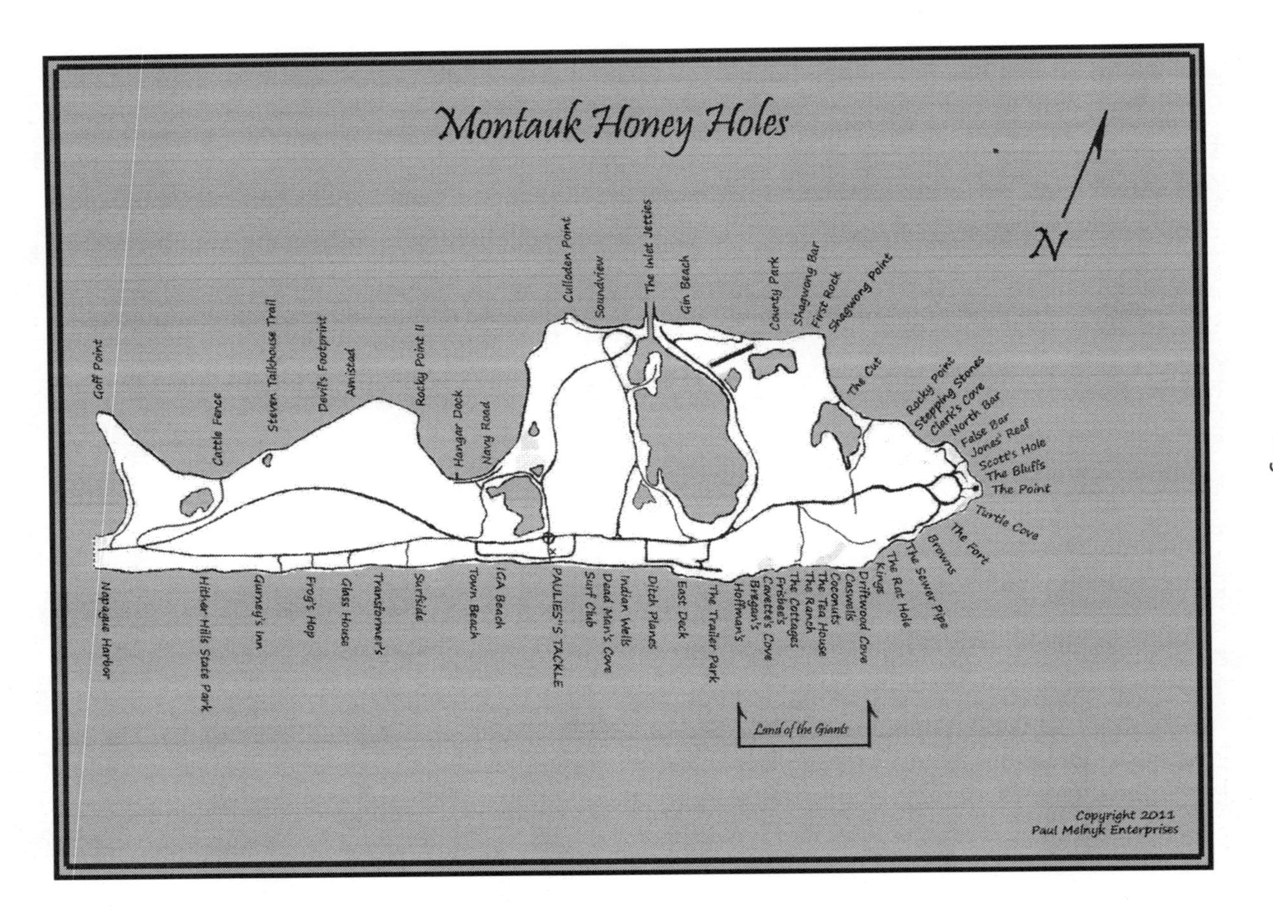
Montauk Honey Holes
N
Goff Point
Cattle Fence
Steven Talkhouse Trail
Devil's Footprint
Amistad
Rocky Point II
Hangar Dock
Navy Road
Culloden Point
Soundview
The Inlet Jetties
Gin Beach
County Park
Shagwong Bar
First Rock
Shagwong Point
The Cut
Rocky Point
Stepping Stones
Clark's Cove
North Bar
False Bar
Jones' Reef
Scott's Hole
The Bluffs
The Point
Turtle Cove
The Fort
Browns
The Sewer Pipe
The Rat Hole
Kings
Driftwood Cove
Caswells
Coconuts
The Tea House
The Ranch
The Cottages
Frisbee's
Cavette's Cove
Bregan's
Hoffman's
The Trailer Park
East Deck
Ditch Planes
Indian Wells
Dead Man's Cove
Surf Club
PAULIES''S TACKLE
IGA Beach
Town Beach
Surfside
Transformer's
Glass House
Frog's Hop
Gurney's Inn
Hither Hills State Park
Napague Harbor
Land of the Giants
Copyright 2011
Paul Melnyk Enterprises

Turtle Cove is at the southern end of Montauk Point State Park. This is a beginner's location with a soft sloping beach that leads to a deep water cove. It is very productive starting in mid-September and is often very crowded with amateurs when the fish are blitzing because of the relative ease in getting there. A well traveled pathway snakes through a natural wooded tunnel through the brush, and leads right to the heart of the area. The western end of Turtle Cove is often overlooked because of the rocky coastline which begins there and extends west for several miles; more on this location later.

The North and False Bars are also located in the Lighthouse vicinity. You must travel west of Jones' Reef on the north side to find these grounds. This is the location of the notorious "Murderer's Row," which is named appropriately, as it is fished by the sharpies. These are superior sites that are very covetous in a dropping tide with a north wind in your face. Bucktails and darters work well here. Patience and etiquette must be observed to fish this hotspot without getting roughed up.

The sand beaches of Montauk town and points west are superior in the early summer, right through to the fall. Many fifty pound fish have been taken from the various cuts and mussel shoals along our sandy coast. A mile west of Montauk village has been holding fish since 2008. This has been a summer hot skishing spot for me. You will need a 4WD beach permit (East Hampton Town) for the privilege to cruise this beach, and during the tourist season, it is forbidden to drive this area during the daytime between 6:00am and 6:00pm. Beyond the resort of Gurneys' Inn, begins Hither Hills State Park, where you will need a NY State Beach Vehicle permit to proceed. East of town are the sites known as Indians', Dead Man's, Ditch Plains and the Trailer Park. These spots are a bit more hard core and require heartier equipment.

Shagwong Point is next on the list. A Sufflok Co. Permit is required to drive the mile-plus beach to this sandy hot spot. Shag is very productive on a dropping tide most of the season. For big fish, work a north east wind. This is another favorite of the hardcore enthusiast. Bucktails are used in the daylight here, with darters, needlefish and bottle plugs utilized in the dark. Beginners should keep to the west end of the Point. For the hardcore, you will find three or four big rocks at the surf zone known as "the rock pile" which begins this hot spot prized by the pros. Storm tides bring great fishing here in the fall. Fluke and blues may be taken from the beach west of the Point during the summer months.

Camp Hero (located within Montauk Point St. Park) encompasses a good portion of the action packed striper coast of Montauk. This is not an easy place to fish, and it does require extensive equipment and a hearty soul to reconnoiter the area; quarter mile walks over rough terrain being common. Brown's is located under the cliff just west of the Lighthouse and is popular for casting live eels from the many flat rocks that set between five and twenty yards from the surf line. Here, blitz action is common in the fall. Night fishing will produce fat stripers. The Sewer Pipe is a rock strewn cove at the end of the access road that may be traveled with a Camp Hero Permit (NY State). It has easy access, so it may be crowded during a day with a lot of action. Just west of the Sewer Pipe are The Rat Hole and King's. These are rock shoals with many good and deep holes that hold nighttime trophies. The daytime scene is known for the blitz action and should be a go-to-location from September till mid October. This is a popular site for the skilled caster, because of its unique beauty and convenience.

West of Kings begins the area known as "*The Land of the Giants*," for obvious reasons. You will have to be able to walk several miles under extreme (rocky) conditions to fish these spots. Driftwood Cove begins the journey, with the Stone House jetty and rocks; a trophy bass location. The sandy beach of the cove is also a good place to throw bait. Just past the cove begins Caswell's Reef, which is very hard core. Eels, plugs and bucktails are thrown in the dark from deep rocks frequented by the hardest of the hardcore wetsuiters to yield gigantic fish. I personally love to skish the Caswell's Reef at the east end and into Driftwood Cove in the dark of night. The remoteness is a draw for me, as are the big fish. Further west is The Tea House, known for its oriental style estate with a sweeping blue tiled roof. Coconuts and Tuma's Reef will be further west still. The Ranch and the Cottages continue our westward trek, with the Cottages being about five miles from the Lighthouse. All these spots are remote and more often than not secluded. These waters are not for beginners or the faint of heart. It would take a week to find your body.

From Ditch Plains, the Trailer Park and points east is Hoffman's (bird shit rock) which features a flying staircase on the face of the bluff. Bragan's Rock is at the eastern end of the reef at this locale about 75 yards from the beach, in seven feet of water. Many fine rocks are to be had for night fishing here. This is also a favorite of mine to skish in the dark. Cavette's Cove comes next. It is very sandy, with a big drop off. Both the east and west ends of this cove hold fish. Church's is the next shoal west. This is the site of an old fishing pier and gentleman's club which was active in the late nineteenth century. There are still several large boulders with holes drilled in them, which acted as anchor points for fishing stands. There is some great fishing here for those who can walk a mile or so in the dark. I have also skished here under certain conditions.

Even more obscure spots exist in Montauk. Culloden, which is west of the Montauk Inlet on the north side, is a favorite for fly casters because the wind is often at your back. The jetties at the inlet of Montauk Harbor are popular for day trippers to cast a hunk of bait. The harbor docks produce bass to 30 inches and 3 pound fluke on live bait which you can snag right at the site. It is a hoot to reel in a doormat fluke as the Viking Star (party boat) pulls away from the dock, loaded with $50 a head fares, gawking in disbelief at your catch. The Cattle Fence and Goff Point are located at the northwest end of Hither Hills St. Park and Napeague (Umbrella, White Sands) are located on the southern Atlantic. These spots can land some quality fish, and are very secluded.

The Pier at Navy Road is a great location to bring your kids for a day of picnicking and dock fishing and is located at the west end of Navy Road. Turn west on Industrial Road (off Edgemere, just north of the Surf Lodge) and then turn right at the sharp bend in the road, just past the lumber yard. Go over the RR tracks to the sound. Turn left down Navy road. There you have it; the site of the pre-war navy base and "Fishangri-la" of the nineteen fifties. With picnic tables, porta potties, a grassy field and a nature trail this is a great place for the wife and progeny.

Freshwater aficionados will find a multitude of hidden ponds and clear water lakes to score a largemouth bass or two. Most often utilized is Fort Pond, located on the northwest end of town. Large carp, pike, perch, sunneys, large and small mouth bass and high-bred stripers are waiting for your hook in this popular body of water.

Big Reed and Little Reed Ponds are located off East Lake Drive and may be reached from the access road near the airport, located on the right side at the sharp "S" bend in the road. There is also a very beautiful nature trail that winds through the woods in this location

(Theodore Roosevelt County Park) with well marked picnic areas throughout.

The ponds within Montauk Downs Golf Course are filled with largemouth bass, but access is denied by the state, so don't fish here.

Within Hither Hills (Woods) State Park is a very productive pond known to the locals as Hidden Pond; a must see for the die-hard basser.

All right, my friends. The spell has been cast; the crystal ball is polished and ready for viewing. Spirits have divulged to me that there is a slob in your future, (*other than your pal that goes by the name of 'dumbass'*), as long as you follow my directions *explicitly*.

You will not hook your fish of a lifetime while sitting in front of a TV. The most rudimentary principle in the universe and the beauty of all great systems are sheer simplicity. You've got to ***cast*** to ***catch.*** Don't think too much. Do it. Then do it over and over, and over again. To conquer the beast, you must sacrifice the most precious and ethereal of all a man's possessions...

TIME...

But ***most*** of all...

*You **need**...*

luck........

Terminal Tackle.

I have been hearing lately, from various friends and rivals, that it is always better to be a 'has-been' than a 'wanna-be'. In truth, I have come to the realization that I prefer to be "it." Within the scheme of things, I have been witness to great catches, and great men who excelled at the sport through pure determination and perseverance. Few of these fellows will admit to this fact that when it comes to fishing, they attack the sport with a gusto that defies logic, yet there they are, stumbling to some far off point in the middle of the night, with the hope of hooking a monster, acting like this is the most natural thing in the world.

What is the point? Will the beast be carved up and canned for the winter larder? OK, there are a few out there who will distribute freezers full of meat to the wanting ones, but for the most part, these fish are meant for bragging rights. The motivation is, more often than not, to hang the fish, to make the Daily Herald. Hell, I myself have often been guilty of this. As a matter of fact, half of this book documents this fact.

There are those who seek a more personal harmony with the beasts. For these fellows, it is the hunt and chase that are most appealing. It is a connection with nature and a desire to reestablish a link with a mentality that is primal to us all to hunt and gather, to commune with the earth and sea. Is this motive any more righteous than those who seek notoriety?

One thing is for sure, the Montauk crew takes the sport very seriously. The combination of being the nexus for the migration of striped bass, and having to contend with some of the most challenging terrain on the planet, tends to make us more intense. There is a pride involved with being able to endure the elements, to deliver. It is what motivates the soul, and as a result, we do not suffer fools well. But in contrast, once we recognize that kindred spark in a neophyte, it is a foregone conclusion that many among us will take the fellow under our wing to "show him the ropes."

The sad part of the equation is that we often kill the fish. Whether it is for the need of attention from our peers or blood lust, these noble beasts often find themselves in the cooler. This is not necessarily an evil aspect of the sport, for as long as the hunter is conservative in his take, the species will endure. But there are those who will wreak havoc on the schools, taking as much as they are allowed, and sometimes even more, on a daily basis. Under such circumstances, the fishery is doomed. As I have matured (*well, gotten older*) I have seen a depletion in the numbers when it comes to the cow bass, and it saddens me to think that one day, the stripped bass will go the way of the buffalo, relegated to a place in history called "once upon a time."

I show no animosity towards the young guns. They are full of piss and vinegar as I once was, obsessed with an insatiable lust for striped bass fishing. Fellows like Milano, Capolla, Blasco and Bruno deserve their day in the limelight, and I would never dream of denying them their moment. As a matter of fact, I get pleasure in seeing their catch swing from the scales. It is often all that is left in the way of motivation for me, now that the years of being bashed to shit in the rocks have taken their toll on my mortal frame, and truthfully, these fellows release *tons* of fish.

I will be the first to declare that I am not finished with the sport of taking the cows and shoving them up the arses of my friends. I am still searching for my personal best, although in truth, those fish that remain within the gray matter of my brain, the ones that have beaten me, are the sweetest memories, as is evident within the pages of this book. The fish that gets away is the one you will remember.

So, as the days get shorter, forgive me for waxing towards sentimentality. I have tried not to make this collection of memories a trophy to myself. My intention was to give you a window into the psyche which turned my life into an obsession. My days in the surf are numbered, as they are for all of us, and I will soon be left to warm that chair with my name on it, in front of Paulie's.

About the Author:

Paul Melnyk is a resident of Montauk, Long Island where he lives with his wife Dawn. Paul is a journeyman cabinet maker whose designs grace the interiors of many of the finest homes in "The Hamptons." He is also a world renowned fisherman and originator of the surfcasting technique known as Skishing, where the fisherman swims into the ocean with a rod and reel to catch fish while treading water.

Paul has been featured in many periodicals and books, such as, Men's Journal, Field and Stream, The Wall Street Journal and "On The Run," a novel by David DiBenedetto. Paul has also been featured on film and television and is a songwriter, and musician.

List of Photographs

Cover, Skishing, by Paul Melnyk
Title page graphic, Fish or Die by, Bill Graff
Vito and George, circa 1994, by Paul Melnyk 19
Melnyk and The Tree Man at the bluffs, by unknown.................. 57
Denis Gaviola, Dave Markley, Paul Melnyk, by Joe Gaviola 65
Jack Yee, by unknown.. 79
Pope Noel on Weakfish Rock, by Paul Melnyk............................. 86
Paul Melnyk's infamous photo, by Domonique Arnould............. 95
Dom Arnould smoking bluefish, by Paul Melnyk......................... 97
Melnyk going skishing, by Dominique Arnould 105
Gary 'Toad' Stephens blowin' his horn, by Paul Melnyk.............115
Melnyk and Toad with fish at Paulie's Tackle, by Jack Yee 117
Jack and Eddie on the beach, by Paul Melnyk.............................133
Frank Blasco with his skished cow, by Paul Melnyk.................. 159
Paul Melnyk with frozen goose, by Dawn Melnyk 193
Atilla Ozturk skishing, by Paul Melnyk 203
Map of the Montauk Honey Holes, by Paul Melnyk.................. 223
Paul Melnyk with cow, by Jenna Melnyk 231
Back cover, Sunset, Main Beach, E. Hampton, by Paul Melnyk

Made in the USA
Lexington, KY
05 February 2012